"*Liar's Winter* is delicious Southern story~~telling~~. ~~Cindy~~ ~~~~

use of dialect along with the ~~~~

tell the second of her Appala~~~~

Marie Everson, speaker and ~~~~

ing *The One True Love of Ali*~~~~

"In *Liar's Winter*, Cindy Spro~~les~~ ~~~~

rivals that of the mountain ~~~~

and loves depended on their stories. I held my breath for most of the
novel, aching with the main character, what happened to her, and the lies
burned into her soul. This is a story that will resonate with many who
will see their own hurts etched into the pages, their own disillusionments
spelled out, their own voices in the dialogue . . . and their faith awak-
ened as the tale unfolds." —**Cynthia Ruchti**, speaker and award-winning
author of 22 books, including *As Waters Gone By* and *When the Morning
Glory Blooms*

"As with Cindy Sproles's first novel, *Mercy's Rain*, *Liar's Winter* captures
flawlessly the voice and setting of a nineteenth-century Appalachian
mountain valley along with a powerful redemptive message. One oft-
repeated word evokes the story's theme—choice. The choice to love instead
of hate. To return kindness for cruelty. To believe, despite all appearances,
that in this world's darkest valleys there truly is a Good Shepherd who
guides, comforts, restores, and ultimately leads us home. In the end, the
liar's winter proves its own illusion, leaving the reader—and the protag-
onist herself—with spring's new life. No light read this, but worth every
inevitable tear and smile." —**Jeanette Windle**, award-winning author of
14 books, including *Congo Dawn*, *Veiled Freedom*, and *Freedom's Stand*

"You will love the voice, the characters, and the compelling story Cindy
Sproles has spun in *Liar's Winter*. You will long remember it. You may be
haunted, even changed, by it." —**Bob Hostetler**, award-winning author
of *The Bone Box* and coauthor of the Northkill Amish series

"Infused with the rich culture of Appalachia, *Liar's Winter* is a vivid journey into a world many of us will never experience firsthand. Lochiel, a girl born with a birthmark that many mountain folk interpret as the Devil's handprint, lives a lonely and loveless existence. Through her realistic and sometimes tragic search for acceptance, we witness the strength of family and the power of a loving God demonstrated through His people. Sproles not only stays true to the beliefs and dialect of the mountain people, she immerses us in their society so completely that we feel as if we've walked in Lochiel's footsteps." —**Virginia Smith**, best-selling author of over 30 books, including *The Amish Widower* and the Tales from the Goose Creek B&B series

"Beneath the hardness of life lies something beautiful. This is the theme of *Liar's Winter*. The story clings to your senses and won't turn you loose, like Cindy's own description of being caught in a spider's web that 'stuck to her like molasses.' Cindy has a unique voice and a shockingly wonderful ability to tell an Appalachian story while weaving the magic of her mountain metaphors. This is another winner, like her best-selling debut novel, *Mercy's Rain*." —**Yvonne Lehman**, director of Blue Ridge Novel Retreat, and best-selling author of over 45 books, including *Hearts That Survive: A Novel of the Titanic*

LIAR'S
WINTER

An Appalachian Novel

LIAR'S WINTER

CINDY K. SPROLES

Kregel
Publications

Liar's Winter: An Appalachian Novel
© 2017 by Cindy K. Sproles

Published by Kregel Publications, a division of Kregel, Inc.,
2450 Oak Industrial Drive NE, Grand Rapids, MI 49505.

The persons and events portrayed in this work are the creations
of the author, and any resemblance to persons living or dead is
purely coincidental.

Scripture quotations are from the King James Version.

ISBN 978-0-8254-4453-1

Printed in the United States of America
17 18 19 20 21 22 23 24 25 26 / 5 4 3 2 1

Dedicated to Yvonne Lehman,
a Southern mountain charm and author of
multitudes of books, who has mentored me without
hesitation and guided me with great love.
Some ten years ago, I stood in awe as she directed
the Blue Ridge Mountains Christian Writers
Conference. I never imagined she would become my
friend and mentor. Thank you, Yvonne, for sharing
your wisdom freely, for welcoming me into your
home, and for the joy of hearing you call me Sugar.

THE FIRST TIME I ever seen that girl she was squallin like a banshee. Her whole face was beet red so I didn't notice her mark right off. She was such a tiny thing. Before I could think twice, I'd picked her up.

Her screams was what brought me to the door of the shack. The door wasn't latched. I poked my head in and hollered, but there wasn't no answer. Probably couldn't hear me over the racket of the baby. I'd been squirrel huntin and left my catch on the front step.

The baby was wrapped tight by its momma's side. Its momma laid real still. "You alright?" She didn't wiggle so much as a finger. If she didn't hear that baby bellerin, she sure wasn't gonna hear me. When I grabbed aholt and tugged that baby outa its momma's arm, her arm flopped and I about jumped outa my skin.

That baby commenced to nuzzle at me and quieted to a whimper. Then I hightailed it outa there. I was smart enough to know I couldn't talk a body back to life. Momma would know what to do with the baby. She needed a new youngin anyway, to replace the ones she'd lost, the ones that kept on dyin when they was born. Momma just sit and stared these days. Hardly ever talked. Havin this youngin would make her happy again. I smiled just thinkin about it. This baby would do just fine. And Poppy would be proud I'd done such a fine thing for Momma.

I forgot my squirrels on the step though. And it was a ways back home. I'd wandered farther than I'd figured. Long before I made it home, I was right tempted to just leave the baby lyin in the woods. My arms was tired.

Wasn't 'til I got home I realized I'd left my gun leanin against that shack.

It goes without sayin that Poppy wasn't happy I'd lost my gun. And Momma wasn't happy when she laid eyes on the mark that spilled down one side of that baby's face. That marked baby for my gun, worst trade I'd ever made. Right from the start, that girl brung me nothin but trouble.

ONE

Summer's Mountain, 1893

"COME ON, DEVIL's daughter. Let me see that demon." Gerald rested the point of his knife just under my eye. I didn't dare twitch. "That Devil marked you when you was born. Burned his mark on that cheek and neck." He eased the knife down my cheek and settled at my throat. "You know, Lochiel, I've often wondered if that mark would cut off. Wonder if we could skin you like a rabbit. What do you think?" I couldn't stop the tremble that crawled up my spine. Gerald often goaded me, taunted me. Sometimes I lashed back with my tongue, other times I just never opened my mouth, never sayin a word. Can't be sure which way made him maddest, but he'd never drawed a knife on me. "Come on, let me see that demon. Show me!"

I could feel the fear in me turnin to anger. I could taste the bitterness like bile crawlin up my throat and into my mouth. If the Devil really was in me, he was hankerin to get out. My mark burned hot.

Then Gerald laughed and flicked his knife away, slid it into his belt. My hand flew to my neck and came away with a tiny drop of blood on my finger.

"That red 'bout matches your face."

One, two, three. Walk away, Lochiel Ogle. Just walk away. But I couldn't. Seems I'd spent so much time listenin to everbody tell me what to do that I couldn't even hear myself no more.

Without me givin it a second thought, one hand clutched his arm and squeezed and the other struck out and clawed his face, scrapin away skin. I gasped and drew back.

Poppy wasn't gonna like that I'd laid a hand to his boy. Never mind that his *boy* was a grown man.

For a second, Gerald's eyes glassed over. He looked confused, hurt. Like he was a youngin again. Then they turned icier than the wind whippin round us. He wheeled around. To go tattle, I reckoned, just like a youngin. Might as well finish gatherin the laundry before Momma started hollerin for me. The clothes was done froze solid.

"Come on. Turn around, Devil girl."

I spun on my heels. A rock the size of a melon smashed into the side of my head. My knees grew weak and a curtain of darkness slowly covered my eyes. I felt my head droop to my chest and the cold bite of the winter snow as my cheek hit the ground.

———

My jaw ached and I could only open my right eye. Overhead hung a boulder just wide enough to shelter me. A small fire smoldered a few steps away. I raised myself up on my elbows, but that small movement made it feel like the ground was spinnin under me.

I come into this world with this purplish-red mark coverin the side of my face and neck, and there was nothin I could do to change it. I knew from the time I bent over the edge of the riverbank and seen my reflection in the crystal-clear water, this curse that covered my face would be my death. Creamy-colored skin, long black curls, golden eyes, and that . . . that horrid mark.

The Devil'd marked me. Leastways, that's what Poppy and Momma told me. Satan burned his mark on me before I was born, so they called me the Devil's daughter.

"You shoulda died. Shoulda been kilt." Momma never missed a chance to remind me I was a stray picked up outa the woods. I'd been left there to die by my real momma. Left there to be eaten by wolves.

A blanket laid heavy on me. Heavier than any I'd ever felt before. I pushed it aside. My head throbbed. I put my hand to it and yelped. A shot of pain was a hard reminder of the rock. My hair was plastered to my head. I took my hand away and saw red on my fingers, remembered the knife. Even with the cold, a trickle of blood dripped over my marked cheek. Blood never seemed to clot over that mark. Was it the heat of hell that seeped from it? I felt a pang of sorrow over what I'd done. I didn't mean to hurt Gerald. He and Momma and Poppy was the only family I knew. And now here I was, left out to die again.

The ground slowly came to a standstill. "Poppy? Poppy, where are you?" The wind whipped and danced around the ledge, whistlin an eerie melody.

I crawled to my feet. Not a soul in sight. Nothin but the tips of the summits liftin like fingers through the foggy mist.

"Poppppyyyy!"

My voice echoed off the summit.

"Aaghh!" I beat my fists against the rock ledge. The pain in my chest felt like someone had ripped me clean down the middle with a knife. And my spirit broke. Shattered into little pieces all over that mountainside.

TWO

MOMMA'S WORDS DUG into my soul like a dog scrabblin at the ground for a rat. They was nothin but an echo, comin back at me over and over. *"You oughta be grateful Poppy saved you. You woulda been killed. So, you pray hard the Devil hisself don't come lookin for you. 'Cause from the day you was born, your soul belonged to the Devil. We tried to save you even after he had done marked you as his."* She was relentless, wavin a cross all round my head. Over and over sayin them same words.

Fear crawled under my covers at night and nearly took my breath while I waited for Satan to slither into the loft and eat my soul, layin claim to me.

I scooped a handful of snow and pressed it into an icy ball. *Cover my eye or bite into it?* I was thirsty, so I bit. The dampness of the snow quenched my thirst, icy water runnin down my throat. Despite the cold, I sweated under my threadbare coat.

A neat pile of sticks and arm sized branches lay to one side of the tiny fire. Shoved into the crevice of the rock overhang was a bag.

On my hands and knees, I made my way to the leather bag. Maybe Gerald had an ounce of conscience after all. Leavin me somethin. But it seemed odd the one who wanted me dead would leave me a nibble of hope. Maybe Poppy left it.

I grabbed hold and opened it. Bread and potatoes. I wanted to cry, but considerin the cold, I decided it was best to keep my eyes dry lest they freeze shut. On the ground, a set of tracks, boots bigger than my feet, marked the mud. I wondered if Gerald had hauled me up here. He surely wouldn't have built me a fire, though, seein how he wanted me dead. Poppy, most likely.

Maybe Poppy felt bad for what Gerald had done and felt some shame. He wouldn't want me dead. Poppy cared some, or I thought he did.

The breeze cut across the gap, tearin clean through me. That's the way it is on the mountain unless you're lucky enough to be on the side that turns its back to the wind. Them hills can shelter a body or open them up to be froze solid.

I fingered the spotty portions of ankle-deep snow. *Another month 'til spring.* The clouds hung heavy. I remember Poppy tellin me these mountains was called Smoky for a reason. On days like this, a body could look across the pass and see a smoky mist of clouds risin so thick you could scratch lines in them.

I pressed my hand over my good eye and shaded a clouded sun. If I could just get my bearings and figure out where the sun sat in the sky, I could get a good idea of the time. From where I stood I couldn't tell east from west but I knew from the sun hoverin overhead it was midday.

"Looks to be close to noon."

The voice boomed from behind a stand of trees and I jumped like a scared cat.

A tall, lanky man stepped into sight, his arms filled with firewood. Jet-black hair streaked with silver hung to his shoulders and the weathering in his face put him about Poppy's age. He leaned and spit a stream of amber juice long as his arm.

"You tryin to figure the time? That's good. Good to see you're up and about." The man came closer. "Cat got your tongue?"

He eased the wood to the ground and untied a dead rabbit from his belt.

I stared as he worked his way around the fire, jabbin sticks into the gaps between the logs. Close to noon. It had been drawin on supper time when I was takin down the wash.

"You was out for a spell. I was beginnin to figure you wouldn't never come round."

He heaved up a large log and placed it in the center of the flame. Embers jumped toward the greyish sky. The fire gnawed at the bark, sparkin and risin high enough to warm my numbed hands. "We need to build this fire up. Get plenty of hot coals to last when night falls."

He took hold of a branch and brushed away the snow. "Don't just stand there starin. Clear the snow so the ground'll heat and dry a bit. Lest you wanna be sleepin on a froze ground again."

Snow spotted the dirt and the midday sun teased us with just enough warmth to fool us. *Liar's winter*—the time when the mountain fights with winter and spring not knowin whether to warm the ground or chill a body to the bone. More times than not, a spring rain would eat up a winter storm and the sky would spit both at the ground. When them storms come, the elements fight 'til one wins out over the other. If the snow won, it would be a deep, wet snow—heavy on the trees, droppin limbs to the ground just to show its might. If it be rain, then it would be a toad choker.

"I see you and your brother had a brawl."

"How d'you know 'bout me and Gerald?"

"Whole mountain knows the legend. A family raisin the Devil's daughter. Keepin her hid away. Course that's just legend. Never knew it was true. Least not 'til I seen her with my own eyes." He kicked a lit log closer to the fire. "I was passin by with my goods when I come upon your little brawl. Kept outa sight. Family feuds ain't none of my business."

"You ain't screamed and run yet. How come?" I crossed my arms and tucked my hands in my armpits. "Poppy always told me if folks saw me they'd either run or turn to kill me."

The man pushed his hat back, his smile as warm as the fire. "You seen many folks?"

"A few."

He nodded. "*A few* ain't many. Don't give a body a lot to judge on, now does it?"

I wasn't sure what to say.

"Well, I reckon everbody has a story." He added a new log to the fire. "Ain't my place to judge. Leastways, that's what my momma always taught us youngins. I figure every soul deserves a fair treatin."

I stepped closer. "You ain't blind are you? I mean, you can see this here mark that plagues me?"

"My eyes is pretty crisp. I can spot a doe huddled in a thicket." He laid down an armload of brush under the overhang, scattered it out a bit.

"Well, ain't you scared? Afraid I'll hex you? Maybe you ought not come too close. I don't know my powers yet."

"I ain't too bothered by you. Don't got much to be scared of." He continued to pack and spread brush on the pile. Then he lifted his foot and stepped into the center of it, crushin it and pressin it down.

"This will make you a warm nest tonight, and we'll pray to the good Lord for rain and not snow." He nodded toward the black cloud hoverin over the summit.

I didn't know him from a hole in the wall. He coulda been a bootlegger for all I knew. A murderer. Rustler. Poppy warned me against the dangers in the world. Especially harborin this mark and all. He said strangers'd just as soon slaughter me as wait for me to conjure up the Devil. That's why I had to hide whenever someone happened by, watchin 'em through the cracks in the shed.

"You got a name?" He tinkered with a stick in the fire.

I pressed a handful of snow against my swollen eye. "I reckon I can ask you the same question. But seein as how you know all about me, I figure you already know my name."

The man stuffed a wad of tobacco between his lip and jaw. He wasn't ignorin me, but he wasn't answerin either. He worked the chaw around a bit, then spit. Still nothin.

I gathered another handful of snow. His silence rankled. My fist squeezed around that snow and I whipped it at his head. "Low-kill. That's how you speak my name. You got it? Lochiel."

The snow crumbled against his shoulder. "Well, Miss Lochiel. Name's Grubbs. Walton Grubbs. I live across the gap."

THREE

"You know, there is a lot in a body's name. My momma is part Cherokee and so she give me the Indian name Blue Water. Means free movin. So I reckon my name set me in life, bein as I'm a peddler and all."

"Your momma is Cherokee?" I'd heard Poppy talk about Indians. He told me stories about them campin on the other side of the ridge.

"Part. Her momma's womanhood was shared with a slave. That made my momma a Melungeon—Indian and slave mixed. And so it's passed on. Been called a half-breed the biggest part of my life. But seein as I carry a wagon of goods, ain't many folks who turn me away. But you, on the other hand"—he pointed a finger at my face. The skin around his nails was cracked and rough from hard work—"you got a mark to contend with."

A burst of heat from within flamed from my face. The Devil in me tryin to work his way out. I tried to shoot fire from my eyes—that's what Gerald woulda called it—but I reckon my swollen shut eye stopped that from workin. "I've heard Poppy talk about half-breeds. You don't look no different."

"Blood that runs through the veins is still blood. It's the man that makes it different. I reckon you know about bein different, though. We're a lot the same."

"How do ya figure that? People call you the Devil too?"

Walton went to waggin his head from side to side. "Lawsey, no. Ain't nobody ever called me a devil, 'cept maybe my brother when I poked at him as a kid."

"There's two of you?" I raised a brow.

"Was. Not no more. My brother died of the fever a few years back." He hung his head.

I leaned toward the fire, facin my palms near the warmth of the flame. "Then I ain't seein no likeness betwixt the two of us."

He cocked his head and sighed. "If you have to know, the Cherokee ain't exactly the ripe pick for a neighbor. With a name like Blue Water, a body can't exactly hide from who they are. That's why I took on Walton. Folks can't tag me like a deer."

If there was one thing that held true amongst the mountain people, it was givin their youngins names that held some meaning. Momma said as much. She given Gerald his name 'cause he come out of the womb demandin to be king.

But my name—my name was meaningless. Like Momma just walked out on the mountain and made up a word to call me. *Lochiel.* Empty. Lost. Nothing. Alone . . .

I'd been cryin as Momma, Poppy, and Gerald climbed into the wagon to ride into Etowah. I reckon I was about five or so. Poppy'd roped me to the porch post so I couldn't wander off.

"This here is for your own good." He looped the rope around my waist and knotted it several times. "Don't you dare take that off," he'd said. "This way you don't wander off where you ain't safe." Poppy always made it his business to keep me safe.

I'd never dared mess with them knots either, not that time or any other.

"You stay close to the cabin," he'd said. "This here rope is long enough for you to get to the outhouse and water trough. You can get in the house, and bar the door if you stand on the chair." Eventually I didn't need to stand on the chair. "You'll be safe tied to the house. Momma left you biscuits. You'll be fine. Remember this is for your own good. People won't take to you bearin that mark."

I'd sobbed into the air and wailed like a wolf at the moon, but Poppy'd just pressed his finger against my mouth real gentle-like and shushed me.

"Now, Lochiel," he'd said. "You get in that house. And remember, there's folks who has things a lot worse than you. You remember that. You got a roof over your head, clothes, and food."

So maybe this was one of them folks that had it worse than me—bein a half-breed and all. I stole a glance Walton's direction. The Devil in me cooled. "I'm sorry. I didn't know."

"And now that you do, does it change your mind about me?" He handed me a chunk of hard bread.

"Course not." How could my mind be changed when I didn't hardly know him at all? He was actin gentle. But maybe he was just plumb crazy. Either way, he wasn't the least bit scared.

I'd finally figured it was Walton who'd drug me to shelter and built me a fire, not Gerald or Poppy.

He ran his finger between his gum and jaw then scraped out the chaw of tobacco and tossed it to the edge of the fire. The coals sizzled as they ate the damp spit.

"There you have it. I think no less of you because of that mark on your face. We are alike."

I bit hard into the bread, my eyes fixed on the fire's flame. I still couldn't figure on how we were alike but the idea had a kindness in it, so I didn't disagree again.

Walton cleaned the rabbit carcass and hung it on a stick over the flame. The scent of fresh-cooked meat made my mouth water.

He grabbed his knife and swiped it clean against his trousers; then in one swift motion, he split the rabbit in half.

"Here." He handed me the stick with my portion. "You need to eat, put some meat on your bones."

At home, Momma'd feed the meat to the men. I got taters, kale, and bread. As I held that stick, I felt the weight of the man's kindness. It felt burdensome somehow.

"See them clouds over the ridge?"

I nodded.

"Looks like rain. A body would have figured for more snow, but them is black clouds. Spring's easin over the mountain. We need to get us some shelter set before the rain comes."

So we ate. Said little. Then Walton burrowed out a spot deep under the rock's overhang. He carried hot coals over and dropped them in.

"In case the fire gets rained out," he said. "Now, you spread your blanket over that brush so it stays dry. Lay on that. You'll need it once it starts to rain."

"Where you goin to rest?" I did what he said.

"Oh, you don't worry 'bout me. I got me a camp just down the mountain a bit."

My chest hurt and it was hard to grab a breath. I clutched the front of my coat. What if Gerald come back? As many times as I was left alone as a youngin, I couldn't bear the thought of bein alone out in the open. Didn't feel safe out here in the open spaces.

He was gatherin stones and makin a ring around the coals. "Now, Miss Lochiel, I'll be within earshot. Don't you worry none." Walton smiled. "You ain't scared are you?"

I stared into his eyes. "No, I ain't scared." It was a lie. But he didn't need to know that the dark got me shakin like a newborn pup.

He patted my shoulder as he walked past and quick as a wink I slapped his hand away.

He paused and looked me in the eye. He didn't look angry. "Now, you listen good to me. We ain't never alone. That's a promise the good Lord made us. We ain't never alone."

I wasn't sure what he meant by that 'cause he was fixin to leave me.

I opened my mouth to speak but nothin come out.

He poured an extra cup of coffee into a leather water pouch. "Keep that close to the coals, and it'll stay warm." He gave me another blanket and a knife.

I watched as he packed up to leave. Like Momma and Poppy readyin the wagon. Only there wasn't no rope on me this time.

"Let's have that question, girl. Spit it out."

I stuttered as the chill in the air set my teeth to chatterin. "Wh-where will I go? What do I d-do?"

He leaned against the rock and shoved his hat to the back of his head. He scratched at his chin.

He pointed to my feet. "You start here." He lifted his hand and pointed over the mountain. "Then go to there. And you never stop 'til you find what feels like home. My best guess is, you'll know it when you find it."

Walton dug into his pouch. He held out the rest of his bread until I took it from his hand. "Stay up under here 'til the rain passes. That little flame has warmed the cliff rocks. That should keep you snug as a bug in a rug." He knelt at my feet. "Lord, I ask for your protection over this young woman. Guide her to the name you have give her. One that has meanin."

I looked around. "Who you talkin to?"

He raised his head. "That's not talkin, that's prayin. Walton Grubbs prays over everthin. I figure you got some smarts about you. It'll come to you. But I'll tell you this. My momma always told me the good Lord is a person you find. But for Him, He's done found you. And you best get to figurin, 'cause you're gonna need the help of the Almighty."

That made about as much sense as a fly in hot butter. He stood and brushed his knee with his hat as if what he'd said settled the matter.

"Since you seem to know it all, you reckon Gerald thinks I'm dead? Or do you think I oughta sleep with one eye open?"

There was no answer. Walton fed the fire and stacked the extra firewood under the ledge.

"Figures," I said, pushin a rock closer to the fire.

A cold wind rushed around the side of the bluff, causin the blaze to flicker. I watched as the flames licked at the bark. I pulled the extra blanket tight around my shoulders.

"I reckon you was right. The rocks is warm from the fire."

"Yep. Well, my momma raised a wise old bird. Now you get you some rest."

Over the mountain, the clouds bumped and rumbled. An echo to the throbbin in my head. As drops of rain commenced to fall, Walton's lanky figure vanished into the thick woods.

FOUR

I AIN'T RIGHT sure when I nodded off. But it was the smell of smoke blowin in my face that woke me. The wind had taken an upturn. Its gusts were like hands fannin at the base of the flame, spittin water into the coals and causin the fire to struggle. Smoke billowed and hung under the rock ledge.

I grabbed a stick and poked the bowl of coals, tossin on a small log to kindle the fire under my ledge.

I could only hope for some mercy from the gusts. My eyes burned, but I managed to clear the white fog from my shelter. I'd never, in my whole life, been off the homestead. Didn't have no idea what laid beyond what I could see from the porch of the cabin, and I was torn between fear and wonderin. Lost is what was and what was to come. Right this minute, in the midst of this mess, my lips was wetted with a drop of freedom and it made me thirsty. Real thirsty.

I looked out into pitch black. No stars. No moon. Just the dark. For all them times I'd swallowed loneliness at Momma and Poppy's, this beat the tar outa them.

My teeth chattered from the cold, and though what was left of the snow seemed to have melted around me, it didn't stop the nippy dampness from seepin into my bones. Odd thing was, outside of the rain, there was no sound. It was like every animal on the mountain had burrowed into a hole to beat the nip.

And here I was. A sorry sight. My hurt eye cracked open just enough for me to peer through. I run my fingers up my cheek, and the tips dropped into the clotted gash above my brow. Walton had tossed me a rag, told me to press it to my head, but it hurt too bad.

I don't reckon I'd ever hated a soul before, but I guess there was a time for everthing. Every throb of my head made me hate Gerald just a little more.

The dirty dog was sly and connivin. I reckon it happened little by little. Once we got in a brawl and Gerald was sittin on me, holdin me down. He was already a man, but still set out to pester me whenever he had an inkling.

"Let me up, Gerald," I screamed. But he pushed my hands harder against the ground. Poppy stood on the porch, smokin his pipe. I squirmed enough to draw my knee up hard, between his legs, forcin him to holler and turn me loose.

Poppy purt near cried over him. "Lochiel, you hurt my boy."

"Aw, Poppy." I'd sat up and brushed my hair back from my face. "I knocked the wind out of the demon. He ain't dead."

That's when Poppy turned on me. "He ain't no demon. Gerald's a good boy. It's you that carries the evil." Poppy gave me up right then and there.

Up to that point, Poppy had kept an eye out over me. Momma made no bones about my place, but Poppy—he kinda kept Gerald at bay. He protected me some.

Poppy gently patted Gerald's scruffy cheek. "Come on, Son. Open your eyes."

Gerald pulled open his lids and, for a minute, I was disappointed that they opened.

"Wipe that smile off your face, Lochiel!" Poppy shrieked at me as he pulled Gerald up into his arms. "What's happened here ain't funny."

"I never said it was funny, Poppy." I tried to lay my hand on Poppy's shoulder, but he shrugged it off like I'd burned him.

"Don't you never lay a hand on me or my boy ever again." That was the last time I touched another person, until yesterday.

It took a good many years before I boiled over and struck Gerald again. Now, here I set, alone on the mountain in a downpour. Maybe Poppy was the one that set me out to die this time.

My stomach begin to rumble as I stared into the yellow blaze of my little fire, my face growin hot from the warmth. I pulled Walton's bag off the stick where it hung and fingered the tie. Inside was two hard potatoes and a towel with some fatback rolled in it.

It didn't take long for me to get a hankerin for one of them taters. Sticky juice dripped from the tater as I scraped away the peel. That knife'd sure come in handy. I stabbed into its flesh like I was guttin a squirrel, then balanced it against a log at the edge of the fire. I never got good at peelin taters like Momma. She'd start at one end and trim the peel like a snake sheddin its skin—twirlin and twistin one long cord.

The tater sizzled as the flames brought its juices to a boil. The scent of the potato spun around my head. Peeled or scraped, it set my mouth to waterin.

I slowly twisted the potato to warm it through. Tears welled in the corners of my eyes. When Poppy shoved my hand away, it broke my heart. I reckon I broke his first by hittin Gerald.

Despite what they was, I loved them. I needed to love, and they was all I had.

There ain't much worse than the dark. The kind of dark I was staring into now. My mind can conjure up some horrible things from the dark. And them times I laid in the corner of the loft as a youngin and tried to hide, the horrors never went away. They just grew bigger.

When Momma and Poppy left me at the house whilst they went into town, I dreaded nightfall most. Alone in the loft, the darkness of night pressed down on me so hard I could hardly breathe. There wasn't a thing I could do but cry. Cry and plead that the Devil wouldn't sneek up the ladder and eat my soul.

In the log and the flame, I could see the face of the Devil hisself, his hot tongue lashin out, tryin to get me. My tater shook on the end of that knife, and I raised my face to the sky.

"Poppy, I'm sorry!" My words quivered and disappeared in the dark. "Please don't leave me up here. Please, Poppy. I've learned my lesson. I won't never hit Gerald again." That taste of freedom turned on me. What I had wasn't much, but it was better than freezin to death.

I called out across the mountain. "I've learned my lesson." But there was no answer, just the sound of the rain. And then my heart broke open. "Don't leave me." I dropped the potato stick and hugged my knees to my chest. Sobs rung out over the ridge as I let loose the wails that ached inside me. "Don't leave me. Don't leave me." My pent-up sorrow spilled on the already wet ground. Tears made their way down the side of my nose and over the busted lip. The salty water burned the cuts, a different pain to ponder on.

My squallin shifted to hummin with each jagged exhale.

And then, after a time, shuddered to a stop.

I wiped my nose with the tail of my skirt and opened my good eye. The Devil's face was gone and just the firelight remained. I picked up the potato. Steam curled and danced in the cool misty air as I gently blew across the vegetable. I twirled the tater and stared into the darkness, waitin for someone to take it from me. No one did. Proof I was alone. For the first time, alone—scary as it was—wasn't the worst thing that could happen to a body.

As I bit into the tater, through the rush of the rain I caught sight of somethin.

"Who's there?" I pulled the knife from the tater, clenchin the handle in my hand. "I saw you. Show yourself."

My heart raced like a runaway wagon. I eased back from the light of the fire. If it was Gerald, at least I had a knife.

A child—a boy soaked to the bone—peeked from around a tree.

"What do you want?"

The child froze like a squirrel spotted by a coonhound, and then he inched toward my fire.

"What do you want?" I repeated.

I ain't sure which of us was the scardest. He craned his head to one side, lookin me over.

"Ain't you got nothin to say? Sneakin around here like a fox."

The boy moved closer, close enough to see me clear, then lifted his hand and gently touched the mark on my cheek. I flinched and shoved him away. There was a minute when the Devil pushed at me to jump at him and scare the whiz outa him, but I remembered what it was like to be scared.

"It's true." His words sent chills down my arm. The boy gasped and, like a shot, tore into the darkness.

Gone. Alone again. Poppy was right. My mark had scared him off. My heart split open. Was this what the rest of my days was gonna be like?

The night drug on, endless as the runnin river. I glanced around the small camp Walton had set up. I'd never had such a thick, warm blanket before, much less two. Momma's quilts was thin and small, never really coverin a body good.

Nobody ever built me a fire. And they certainly never allowed me a full potato to myself. Everthing at the table was divided. Poppy and Gerald gettin the most and Momma and me gettin less. And bread, well, I got good at sneakin a biscuit from the skillet.

Yet there I sat. Rain dousin the ground, and I was pretty dry. I had a blanket under me, and one around my shoulders, food to myself, and not a soul naggin at me about the mark on my face.

I was alone—a good alone, I think. There was somethin freein about just cryin it out. When a body's done, it's like a weight is lifted. I was on my own with no promise of how long Walton would be around. I'd best pull myself up by the bootstraps and take charge.

I unlaced my shoes and leaned my feet against the warm rocks around the fire. They tingled and twinged. For a minute, I wasn't sure if it hurt 'cause they was gettin burned, or if it hurt 'cause they was gettin thawed. I decided on thawed.

I can't say I begrudged Momma and Poppy. After all, I wasn't their child. They was good enough to pick me up and keep me from dyin. And I ain't ungrateful. They protected me from people who might've killed me.

But this here man, Walton, he was different. What was in it for him? Why'd he feel the need to help me?

There was more questions than there was answers. I didn't understand his kindness or his purpose. And as much as I wanted to run from this old man, there was somethin about him that drew me in. Maybe it was because he said we was alike. Him bein a half-breed. I reckon he knew what it felt like to be shoved away. I pulled the blanket tighter around my shoulders.

I can't figure this. I can't make out how come this man wants to help me. Better yet, he don't seem to want nothin in return.

I slipped my feet into my boots and tied the strings. For the first time since fall, they didn't ache from the cold. The rain picked up and thunder rumbled through the valley. By mornin, there'd be little snow left on the mountain.

I stoked the fire once more, this time droppin on two good-sized logs. *That oughta last 'til mornin.* With my belly full, my feet warm, I was dry under the ledge.

Walton had done me a favor. I reckon I owed him. My eyes grew heavy and though I was wary of fallin asleep, my head was tellin me to rest.

A howl echoed off the summit. Then a second, and a third. Darkness outside the glow of my fire closed around me like a fog. The wolves called to the wind. A crack of lightning lit up the mountain and I could see the outline of the wolf standin, rain washin over his fur, head arched and nose to the sky, howlin, callin out to the pack. Waitin.

Waitin for me to close my eyes.

FIVE

"Git up! Now, Lochiel! We ain't got no time to tarry. Lochiel. Git up!"

I come off the pile of brush like I'd been stung with a brandin iron.

My heart skipped. "What's goin on?"

"They're comin. Help me. Quick." His voice was a hoarse whisper as he kicked at the coals. "Grab your things. Get anything that looks like you was here."

"I ain't got nothin. There ain't a thing somebody could hook to me. Who's comin?"

Walton grabbed a handful of tater peels and mud, then waved it in my face. "I said get anything that looks like you was here. I mean *anything*."

He commenced to heave the brush and limbs he'd collected for the fire over the side of the mountain. I stood starin, dazed.

Walton grabbed my arm and shook hard. "Lochiel, lest you want to meet your maker in the next few minutes, hop to it." Gerald must be on the hunt. And the prey was me.

Walton put the leather bag filled with food in my hand. Then he pulled his knife from its sheath and yanked up the tail of my dress.

I screamed but couldn't force my legs to run.

"Hush. I ain't gonna hurt you." He rammed the blade into the material and cut until the dress that hung to my ankles now dangled just below my knees.

"You need to be able to move fast." He pressed the scrap into my hand. "Put that somewhere."

I stood gapin at him.

"Look at me." Walton clapped his hands in front of my face, his voice sharp. "You stop this manure. Pay me some mind. I'm tryin to help you. Now listen to me."

"Alright."

"There was a youngin on this mountain last night. Did you see him?"

"I talked to him."

Walton slung his head from side to side. "Ay, law."

"What? What's wrong?"

"He was a sentry for Gerald. Sent up the mountain to see if you was alive or dead. I reckon you failed the dead part seein as you're still standin."

"You mean Gerald wasn't sure I was dead?"

"Well, are you?"

"Of course not."

Walton worked like a beaver gnawin at a tree to clear the campsite. "He needed to be sure you was dead. Cover his tracks. So he sent a youngin up to do his dirty work. I followed him a piece 'til I saw him meet up with Gerald. You was lucky the rain was heavy last night. Held him off a bit."

Fear crawled up my spine like a spider.

"Gerald has convinced a posse that he's found the Devil's daughter and for their families to be safe they need to hunt her down. Put an end to her. They're headin up the mountain. They're lookin for you. I done seen you knocked silly once by him. Got no plans of seein it again."

He glanced around the camp. With a piece of bush, he swept away any signs of fire.

"You *saw* Gerald hit me?" Walton glared and motioned for me to help.

I stuffed the blankets under my arm. The mud on the mountainside would easily fill in our footprints.

"That away." Walton pointed to a dense stand of trees. "Go!"

I'd never felt like an animal before. Leastways not a hunted one. Is this how a buck felt to be hunted? It wasn't the time to ask questions.

Now I ran.

Briars snagged the skin around my knees, tearin shreds of flesh from my legs. Warm droplets of blood oozed from the nicks and poured down my calves.

The woods on top of the summit were thick. Limbs—even after the

storm—still hung low, bent downward from the weight of the winter
snows. Evergreens scratched at my face as I plunged through the thicket.

"Don't slow down."

I didn't argue. Whatever Gerald had in mind, I didn't want to stick
around for it. He was none too nice last time. The gash on my head proved
that. My lungs ached for air, but I pushed through the forest. In the back
of my mind, I was makin a list of things that didn't add up. Things like
why this stranger was helpin me. Why he wasn't scared of me. Why he
cared that someone was tryin to kill the Devil's daughter.

Walton wrapped his giant hand around my elbow and edged me
around a large boulder. The strings of my boot hung up in a stand of
thorns, takin my feet out from under me. What little wind I had in my
lungs was shoved out.

"Get up. Come on."

I tried to stand, but the giant thorns were like a bear trap. They dug
into the leather of my boots, holdin me tight while the trappers made
their way to the catch. Fear bubbled in my gut, forcin me to panic, but
Walton come behind me and grabbed under my arms.

"When I pull, you shake them feet with all your might. You ready?"

I nodded, my chest heavin and my lungs burnin.

"On three. One. Two. Three."

I kicked with all the might I could muster. The prickly vines snapped
and I was free.

"Now, come on. Ain't much farther."

As fast as we'd run up and over the summit, we headed down the other
side, grabbin at saplings and small pines to hold steady.

"Where we headin?" I wrapped my arms, blankets and all, around a
tree to keep from slippin over the edge of the mountain. My foot dug
into the wet, ankle-deep pine needles. As I hugged a sapling, the sun
came peerin over the edge of the mountaintops. "East. We're headin
east?"

"Yep." Walton hesitated and took in the mornin sun. "Good Lord
paints a new picture every mornin. It's a sight, ain't it?"

"You got time to look at the sunrise?" I snapped.

"A body has to catch a breath. Might as well look at somethin beautiful."

Walton stooped a bit, hands on his knees, breathin heavy. So I looked back toward the east.

Clouds strung across the sky, meltin from purple to pink, and then streaks of orange and yellow bled in—just like somebody had dipped their fingers in the sun and dragged them across the sky.

I took in a deep breath of clean air.

"Let's go. Move. The good Lord will forgive us for not gawkin any longer." Walton stepped around me and lifted his finger. "There. Behind them trees there's a clearin. I got my wagon and horses hid down there."

We worked our way down to the clearing. Though I had not yet heard Gerald or his posse, I found myself, for a second time, relyin on this stranger. I couldn't put my finger on how that made me feel.

Walton's chest heaved from the long run and his voice seemed to stick in his throat when he spoke. Still, he never slowed and he didn't let me tarry neither.

"I reckon you managed to make an enemy yesterday." Walton pushed a dead limb to the side.

"I think we was enemies long before yesterday. I just never stood up to Gerald before then."

"You believe that story, don't you?"

"What story?" I grunted as I tripped over a hidden stump.

"You believe the legends. All that mess about bein the Devil's daughter."

I stopped. "I carry the mark. Had it when I come from my momma's loins, so I was left out to die fresh outa the womb."

"Hogwash."

"My momma feared for her life. Said she thought if she didn't kill me, I'd hex everone on the mountain."

"How do you know what your momma thought? All you know is what you was told."

We broke through the dense forest into a field. The tall grass had browned through the winter snows. I stepped into the foliage.

"No. Stop." Walton huffed and motioned toward the clearing. "Walk the edge of the woods. Don't get in the field. Your prints will hang on. The horses and wagon are on the lower side."

I realized how dumb about the world I was. I could cook up a mean mess of collard greens and onions, but I had hardly been past the river. If a body tried real hard, they could throw a rock to the riverbank from our house. My smarts on the world outside stopped at the end of that rope Momma and Poppy tied me with.

We edged along the tree line, spotting the wagon in the lower field.

"Where's the horses? There ain't no horses."

"Simmer down. You don't think I'd leave my team out in the open, do you?"

He bobbed his head toward the patch of wild hay where two black horses grazed.

"They're beautiful." I inched toward one mare, my head just to her shoulder "I ain't never seen a horse this big."

"Them's workhorses. Built to pull logs. Now stop gawkin and untie them reins."

I untied the horse's reins and led her through the woods to the wagon. Walton walked the other one along and lined the horses up side by side. Puttin the leather straps in his mouth, he leaned and heaved the yoke upward. It was a sight to watch as he flicked his head to the side, tuggin on the reins. The horses slowly backed into the yoke. He hitched the leather straps to the harness and slipped the bridles into the horses' mouths. He motioned me into the wagon.

"Ain't you plumb useful? Hitchin them horses all by yourself."

"Body does what a body has to."

Walton smacked the reins and the horses groaned as the wagon loosened from the mire. Sweat beaded in the deep crevices of his forehead. He hauled off and spit as the wagon pulled free.

It seemed the time to ask some questions. How did Walton happen to see the boy? How'd he know to follow him to see what he was up to? "Didn't you sleep at all last night?" I asked.

"Lochiel, you ask more questions than a youngin and all at the worst times. There'll be time to answer questions, but right now ain't it."

"You're sweatin." I offered him the scrap he'd cut from my skirt.

He took it and swiped his face with it. "Did *you* sleep?" he asked.

"Them wolves howlin didn't give me much chance."

"Rest ain't all it's made out to be. Especially when a body's on the run."

"Poppy always likes it when it rains. Says it gives him a good night's sleep. I reckon all it gives me is cold hands."

Hounds howled on the upper crest of the mountain. Their voices callin out to the hunted. The hunted, meanin me.

Walton slapped the leather reins against the horses. "Haigh there, horses. Haigh!" The wagon jarred and we commenced to rumble across the bumpy field and onto a backwoods path.

The dogs howled again. I could tell by their bark, they'd picked up my smell.

Walton reached over the seat into a wooden box. He pulled out a shirt and overalls.

"Crawl over and put these on. Do it now! We got to rid them dogs of your scent."

I bounced into the bed of the wagon and ripped my dress over my head. I pulled on the shirt and overalls.

"Stuff them old clothes in this bag. When we cross the shallow of the river, you throw that bag as hard as you can into the rush." Walton drew the team to a halt and jumped onto the ground. Snaggin a good-sized rock, he shoved it at me and crawled back into the seat.

"Put that in too, so the bag will sink."

We rounded a sharp bend and there in front of us lay the river. The horses splashed into the water, and the wagon jumped the riverbed like skippin rocks.

Halfway across the river, Walton squalled. "Do it now! Throw out that bag."

I spun the strap of the bag and let it fly over my head into the hard rush of the river. The rapids swallowed it like a hungry bear.

For the time being, there was no sign of me to be found.

SIX

THE HORSES' BACKS shined as flicks of perspiration caught in the wind, damping my face as we raced along the gap. Walton pushed them hard to put some distance between us and Gerald. My rear was sore from all the bouncin around on the wagon bench.

"That there turn is Sulton's Bend. It's a hard turn. Hold tight. We ain't slowin down 'til we get to the other side." Walton was right. When we took the turn at Sultan's Bend, the wagon tipped up on two wheels. The goods in the wagon rattled and clanged until we come upon a smooth path. We'd made the turn in one piece.

"Whoa there, team. Ho." With a lurch that nearly slid me from my seat, the team slowed to a halt. "You did me good, mares. I reckon you earned a rest."

Walton climbed from the bench and gently patted one horse's rear, then worked his fingers up her back. His arm slipped around her neck and he pulled her head close to scratch her nose. I could hear him whisper praise as he stroked her.

"You love them horses," I said, standin to stretch my legs.

"Man can't have a better friend. Both these gals have been better to me than a house full of wives."

I wasn't sure if I was supposed to laugh. It sounded like Walton was bein funny, but then it didn't. My curiosity got the best of me.

"Ain't you got no wife?"

Walton eased around the second horse. "I try to love on my gals equal. They're hard workin."

"That tells me you got no desire to answer." I rubbed my sore hip.

"I reckon you figured that about right." He scrubbed his hands together then shoved them into his pockets, made his way back to the wagon. "We got a minute before we need to make our way across the gap. There's some sourdough bread in that box behind you."

I twisted and heaved open the heavy slat lid. The tart smell of yeast crept from the box.

"Woowee, that makes my mouth water."

Walton swiped his blade on his shirt, then sliced a thick piece of sourdough. "Sorry there ain't no time for coffee. We need to put as much betwixt us and Gerald as we can."

"Where we headed?" I bit into the tough crust.

"Thunder Mountain, thereabouts. I have some friends who might take in a couple of misfits."

"I'm much obliged for your help." That's the kind of thing Poppy would say when someone would come our way to help patch the roof or lend a hand layin fence. Whenever someone come by, I knew I was to hustle out of sight, into the loft, the shed, or the root cellar—whatever was quickest at the time. But I found spots where I could still peek out or at least listen.

"Not to worry. I saw a need and stepped up."

"It's mighty kind of you. Takin a woman under wing who's all busted up." I eyed him to get a hint of what he wanted.

Walton dug the heel of his boot into the ground and burrowed out a hole. He cracked open a rimmed barrel in the wagon and ladled out some water for the horses.

"We'll let the girls cool down and then be on our way."

From the narrowed-out holler where Poppy's cabin stood, there was little else of the world we could see past our homestead, yet I could look up and see the mountains were beautiful. The air was fresh, like the smell of clothes off the line. Sunshine and river water add a scent to a shirt that, when a body closes their eyes, draws a picture of white, puffy clouds. And if Momma had a fire brewin close by, them shirts would have a hint of applewood.

"Walton?"

He raised his head from between the horses. "Yeah?"

"I don't mean to seem hateful toward Momma and Poppy."

"What in tarnation are you talkin about?" He stepped over the guide board and leaned against the wagon.

I glanced toward the footrest. "I know Momma and Poppy did their best. And well, me and Gerald has always been like melted lard and water, never mixin. But they always give me what I needed, protected me from strangers, never raised a hand against me."

Walton commenced to pace along the side of the wagon, like he had somethin on his mind that was achin to get out. He took in a breath and wheeled around with his fingers curled into a fist.

"You feel sorry for them?" His fist thumped the side of the wagon, and I jumped.

"Rumors was there was a marked child, hid away, made out to be a slave. I hear folks down near Chattanooga talkin 'bout slaves. That's what it sounds like you was—a slave. Then that Gerald nearly kills you and he drops you off on the side of a mountain like a dead animal left to rot. There ain't nothin for you to feel grateful about." Walton's voice rose. "Good land! Their son is huntin you like an animal. You need to toughen your hide."

I stared eye-to-eye with Walton. His nose flared. He seemed pretty sure of what he was sayin. But I couldn't say as I agreed. They saved me from bein killed as a baby. Took me in, give me a home. They was the only family I had—despite their fear of me.

I pressed my hand into my hip. "Who told you rumors about me? Ain't many ever come around the homestead. I was always real careful not to be seen."

Turnin away, Walton edged around the front of the horses and readied them to move.

"I asked you a question."

"I heard." His voice sounded hard.

He swiped at his eyes with his kerchief, and then snatched up the reins and scooted onto the wagon seat.

I had to decide what to do, quick. Didn't seem I had much choice. I clambered up next to him.

"You best be holdin on, this ride's about to get bumpy." I sensed his anger with me. Maybe I seemed ungrateful.

Walton was hidin somethin. He knew things I didn't know. Yet he was harborin them details to hisself. Why would this stranger help me unless

I had somethin he wanted? I couldn't guess what that would be. I hardly owned the clothes on my back.

Walton cracked the reins and the horses bolted.

"Haigh there, horses. Haigh!" He whistled and the horses took to running.

"Where we goin?" I slipped my fingers through the slats in the seat and gripped tight as the wagon bounced over fresh clots of red clay.

"I done told you. Thunder Mountain. They're a different breed of folks over there."

Bein as I'd never seen the trees past Poppy's homestead, it ate at my soul not knowin where we were. Now that's somethin that'll gnaw at a body.

There was times I could hear Momma and Poppy talkin as I huddled against the warm stones of the chimney in the loft.

Momma's voice rose a bit. "Can't nobody know. Not a soul."

I'd wondered what Momma and Poppy was connivin. They never said my name, but then they didn't have to. I guessed they was speakin of me. Their voices softened, the words become whispers. It seemed my life was nothin but hidin and secrets.

From a fog I heard Walton say it again. "Hey, Lochiel. You with me?"

His words give me a start, woke me from my daydreamin. I nodded, not darin to share my thoughts.

"They're different on that side of the mountain. Good folks."

"Different from what?"

"You'll see."

Walton slowed the horses to a walk as we headed through the gap. Oak trees leaned in from the banks of the mountain, forming a shaded tunnel for us to cross through. The farther we traveled, the darker the path grew. The trees soon became the forest, filled with odd sounds echoin into the shadows. The last of winter hung tight in the trees.

My teeth clattered together like woodchucks tittering.

Walton pulled the reins to the left and the horses turned up a nearly hidden pathway. The yellow eyes of a deer gleamed in the brush.

"You gonna tell me where we're goin or not?"

"Edna's place."

"Who's Edna? Is this Thunder Mountain?" I pulled my arms tight around my body.

"It's one side." He swatted at a willow branch poking into the trail. "Edna's kin. I'm sure she'll take you in. I stop around to her place three or four times a year. She's a good woman."

Take me in? Once again, I found myself lost. A soul with no home.

"Reckon this Edna will stand in judgment of me? I *am* marked. Maybe she oughta be afraid I'd hex her. Maybe you oughta be afraid." My words seeped out snide-like.

"Edna don't see nothin but the heart. She cared for me when I needed it and when I didn't."

At last, a tidbit of information about hisself slipped out.

"She don't mind that you're a half-breed?" I felt a twist of spite as I uttered the words.

Walton leaned over the buckboard and spit. "Ain't quite got you figured yet. One minute you're feelin all guilty and mush-mouthed about the Ogles and what they did for you. The next, your tongue is like a snake."

I reckon he was right. My heart was close to the surface. There was so much I didn't know. So much I couldn't understand. Things kept from me. I didn't even know how I was supposed to feel. The Devil in me come to a boil and when I lashed out it was like tossin a pot of steamin water.

"What does a half-breed stranger want with a marked woman? You plannin to peddle me?"

I wanted my words to sting and burn. I wanted to hurt. And I reckon I had managed that. Still I was sorry as soon as the words left my lips.

Walton shook his head.

"I walked away from Edna once. Anger can do that to a person. Blame will too. She loved me despite myself. And when I come to my senses, she took me back in."

I wondered if Edna was his wife.

"She took you in?" My heart went gentle. "Was you injured?"

Walton rolled his eyes. "No, I wasn't hurt. Leastways, not my body."

"What then?"

"Ain't none of your business. All you need to know is Edna is a good woman. She don't hold no judgment over nobody. She taught me about the good Lord. Set me on the right path." A smile come across his lips. "I ain't sure she can heal nosey."

The wagon rounded the bend and a small field of tall grass opened. Sun-warmed air hovered over jonquils peepin out of half-frozen ground. On the back side of the field sat a tiny cabin. A woman stood hangin clothes on a line.

"Blessed be the tie that binds. Our hearts in Christian hmm . . . " Her voice, a sweet high pitch trill, carried across the field.

"What's the old woman got that can help a child of the Devil?"

Walton turned to me and reset his hat. "She knows your real momma and daddy."

SEVEN

YOU COULDA BLOWED me over with a feather. I sat shoulder-to-shoulder with Walton, speechless. There wasn't a word one that come to mind. *My momma?* I didn't know whether to jump for joy or be madder than the dickens. *My daddy?* The Ogles had never made mention of me even havin a daddy.

The wagon come to a halt and the woman dropped a wet skirt back into the basket. She shaded her eyes to see who rumbled down the rocky lane to her quiet homestead.

"Walt? You dawg. That you?"

"Yes'm. Nobody else it could be."

The woman lifted her skirt and took to limpin in a half run across the field.

"Lord have mercy." She wrapped her frail arms around Walton's neck. Tears squeezed from the corners of her eyes. "I'll be. My boy. You're a sight for sore eyes."

"My boy?" The words slipped out before I could stop them. "This is your momma?"

Walton lifted her from the ground and spun her. "Hello, Mother."

Mother? I'd only heard that name one or two times in my life. *Mother.* It sounded respectful, yet gentle. Kind, yet powerful.

I watched as the woman took Walton's face in her hands and twisted his head from side to side.

His mother knew my mother. "Why didn't you tell me she was your momma?"

Walton smiled. "Would it have changed anything 'cept maybe to let you judge her before you met her?"

40

"Oh, lordy, ain't you a sight. I'm beside myself." She pulled him close and kissed his forehead. "And how have you been?"

"Finer than frog's hair. Workin to keep a shirt on my back. Peddlin goods all over three mountains. Speakin of . . . I brought you somethin."

Her face lit like a winter flame. "You brung me somethin?" She clapped her hands.

Walton reached into the wagon and brought out a woven blanket. I'd never seen the likes of it. Colors of the rainbow stretched the length of the fabric. Blues bluer than the summer sky on a clear day. Yellows brighter than the heart of a daisy. Greens that rivaled the fields on the summit.

"It's beautiful." She fingered the blanket and then brushed it against her cheek. "And so soft." Her eyes closed as she savored the feel.

"Mother, Miss Edna, I'd like you to meet Lochiel Ogle." He turned her gently toward me. "Lochiel here needs your help."

Edna's eyes fixed on my mark. She followed it up the side of my face, furrowing her brow as she stared. She took a step toward me, and I stiffened.

"The mark." The words whispered from her lips.

Slowly, Edna paced a circle about me. When she paused in front of me, she reached out to touch my cheek.

My head jerked back.

"It's alright child. I got no plans to hurt you."

It wasn't somethin I was used to, a body touchin my face. Feelin the mark that crawled down my neck. Poppy had always told me folks would just as soon kill me as know me.

The woman looked into my eyes, and then she took hold of my shoulders. Edna's hands were scrawny, but her grip was strong. I tried to pull away, but she wouldn't turn me loose.

I grabbed her wrists, panic pushin through me. She pulled me toward her.

"It's fine. Shh. Let me hug you. I promise I won't hurt you."

I glanced at Walton. He nodded an approval. "Edna loves to hug. She could make a wild cat feel loved."

I could see her gentleness. Her intention good. Still I stood stiff, horrified of what was to come. Her grip loosened and she smiled.

"A hug can wait."

Edna stepped close to Walton and whispered, none too quietly, "Miracle child. She's alive."

Walton took his mother by the elbow and nudged her away. "Lochiel here needs a place to stay for a while. I can vouch that she's a worker. She can cook, clean, work the garden—"

"She's welcome here."

My legs grew weak beneath me. Here was a woman who appeared to know me, even seemed amazed to see me—who called me a miracle child. It was too much to take in.

My head begun to spin and before you could say Johnny Appleseed, I went to my knees.

"I don't want to hurt you. What if the Devil comes out in me?"

Walton rushed to my side while Edna hunkered down in front of me.

"You look here at me, Lochiel." I raised my head to see her wave Walton away. "There ain't no devil in you. It's a mark. That's all. A mark."

It was like she was blinded to my affliction.

She just sat right there with me, lookin at me like she was hungry. Her hands fidgeted. I could tell she wanted to put her arms around me, but she didn't. Instead she just spoke kind words.

Walton took the wagon on to the house and unloaded supplies. After a time, Edna stood and started toward the house. She paused, looked back at me, and tipped her head, invitin me to follow. Two puppies bounced around her feet as we neared the porch. They growled and grabbed at her skirt tail, vyin for attention. Momma would have shooed them out of her way, but Edna bent and scrubbed their backs.

"Puppies is like youngins; they need a little love and guidance from time to time. This here's Otis and that black and grey one is Rufus. I brought them up from the river. Ain't sure if somebody tried to get rid of them or if they was lost from their momma. But they needed care. So here they are. I tend to take in all the strays."

There was still no words. My mouth just couldn't speak. Arms full, Walton pried the door open with the toe of his boot and held it for Edna. I followed her inside.

"We're pretty simple around here, but I do keep an extra blanket or two just in case somebody drags in." Walton plopped his load on the table and she patted him on the back. "I reckon you'll find you a warm bed in the hayloft tonight."

"That's fine. That stove still out there? I'll stoke it tight tonight."

Edna cackled. "Indeed." Walton bumped the door open with his knee.

I stared at this woman. Hair black as coal, streaked with strands of white—whiter than the winter snow—hung to her waist in a tight braid. Tiny wrinkles creviced her golden brown hands. But her eyes—they was river blue. Clear as the water and tender as the mourning dove.

I remembered Walton said his momma was half Cherokee. I'd never seen an Indian, but Poppy had told me about them. About their brown skin and dark hair. She looked like how I imagined, except for those blue eyes.

"Come here, child. Let me look at you." She wagged her finger toward a tiny stool. "Lordy, lordy. I never."

"You never what?" I snapped.

"I never figured on seein you."

My stomach twisted in a knot. I didn't know her, and didn't know Walton either. How did they know me and why would they never think they'd see me? Edna knew my momma—my real momma. So what'd they want with me?

"Simmer down. I got no reason to harm you."

I eyed the stool but didn't sit.

"Come on, now. Talk to Miss Edna. Let me hear your sweet voice."

"Ain't sure I got anything to say."

"I imagine you got lots to say. Tell me your name again."

I wrapped my arms around myself and shivered.

"Oh, baby girl, you're cold. We can fix that in a heartbeat." She headed to a pantry. "I got just what you need to warm your bones." She pulled a thick quilt from the shelf.

"Here we go. I done quilted this one back last year before winter hit. It's filled with down." Edna draped the quilt around my arms. "This ought to warm you. We'll get Walt to bring up that fire. Tell me about yourself."

"Mother." Walton pushed back through the door, knocked the muddy snow from his boots. "Let the girl alone. She's been through enough."

"I can see she has." Edna reached toward the gash above my eye. "That's awful deep. I reckon we might oughta sew that up."

"Sew it up?" I backed away. "It's alright. Ain't bleedin no more."

"Aw, sit down, Lochiel. Edna here is known for her doctorin skills." Walton stoked the fire. "It'll be alright. Trust me."

I sat and crossed my arms to keep them from seein my hands shakin. No doctor ever come around our place. Momma didn't put no stock in them. "Trust you? I don't know you. And I still ain't figured why you'd want to help me."

Walton took hold of the stool I was sittin on and scooted it toward him. "Look, I know you're scared and you don't have reason to trust us. I suppose I can understand that bein as all you've been through. But I've yet to hurt you, to lay a bad hand against you. That oughta mean somethin. We ain't gonna hurt you. Now let Edna doctor up that cut."

"Scared? I reckon you got that one right."

His voice sharpened. "Listen to me. Gerald knows you ain't dead. And he's on the hunt for you. It don't matter if there's anything in this for me or not. Which there ain't. What matters is savin you."

I sat real quiet-like—just like a deer standin motionless until the danger passes. "Alright."

Edna drew a bowl of warm water from the pot hangin on the fireplace hook. She tore a strip of fabric the length of her arm, then gathered her sewin basket at my feet.

"Walton, there's some yarrow hangin in the smoke shed. Grab me a stalk of that yellow one. I'll make a mash outa that so I can numb this cut." She smiled. "I can fix it so it ain't gonna hurt too bad to stitch you up."

"Stay right there. Hear me?" Walton's hand went up. "You understand me?"

"I understand." My mind swirled thoughts of what might happen to me if I did try to move. Would they try to kill me?

Edna handed me a warm cloth. "Hold that right against that cut while I start my mash."

I pressed the rag to my head.

Within minutes Edna had ground the dried flower into powder. She added water and mixed it into a paste.

"Let down that cloth now and hold still. This might sting a little, but before you can say horse hair, it'll stop." She reached to smear the yellow mash over the cut above my eye. I clamped my fingers around Edna's wrist. I could yank it away if she tried anything funny. It felt boney, fragile, like I could snap it if I tried.

"Don't you worry. The good Lord tells us to worry not. Cast our worries on Him. I ain't gonna hurt you, child. Trust me."

Trust me. When Gerald said that, it was right before he stirred up some mischief.

BRINGIN THAT BABY *home was somethin I come to regret most every day.* *Even when she was nowhere nearby, she could get me in trouble, the Devil in her was that strong.*

Once me and Eckert Job was out rousin some quail. Six birds hung off my belt, but he'd shot four of 'em. I knew I'd never hear the end of it.

"You think you're somethin, sportin them birds. Most of 'em is mine." *Eckert shoved me, makin as though he was gonna snatch the quail off my belt.* *"You can't hit the broad side of a barn." He pushed my head down. "That's why you're carryin the birds, 'cause your hopeless shootin 'em. 'Member last time—"*

There was nothin that would hush Eckert up, so I balled up my fist and planted it in the side of his jaw.

Eckert picked hisself up off the ground and rubbed his jaw. "What was that for?"

"You can have the two birds you shot. The rest is mine."

"Liar. You know I shot them birds. You ain't nothin but a liar."

"I'll give you some truth to chew on." I eased next to him and hushed my voice. "I was out huntin three, four years back and snatched a baby right outa her momma's arms. Brung her home. Got the mark of the Devil on her. She's talkin now—speakin hexes."

Eckert took a step back and I smiled. I'd put fear in him. It wasn't true— that she was speakin curses—but Momma said she might and that we'd best be right careful.

"Ain't no wonder you ain't right."

"What do you mean, ain't right?" My fist balled up again.

"Daddy told us a story he'd heard down the mountain. Said there was a marked child wanderin the woods, livin with wolves. You're meaner than a snake and now I know why. You're hexed. Wait 'til I tell my daddy. He's gonna—"

I punched Eckert again. And when he fell I kicked him in the gut to buy me some time to think.

Now I'd done it. I was never to speak about Lochiel. Her curse would fall on me, Momma said, if a single soul found out. Like havin a demon sister weren't trouble enough.

I watched Eckert roll on the ground whinin.

"Aw, shoot," I said, offerin Eckert a hand up. "I was just tryin to scare you. Shut you up. Ain't nothin but a story. You take the birds. But if you say anything about that story, I'll see you pay. Trust me, I'll see you pay."

Eight

Thunder rumbled over the mountain, and a rush of wind threw open Edna's door.

"Lord have mercy. Bolt that door, Walt. Looks like they's a mighty big storm blowin in." She'd finished with the paste and was waitin for it to take hold. My hands fidgeted in my lap.

Walton pushed the plank door shut and twisted the square of wood nailed to the facing. "That oughta hold it for a spell."

"Shew, that wind is cold. You best make you a pallet on the floor in here. It's gonna be too wet and cold for the barn loft." Edna tightened her shawl around her shoulders. Her eyes bored a hole into my soul as she extended her hand toward my chin. It was her way of testin if she could touch me, if I'd allow my Devil to be tamed. I tilted my head and she took my chin in one hand.

"That paste is about dry." She pressed the fingers of her other hand against the cut over my eye.

"Mm, mm, mm." Edna shook her head. "That's a nasty gash." She commenced to push her needle through the skin and pull it tight together. The sting forced a tear out of my eye and down my cheek.

Edna cocked her head to one side. "You feelin that?"

"A little."

"Then I best be makin my stitches hurried before that mash wears off."

I tried not to squirm as she worked to close the gap above my eye. It was hard to let Edna touch my face. She was tryin to be gentle, I could tell, but each time she touched me I felt a sting. Strange as it was, the sting was in my chest.

"A nasty gash." She blotted a drop of blood from my brow. "Yep, right nasty. Gonna tell me what happened to make a dent on this purty face?"

Purty face? She'd called my face purty. I felt my skin grow warm. Gerald's words seeped into my mind. *"Look ahere. The Devil's done burned your face hard with his mark."*

"Did you fall?" Edna continued to dig at me.

"I riled my brother."

"And did you do somethin to raise the hair on his back?"

"Mother." Walton stepped toward Edna. "She's had a rough go. Reckon we oughta save all them questions 'til she's had time to rest up?"

He winked at me as he handed Edna a damp cloth to wipe away the dried mash and blood.

"Edna here is a granny woman. She fixes what ails a body. She just ain't mastered overcomin nosey. Seems she's a bit like you. Nosey, that is." Walton kissed his mother's hand.

"Much obliged," I said, grateful Walton had pulled the reins on Edna's questions. "Thank you for takin me in and fixin my eye. I promise I'll work off your kindness."

"Child, what are you talkin about? You don't work off kindness. Kindness is from the soul. It's gived 'cause it can't help but be gived."

The words Miss Edna shared was words I felt needed to be remembered. *Kindness is from the soul. It's gived 'cause it can't help but be gived.* I marked those words in my heart.

Edna tied a strip of fabric snug around my head, then brushed her fingers through my hair, shapin the strands into a bun. I sat so tensed up that my jaw hurt worse than my head.

"Hold that right there." She guided my fingers to the bun, mumblin as she dug through a cupboard drawer, finally pullin out a small crocheted circle and a stick. "There it is. This'll help keep your hair pulled back."

Edna fingered with the bun she'd twisted on my head and pressed the crocheted circle over it. She pushed the stick through and secured it against my head.

"There, perfect." Edna stepped back and smiled. When her lips parted, I could see a string of straight, white teeth. Those beautiful eyes, bright and full of happiness. When Walton stood next to her, I saw a resemblance. The same smile, the same leather-colored skin, the same kindness.

Walton gently rubbed his momma's shoulders, and I could see how he loved her. And from her eyes always lightin on him, I could tell how much she loved him.

It's funny how a person don't know what they is missin until they see somebody else who has it. I was sure, though Momma wasn't always kind to me, that she loved me a little. She'd have to, just to raise me. When Poppy brung me home, she didn't shoo him back out the door to put me back where he got me from. But as I watched Walton and Edna, I saw what I'd had was different from theirs. And that made my heart ache just a little. Momma and Poppy loved hard and if what Edna and Walton had was right, then what Momma and Poppy had was wrong.

Edna set a bowl on the table and ladled out some stew. "You need to eat somethin, child. You're skinnier than a post."

The scent of the stew made my mouth water. But hungry as I was, the sadness I felt filled my belly, shoved out any room for food. Before I could put a taste of stew to my tongue, I felt a wave of tears rise up in me.

"Miss Edna, I'm grateful. For this stew. For you stitchin up my face. But right this second, I—I—can't—"

The words stopped up in my throat as the walls of that cabin closed in on me. I come to my feet, fightin back the flood of tears.

I rushed to the door, twisted the block that held it shut, and tore onto the porch. Lightnin flashed across the night sky and the wind went to stirrin. It spit flakes of snow the size of my palm that stuck tight to my skin. I run into the field as the snow turned into a drivin rain.

The Devil inside me was keepin me from drawin breath, pressin his way up my throat, chokin the life outa me and tearin at my chest.

My foot dropped into a hole and I gasped a breath as I fell face-first into the muddy field. There I lay, soakin wet, rain peltin me like I was bein punished. A hand took my arm and lifted me upward.

"Peace, Lochiel, peace."

Walton scooped me into his arms and carried me back to the house. There was no energy left in me. I was spent. Lightnin popped around us, fillin the sky with an eerie tint to the darkness. My skin tingled from the icy beads of water. Winter wasn't over, and my heart felt as empty and cold as the liar's winter that laid in wait.

Edna shoved a quilt at Walton. "Set her there. And hold this here blanket up so I can get her outa these wet clothes."

Edna stripped me down to my naked shell and wiped the mud away. She slipped a nightgown over my head, then gently backed me to the bed. She helped me onto the hay-filled mattress and covered me, snuggin me tight under the heavy quilt. My body burrowed into the bed, its depths wrappin around me like a warm cocoon. I wasn't sure what peace felt like, but if this was it, I liked it.

Edna brushed strands of loose hair back from my face. "You rest, child. Just rest and the good Lord's blessin will cover you."

Bundled in a quilt stitched by the bent and gnarled fingers of an old woman, I rolled to my side. A small mirror sat on the table next to the bed. I supposed when you have a son who peddles across the mountain, a few trinkets along the way is a given. And though Edna's belongins were slim, I could spot the goodies Walton gifted her.

My hand eased from under the blanket, crawled across the covers like a spider. I rubbed the edge of the mirror with a knuckle. Wrapped in a small copper frame, the mirror caught the glow of the fireplace. There— starin back at me—was the Devil's daughter. The color of the red mark mixed eerily with the yellow of the fire and tinted my face orange. My eyes, a golden color, glowed like a cat in the dark.

It was no wonder folks called me evil.

I pulled the heavy quilt tight around my neck. I could make out Walton talkin, his words so quiet I couldn't understand them, but at that moment it didn't matter. I remembered an old threat from Gerald—*"You better sleep with one eye open."* And I realized that's what I did every night when my head rested on the floor of the loft. Walton's voice muffled into the sounds of the fire crackin and poppin. I was warm, comfortable, and I could sleep with both my eyes closed.

Nine

I WAS WALKIN down the mountain path, a hoe slung over my shoulder. I heard the warnin of a rattler, and when I finally fixed my eyes on the beast, its tail was quiverin and its head was dancin, darin me to set my foot into its coils. Them rattles sent chills up my spine. I stopped dead, one foot raised and ready to step square into the middle of that rattler.

It was like there was a heavy rock tied to my foot, pullin down toward the bobbing head of the snake. I strained with all my might to keep my foot away, but that rancid snake drawed back, fangs extended, and made a strike, snaggin my leg.

I ain't never felt a pain like when them fangs pumped their liquid fire into my flesh. I swung the hoe, catchin the snake and loppin off its head, then struck it again for good measure.

I jolted from sleep, hair pasted to my neck. The small cabin glowed a dull yellow. Edna's feet was propped on the hearth. Her arms crossed as she sat leaned to one side in the pine rocker, head slouched to her chest. Her chair shifted with each breath she took.

In the far corner of the cabin lay Walton, stretched long on a pallet of quilts his momma had made.

I run my hand down my leg to feel for holes left by the serpent. Nothin. It was just a dream. The same one that haunted me most every night since I was a youngin. I leaned my head against the wall and closed my eyes. The Devil was still fightin to seep out. I raised my hand to my cheek and rubbed hard.

Maybe today would be the day this snake would shed her skin. Maybe today, this mark would peel off and I'd be free from the curse. I pushed my fingernails into the skin and dragged them hard down my face and neck.

A soft hand took aholt of mine, its fingers wrappin gently through my own. "Shh, baby girl. Shh. Don't be scratchin that purty face. A mark is just a mark. A body has to look past that. And when they do, they see golden eyes that shine like a mornin sunrise."

Edna pulled my hand from my cheek and tenderly brushed my knuckles against her face. The rooster's crow rang across the mountain. She grinned and pointed toward the pink glow of the morning sun squeezin through the shutter.

"Mornin's come. See, baby girl. You slept the night through before you let your dreams get aholt." She patted my face and loosened the hair clingin to my neck. Her smile was a balm. Edna balled her hand into a fist, liftin it toward the ceilin. "Yes, Lord. You are mighty. You have brung us through the night." She turned to me. "Now, you tell Miss Edna what troubled you whilst you slept."

My voice left me as I tried to speak. Not a peep came out.

"Now, child, take yourself a deep breath. Look around and see— whatever haunted you in your dreams ain't here. You're safe."

"I've had this dream for as long as I can remember." I woke up, the sweat pourin down my face.

"Well, now, that's all it was, wasn't it? Just a dream."

I wasn't so sure about that. "Yes, ma'am, I reckon it was."

"Dreams lose their power when you speak of 'em. You tell Miss Edna your dream, and it'll loosen its hold on you." Her eyes drew me in to where I just wanted to believe everthing she said.

"I dreamed a snake bit me and when I lopped off its head, it grew another. It was a rattler shakin them rattles at me, rearin to strike."

"Hmm, hmm." She shook her head. "Snakes is ugly creatures. But you know, they ain't all bad. Some of them is good to have around. If it wasn't for them black snakes, I'd never keep the critters out of my 'maters. But you go on. Tell me the rest of that horror."

"I guess that was it. I'd scream at that snake, and then wake up. Then Momma would holler at me to pull the covers back over me. 'Go back to sleep,' she'd say. 'That's the Devil seepin out,' she'd say."

Edna's eyes closed and she pressed her hand tight around mine.

"Oh, Lord," she whispered. "End this child's fear. Take it from her."

This was the second time somebody had prayed over me. And though I wasn't real sure what or who this *lord* was, he had yet to take my fear. I'd have gladly give it to him. Still, I'd learned enough manners from Momma and Poppy to know I should be thankful, even if I didn't understand what they was doin.

"Lay down, child. Try to rest a bit longer. I got mornin chores to do, and then I'll start us some breakfast." She gently nudged me back down onto the bed. "Rest a bit longer."

I wanted to rest. For years I'd longed for a good, sound sleep, and though my eyes would shut, there never seemed to be a minute the muscles in my body let loose. That is until last night. I laid starin at the ceilin, amazed that Miss Edna was right. I'd slept most of the night away before my dreams got aholt of me.

The door creaked open and I heard Edna slip out. "Woot, woot. Come on, girls. Miss Edna has your meal. Chick, a chick, chick, chick. C'mon now."

I could hear the chickens chatterin outside. Walton raised hisself off his pallet and laughed. He pushed open the rickety shutter hidin a tiny window.

"Lochiel, rise and shine. Start your mornin off with a chuckle. Come watch Miss Edna dance with the chickens."

I eased out of the bed and made my way across the darkened cabin. Sure enough, there was Miss Edna, spinnin in circles, basket in hand, flingin corn all around her. A laugh rose in my belly, workin its way out. For with every turn Miss Edna made tossin corn, them chickens run around in circles with her. That's when I learned there really was such a thing as a happy chicken.

———

I pulled my boots on and tied the tattered strings. My mouth felt like there was tin on my tongue. Walton swiped his fingers through his hair and hung his hat on a nail by the door.

"Glad you're back. I'll bundle up and head to the chicken coop." Edna slipped one arm through the coat Walton pulled off. She let out a rowdy laugh. "I done forgot just how big you are." She stretched out an arm, sleeve coverin her hand. "But it's warm."

I watched as Walton wrapped his arm around Miss Edna and gently hugged her. She smiled up at him as he adjusted the coat, her boy fussin over her. I wondered what it felt like, to have a momma's tenderness. Watchin them made me feel like I was spyin, so I turned away.

I poked the coals in the fireplace until they glowed a bright red, then added a small log. The heat from the coals lapped at the bark, quickly takin hold and turnin to flames. The least I could do was put the coffee pot on the hook and grease down the skillet for the eggs Miss Edna gathered.

A small shelf filled with jars and cans hung close to the fireplace. To one side stood a small cabinet stacked with tin plates and a few coffee cups. Wooden forks and spoons lay neatly beside crocheted rags. A worn book with yellowed pages lay on the table. I'd never held a book. Poppy had a book he wrote figures in, but I never touched it. That was the closest I'd ever been to seein one.

I stretched out my hand to touch the gold letters on the front, but my hand just wouldn't do what I was tellin it to do.

"You know how to read?"

I snatched my hand back. Walton stood chewin on a hickory twig.

"You scared the whiz outa me." I clasped my fingers together and twiddled my thumbs.

"Well, do you know how to read?"

"Uh, no. I mean, I know some letters, but I ain't never been to school."

"Come here. Let me show you some things." Walton pointed me toward a chair by the table. He slid the book close to me. "There. Go ahead. You can touch it. I promise it won't jump up and bite you. Can't say what will happen to your heart once you learn to read it though."

I clasped my hands tightly together. "My heart?"

Walton's teeth shined as his lips parted in a smile.

He laid his finger on the leather of the book, tracin around each letter. "B-I-B-L-E." He uttered the name of each letter. "Now, you trace it and we'll say it together."

I moved my finger slowly over the letters. "B-I-B-L-E." The letters were cool and smooth.

"That's real good, Lochiel. This here is the Good Book. The Bible. There's lots of good stories in this here book. Lots of truth."

I repeated the letters again and said *Bible*. "That ain't so hard."

"Lots of things ain't hard if a body has a chance to learn them."

The door flew open and Miss Edna tore through. "Ain't no time, Walt. Hide the girl. Folks with dogs is comin up the lane." She tossed her basket of eggs on the table.

The sound of hounds echoed across the field. I knew them howls. I could almost figure which bark belonged to which dog.

"That's Gerald. I know his huntin dogs when I hear 'em howl." My heart skipped a few beats before it started to race. "He'll kill me."

"Don't you worry none. We'll take care of you." Edna took Walton by the arm. "Help me open the floor."

"Gerald is like a dog hisself," I said. I shoulda been runnin off but my backside felt stuck to that chair. "He gets somethin on his mind, he's like a mad dog with a bone. You can't pry it outa his mouth."

"Hush, girl. Hush. You'll be fine." Edna pulled a small rug away from the edge of the bed and Walton slipped his knife between the floor slats, quickly liftin them out.

"Get in, Lochiel. Get in. And if things ain't right in a while, you watch yourself and crawl out the back side of the house at dark."

Walton got me unstuck from that chair and helped me into the small hole leadin under the house.

Before he gently pressed me to my knees, Edna kissed my head. "Don't you worry none. You'll be fine," she said. The rain from the night before had washed under the cabin and stood in puddles. My hands sank into the muddy ground.

"Don't matter what you hear, don't you open your mouth." Walton's voice from above was muffled. "You stuff the tail of your skirt in your mouth if you have to. But not nary a peep. You hear?"

Hidin was somethin I was used to. Poppy never hesitated to run me into the root cellar if somebody come toward the house. "Can't let nobody see the Devil's daughter," he'd say. "They's liable to shoot her." Same as now. Nothin changes.

"Just practice spellin that word you learned," Walton said. "But practice it in your head. We'll learn a few more later." He was tryin to calm me but the tone in his voice said otherwise.

I was on my stomach and Walton fit the planks back together. What little light filtered into the hole faded when the rug was put back. I heard the thump of a chair on the rug. The cabin door creaked and then things grew quiet.

I inched on my belly toward the back of the house. The ground under the fireplace, though wet and muddy, was warm. I pushed a dried piece of wood to one side, and my worst nightmare come true.

TEN

I CAN'T COUNT the times I'd dreamed about that blessed ole rattler, and though it always scared the tarnation outa me, it was at least, as Edna said, in my dreams.

This time the varmint was real.

I jerked backward, knockin the fool outa my head on the floor of the cabin. My head hit so hard it addled me, but I quickly snagged the branch next to me and shoved it at the snake. The rattles grew louder, so I shoved the branch harder. It took a second, but I reckon that rattler figured wastin his poison on a stick was foolish, so he slithered out from under the house.

I rolled to my back and rested my arm across my mouth to keep from screamin. It seemed I'd come face-to-face with one of the demons that haunted me. As I laid there gettin my wits about me, I felt myself grow a little cocky. *Hateful beast. Scared of a branch? Nasty thang. That'll teach you to mess with Lochiel Ogle.*

I stretched my arm toward the branch and pulled it tight to my side. *You stay right here. I can see right now me and you are gonna be good friends.* I hugged that tree branch despite it makin me feel a tad foolish.

From the far side of the house, I saw Walton's wagon roll past and into the deep, dark part of the woods. The dogs howled and barked as they made their way up the twisted lane. I pressed the side of my wrist into my mouth.

Like Poppy said, people would just as soon kill me as look at me. This time it was my own brother.

I never saw Walton come back from the woods so he either took to hidin himself or he'd left me to fend on my own. I heard the scrape of

Edna's cane-bottomed chair across the planks of the porch. She was singin
to them two puppies of hers, all the while shooin chickens off the porch.

"Lochiel, I know you can hear Miss Edna. Them men is 'bout here.
You keep yourself hid, and you keep quiet. You hear me?'

I said nothin. There was just a long pause of quiet. Miss Edna went to
gigglin. "That's my girl. You understand what it means to be quiet."

And I did understand. There were times Poppy would run me into the
root cellar and then holler at me. If I answered, he'd open that cellar door
and bust my backside. "Lochiel, be quiet means be quiet," he'd say. "You
don't answer a'tall. Answerin might mean the Devil takes you sooner than
later."

I couldn't help but think Poppy cared a little for me. He'd bust my tail
end every now and then, but he never laid an ill hand toward me. He'd
whip Gerald every once in a while too. So I knew when it come to disci-
pline, Poppy thought no more of Gerald than he did me.

The howls of them dogs soon found their way to Edna's knees. I could
hear her fussin. I shoulda been cold under that cabin, since there was still
a snowy mix of rain that fell the night before. But sweat beaded on my
forehead and when I swiped my face, mud covered my cheek.

"Git off my porch. Git!" There was a thud, then a yelp, and I figured
Edna took her foot to the ribs of one of them dogs.

"I'd thank you to corral your hounds!" Edna's heels clicked against the
porch.

"Howdy, ma'am. Name's Gerald Ogle."

"Well, Gerald Ogle, git your hounds off my porch and we might talk."

He whistled and the dogs come to his feet. "I'm lookin for a girl, 'bout
nineteen. She's run away."

The sound of Gerald's voice made the bile in my stomach rise into my
throat. I twisted to peer through the rungs of wood that hung from the
porch to the ground. A silver tip on Gerald's boot caught the mornin sun,
castin a light under the cabin. I knew them boots and I'd felt them silver
tips more than once when they'd slam into my leg.

Where was that rattler when I needed it? I squeezed my eyes closed and
tried to conjure some power over that snake. But nothin happened.

"Run away?" Edna said. "What's she runnin from?"

"Well, ma'am, that's what has us bumfuzzled. My momma and daddy raised her from a baby. She was a youngin cast out. And this is the kind of gratitude she shows. Runs off without a word. My folks is beside theirselves."

I wanted to come out from under that porch and beat the tar outa Gerald. Lyin was one of his best gifts, and today was no different. Deceitful words fell out of his mouth like water over a rock.

Like when I was pullin corn from the garden and Gerald went to whippin his knife around, jumpin at me. Sliced a gash in my arm as long as your hand. When I tried to tell Poppy what happened, Gerald told Poppy I was makin some sort of spell and cut my arm for blood.

I run my fingers over the bandage on my brow, the reminder that Gerald had no understandin of truth whatsoever. *Runaway, my foot. How 'bout this gash? How 'bout left for dead?* The Devil in me boiled.

All sorts of ideas rushed through my head layin under that cabin, and hearin Gerald's voice again give me reason to fear, and reason to doubt. Was Walton's help a lie? Did he trick me into runnin so he could claim the Devil's daughter?

But Walton and Edna has been nothin but kind to me. I pushed the doubts away.

I might not be the ripest apple in the basket, but I knew better than to believe anything Gerald said was truth.

I laid still and never uttered a sound. There'd come a time when Gerald would get his own. His lies would come around and haunt him.

"My hounds lost her scent back down by the river. My best guess is, the girl crossed the river on foot. She'd be wet and cold, lookin for some dry clothes. You ain't had nothin go missin from your clothesline, have you?"

I heard Miss Edna sigh. "Boy, do I look like a body with extra clothes to hang on the line? I got my nightshirt and these rags to my name. So, no, I can't say that a thang has gone missin off my line."

Gerald chuckled. I could see his dogs dancin around his feet, whinin and bawlin until he pulled a piece of cloth from his pocket and let them smell it.

"I'll be movin on." He took a few steps and stopped. I knew what was comin. Gerald always longed to be the one that ruled the roost.

"I trust you is tellin me the truth." He scrubbed the toe of his boot into the wet ground.

"Since you don't know me, all you got is trust. But you're welcome to look around the place if you don't feel like an old lady can be trusted. There ain't nothin round here to hide or no place to hide in."

"You live out here by yourself?" Gerald's voice faded a bit and I reckoned he was eyein her place.

"I do. Married a white man better part of forty years ago and he up and died from the plague. Ole dawg left me stuck in the side of this mountain. I make my way down to Chattanooga every fall for a few supplies to get me through the winter. My Cherokee family keeps me in corn and meat. Is that enough for you or do I need to send you up the mountain to their camp for proof?"

Gerald cleared his throat and spit. "Naw. I reckon you're tellin me the truth. But just so you know, I ain't a man that likes liars. And I have a way of findin out if folks is tellin me a yarn."

Edna stomped across the porch and down the steps. Her tiny feet went toe-to-toe with Gerald.

"And I ain't right good at havin threats throwed at me. I don't take well to hounds, whether they walk on four legs or two. I'd offer you breakfast, but I'm feelin your welcome is done. Now, hightail it down my lane. If you need proof, you make your way on up to the Cherokee camp, and if you and them dogs is lucky, they'll guide you over the pass."

I supposed there was a standoff since neither feet or words moved for a minute.

"Thank you for your time. I'll be back this way soon and check on you. An old lady up here alone. No way to protect herself."

Edna's feet passed by the edge of the cabin and back onto the porch. I heard that chair squall across the porch and then the scrape of metal against metal as she cocked her shotgun.

"I'm obliged, but I've been fine for years, and I reckon I can manage a few more."

"Yes, ma'am. I'm sure you'll be fine. Simmer down now." Gerald's feet lifted off the ground as he mounted his horse. "Hunt dogs. Hunt."

Them dogs tore down the lane—all but one that stuck his nose in the air, circled twice, and made a beeline for the porch. He went to diggin and scratchin at the dirt by the porch steps, and I scrambled farther under the cabin.

That hound had my scent.

If that dog dug me out, Gerald would kill me and most likely kill Edna too. He was never a man with scruples, and though I'd never seen him kill a body, I sure as whiz didn't doubt he would. Especially since he'd smashed my head with a rock and hauled me up the mountain, leavin me for dead. One thing about Gerald, he was never good at losin—be it a game of tag or a buck he was huntin. He always made himself right in the middle of a scuffle, no matter what it took. If he wanted somethin, it become a challenge to get it. He'd plot, connive, lie, and cheat, but he'd get it.

Once he got what he wanted, the prize meant nothin. He reminded me of a mountain lion playin with its prey. The joy wasn't in the meal, but in the hunt, in the torture of the animal bein stalked. It was in the kill. All Gerald wanted was the kill.

That blasted dog kept howlin and scratchin at the dirt until I heard Gerald holler and dismount again.

"You found me somethin, Red? Whatcha got, boy?"

I pushed my newfound friend, my tree branch, betwixt me and the front of the porch. And for the first time since I'd crawled under the house, I heard the sound that sent chills down my back.

The rattles of that ole snake went to quiverin.

He'd slithered away from me earlier and must've made his way around to the front of the cabin. That or I really did conjure him up. More likely, he liked the warmth of the fireplace above the floor too much to crawl far. But the head of that rattler perked and the ole boy rared up, his spine straightenin, and his hiss grew louder.

The more that dog dug at the ground, the more that rattlesnake riled, until just as Gerald bent down to peer under the porch, it hauled off and struck. Not one, but three swift strikes. That dog went to yelpin and Gerald jumped back, landin on his backside.

"Good lord amighty. A rattler. Did it strike my dog? Red! Here dawg. Come on."

Edna hollered and laughed. "Well, Mr. Gerald Ogle, meet my protection."

"I reckon you think that's right funny." Gerald checked out his hound then mounted his horse and took down the lane after the rest of his pack.

"I suppose you'd be right about that, ole boy. I suppose you'd be right." Edna's footsteps clicked across the porch.

I wiggled toward the side of the porch before Miss Edna's warnin to stay hid for a spell longer pierced my memory. So there I laid, pullin and scrapin my way through the mud toward the end of the cabin. That rattler had since made his way clear of me and my branch. I reckon he'd had all he wanted to mess with for the day. In the back of my mind, I wondered if I'd really conjured up a snake.

Eleven

My teeth clicked together like a crow clippin at an ear of corn. I'd laid under that cabin the better part of the day. The cold had no mercy on my hands or fingers. They was numb and my nose was runnin like a sugar tree. I rolled to my back and buried my fingers under my armpits. After runnin for my life, was I to lay here in the mud under a cabin and freeze to death?

I dozed off, then jarred awake. If I crawled out from under that house too soon, I would die. If I continued to lay under this cold cabin, I would die. Didn't look like I had a better-of-the-two choice. I reckon death could be the better of my choices. Leastways for everone else. So I laid still and held an inch of hope that Miss Edna hadn't forgot me.

It wouldn't be the first time I was forgot. Old man Martin come across the mountain to trade some furs with Poppy. Poppy shoved me in the feed shack out back of the cabin.

"Lochiel, get in there. Shut that door," he said. The sun was hot that day and Poppy and old man Martin tangled and dickered over them furs, 'til I grew so hot I couldn't breathe. My mouth dried up like cotton and the sweat stopped beadin after a bit. *Don't you make a sound.* And I didn't. Hours later Poppy remembered he'd pushed me in the shack. He bolted in the door and scooped me up, then give me a good dunkin in the river to cool me down.

"Surely, you ain't forgot me too," I whispered.

I peered from under the porch as the oak tree shadows edged from one side of Edna's house to the other. The sun was gettin lower. My mind was workin slower and slower. Memories mixin heavily with dreams. Too stiff for even the Devil to worm outa me. Suddenly, them boards by the bed popped loose and opened. Walton's arm come through that hole and grabbed me by my hands and pulled. *Freedom*. A second taste.

"Lochiel, I'm prayin to the Lord you ain't froze solid. But them hounds have been all over the side of this mountain. We couldn't chance you bein fount."

"Get her out," Edna snapped. "I done got water boilin over the fire. I'll strip the child down and wash her clean."

My arms were slow to reach, but I managed to grasp Walton's hands. He took hold and lifted me into the cabin.

I fell into his arms shakin like a tree in a windstorm.

"I done got the blankets strung at the side of the house. And I got a stool behind 'em. Let's get her out there and I'll rinse her down."

My head rested against Walton's chest and one arm draped over his shoulder as he carried me outside and set me on that stool behind them blankets. Queer as it seemed, with Gerald out there huntin me down, I felt safe and protected.

Walton stepped away and Edna unbuttoned my dress and pulled it over my head.

This was the second time Miss Edna had stripped me down to the skin. All I had left when Walton found me on the mountain was my privacy. Now that was gone, and I reckoned at this point, it didn't rightly matter.

"Walt, you go wash the mud outa these clothes. I got a bucket filled with hot water inside." Walton scooped up the muddy clothes and headed to the cabin. "And wring 'em out good. You can hang 'em in front of the fireplace."

Edna touched her elbow to the water. "That's just right. Hang on and we'll wash you off." She ladled warm water over my head and streaks of red clay ran down my face and chest. Needles pierced my skin as the warmth of the water thawed me.

"I thought you"—my voice quivered—"forgot me."

"Lordy no, child." She handed me a bar of lye soap. "That rotten brother of yours kept combin this side of the mountain. Them dogs howled and barked the biggest part of the day. I couldn't take no chances."

"I—I'm gra-grateful." My jaw was so stiff I could hardly speak.

"Shh, shh. None of that now." She scrubbed my hair while I washed my face and arms, and though the air was right brisk, the tepid water felt good. When we was done, Edna yanked one of them blankets around me and tied it tight. She took what water was left in her buckets and rinsed out my boots.

"Now there. Let's get you in the cabin and warm them fingers and toes by the fire."

"Miss Edna?" I wasn't fixin to argue but my mind couldn't rest.

"What is it?" She wrapped her arm around my waist to guide my steps. Even with her arm around me, I could feel her list to one side and hobble. Sometime maybe I could ask her what caused her to limp.

"Why are you and Walton helpin me? I'm marked. I belong to the Devil. Why not just let me die?"

Edna stopped in her tracks. "You listen to me. And you listen good. I knew you when you was born. I helped bring you into this world. And when you was stole away, well I just—"

"Stole away?" My breath caught in my chest. "My momma threw me out on the mountain for the wolves because of this mark."

"She did no sucha thang. I was there. When I run to get the pastor to pray over you with that mark, you was stole right outa your momma's arms."

"But—Poppy said—"

"You can't believe all you hear. You can't believe all you're told. Shoot, you don't have to believe me. Sometimes even them folks that care about us maybe don't tell us the truth. But I promise, I ain't tellin no lie."

"But—"

"There's time for answers. And I'll give you every one, but right now, you just take in the truth I told you. Just that bit is a lot to swallow. Be thankful Walt found you. We start with bein thankful."

My heart wanted to believe Edna, but my gut didn't have the gumption. It was enough to get bashed upside the head with a rock, left for dead, saved—now three times—by strangers . . . but to find Edna was there when I was born. My momma didn't throw me out. She was right. It was a lot to take in.

Seems they knew me but I still didn't know them. Then they tell me Momma and Poppy was liars, that I was stole outa my momma's arms. What kind of person does that?

There was one thing for sure. Edna wanted me to take in what I was told.

Now I had double the questions.

It's odd how your mind gauges trust. It's like havin a rope tied to your waist and bein lowered down a cliff inch by inch—just enough so you can get your footin before you edge on down. Edna seemed a good woman. She'd risked her life for me. She was bound and determined to give me what I needed to know, a bit at a time. Bit by bit so I could chew on it, get aholt of it.

I reckon she kept on talkin for a spell, but my mind wandered off, forcin her voice to mesh with the roar of the nearby river. All I could think of was them words, "stole away."

Stole away? How could that be? Poppy found me in the woods just before I was ate by wolves. My head was churnin with this so-called truth Edna had spit out.

"Your Poppy cocked his gun and fired in the air, scarin them wolves and scatterin them across the side of the mountain," Momma had told me, snappin out a shirt before hangin it on the line. "He saved your hide. You need to learn to be grateful for what was give to you." She pointed her finger at my face. "He chose life for you. It coulda been death."

Momma told me that more times than I could count, especially when she wanted me to do somethin I didn't particularly want to do.

"You should be beholdin to the both of them," Momma'd say. "They risked their own souls to save you."

I rubbed my hand over my cheek and neck. The more I thought through what Edna said, the more my heart ached. The more my words left me. The more I stared into the blackness of my past.

The pieces didn't fit together. Nothin fit. Nothin. Everthing seemed outa kilter. I needed to ponder on what Edna had said, but pain was cloudin my view.

"Open your mouth, Lochiel. Let me give you a bite of soup." Edna run the spoon under my nose. The smell of beef stew filled my senses. "Come on, girl. Open up. You ain't eat a bite in two days."

"Reckon she's still cold?" Walton gently laid another blanket across my lap.

"The child has been through a lot, Walt. And she's full of questions. It's an awful state to be in when you can't figure what's happenin. 'Specially when you ain't rightly done nothin wrong."

I opened my mouth to speak but Edna poured a taste of stew onto my tongue. My eyes closed as I took in the scent, savorin the taste of tomatoes and beans—a flavor I'd not had in some time. But as soon as that food went down, my stomach twisted. Edna lifted the spoon to my lips a second time, and I took hold of her hand, gently pressin it toward the bowl. I wanted more, but as good as that stew tasted, it turned my stomach.

I suppose life can manage to sour anything.

What had I done to deserve this curse? Tears pooled, but not a one fell. It was like the rest of me, frozen in place. This was a lot for a body to take in.

Walton pushed the bowl away and laid the leather-bound book in front of me. He took my fingers and traced the letters.

"Remember? I told you this was the Good Book. B–I–B–L–E."

The tips of my fingers flowed over the letters. "I—I remember."

Edna jumped to her feet. "Oh, Lord, she spoke. Lochiel, child, what can Miss Edna do for you? Let me get you some coffee." She scurried around like a mouse after a kernel of corn.

"I know this has been hard on you." Walton pressed his hand around my fingers and squeezed. "But things is new now. You're free."

Free? From what?

I looked into Walton's dark eyes, his face. Whiskers lined his jaw and chin, and his black hair was sprinkled with streaks of white. Just like the last of the snow dustin the evergreens.

His skin was golden brown and his hands bigger than any I'd ever seen. This man, strong and wise in his ways, looked at me with a gentleness I couldn't understand.

There was a time when me and Gerald was just youngins—I mighta been six. The winter had dropped its last snow and Poppy stoked the fire 'til the flames belched like a overfed hog.

Momma had pulled Gerald close and snugged him under her arm.

He squirmed a bit at first but she'd brushed his sandy blond hair away from his face, gently rockin him, and he settled down. I could see the square line of his jaw and the shine of his deep blue eyes as I sat to one side watchin.

A smile'd found my lips, and I rocked in time with Momma as she swayed gently side to side, hummin to Gerald. Gerald looked content for once.

The look in her eyes was tender, and I could see the love she had for her boy. I'd inched my way across the cabin to her side.

"Go to bed, Lochiel." She'd nudged me away with her elbow. "The loft ought to be good and warm. Go on now."

My heart stung, but I'd held on to that tender look she give Gerald that once.

I'd crawled under my quilt on the floor and wrapped my arms around myself. My eyes closed as I rocked to and fro. In my imagination, I pretended it was me that Momma was holdin tight. I saw that gentle stare in my head and made it all my own.

My hand went to my face, slid down to my neck. I couldn't get my mind to hold on to the idea that I was stole away from my momma. It didn't make sense. Why would Poppy have taken me in if it weren't to save me? "Why would Poppy lie to me?" I must've said that last bit out loud because Walton answered.

"Well, the thing about lies is, they ease the pain. They're the words we want to hear, not always the truth. I wouldn't have told you the way Edna spit out the words. But I know what she was tryin to make you see. There's times we just need unbridled truth. Hard as it is to swallow, it goes down easier by the spoonful."

He placed his bear-sized hand on my shoulder. His words softened. "Truth sometimes hurts. It hurts when our eyes get opened and we find things we ain't bargained for. But in the long run, the truth brings the greater reward. The truth always sets a body free."

My chest ached like someone stabbin a knife in and twistin. I sure didn't feel free.

TWELVE

THE SUN HAD made its way across the sky and set over the summit three
more times by now. Each time it was like drawin in the soft red mountain clay. Lines of color pushed across the sky, changin as the breeze
blew past. Reds, purples, and soft yellows streaked the mornin sky. In
all my years, I'd never really looked up as the sun rose. But Miss Edna
and me was up each day before the sun peeped over the mountaintop.
The mornin's smoky mist blurred the sky as it burned away like freshly
damped embers—gone as fast as it come.

"See that line across the night sky?" Edna's boney finger pointed toward
the summit. "You watch that. It's gonna be a beautiful color in a bit."

"Miss Edna, every mornin you stand on this porch and wait. Why?
What about your work that's waitin?" For Poppy and Momma, work
always took priority over the pleasure of a risin sun.

Edna took in a deep breath. The air was brisk, but it didn't burn your
chest like it did when it was really cold. She sighed as she let that same
breath out. The scent of coffee wafted upward, swirlin around me and
makin my mouth water.

"Ain't nothin better than risin with the good Lord every day. A body
has to stand and take in the blessin of the day. Say a little prayer. Be grateful for a moment."

She lifted the tin cup to her lips and gently blew the steam. The coffee
gurgled through her lips.

"You do this even in the dead of winter?"

"Even in the dead of winter. Don't change nothin. Cold or hot outside,
the sun still rises. Still offers me a new day to fix what I messed up the
day before."

I watched as she lifted her free hand to the sky and whispered words to the Almighty. Her lips moved in rhythm to the bird's song that echoed through the valley. She was the gentlest soul. Her spirit, even when she was huffy, always led her to kindness.

"Miss Edna, what do you say when you whisper them words to the good Lord?"

She cracked one eye open and lowered her hand. Them beautiful teeth gleamed in the mornin mist.

"I look at that beautiful sky, and I tell the Lord thank you for watchin over a sort like me. Then I give my words to Him, so I say good things. I ask for wisdom so I do the right thing. And the good Lord is kind 'cause He gives me them answers every day."

She closed her eyes and lifted her hand again. The more I watched her, the more my own hand itched to stretch to the sky. *I don't know You, Sir. But I'm surely grateful for Miss Edna and Walton.*

Strange enough that I'd take to someone I couldn't see or hear. But I saw in Miss Edna somethin I longed for. Peace in the moment. I wanted that peace.

———

The mornin sun dried the dew in the field. After two more days, it finally dried the water Miss Edna'd poured into my boots. There was work that needed to be done and with that hobble, Miss Edna had a rough time doin it.

Walton hitched his team to the plow in the barn and headed into the back field to lay some rows for plantin. He threw one set of reins over his shoulder and held one set in his teeth. Though the field had been planted hundreds of times, the ground was hard after the winter.

I was no closer to knowin about who I was than I had been a few days prior. Miss Edna brushed off my questions by sayin, "In good time." And I didn't dare ask Walton. He'd made it clear I'd know when the time was right. I'd begun to wonder if there was anything more to know. If all this was just made up or if they would ever give me more than a morsel to chew on.

It was strange, goin to bed at night, warm and cozy, then risin to walk where I wanted to on the farm. There wasn't a soul who forced me to stay close to the house or go no farther than the river. I could walk where I wanted. Sit where I wanted. Eat and know my stomach was full.

Maybe it made me a traitor, a daughter that'd turn on her own folks, but I was startin to think I really was nothin to Momma and Poppy.

I pushed open the barn door and grabbed three pouches filled with seeds. I draped them one at a time over each shoulder and headed to the garden. The back field was a short walk from the barn, and it only took a few minutes to make my way into the soft turned dirt.

"You broke them clods of dirt up good."

Walton tipped his hat and kept callin his team to move ahead.

My feet sank into the rich soil, black dirt tinged with red clay. "Ain't it still a bit early to plant?"

"For most folks, plantin is another two months away. But Edna plants, then we cover the garden with a thick layer of hay. Betwix that and the good Lord's mercy on an old woman, things grow real good."

"To each his own." I shook my head and slipped my hand into the brown bag.

Walton called out to me as he passed on a row. "Drop them seeds about a foot apart. Them's corn in the brown bag. Beans in the white one. Lettuce and such in the dark one."

I dropped the seed into the row, measurin by my foot and gently coverin them. "How many rows of corn?"

"We'll make fourteen. Two for 'maters. One with cucumbers. Leaf lettuce over there and then ten rows of beans."

"Ten rows of beans? It's just Miss Edna. How many beans does a little old lady eat?"

Walton pulled the team to a halt, dragged his handkerchief from his pocket, and wiped the sweat.

"It ain't about what Miss Edna can eat. It's about what she does to make a livin. She cans them beans, and I carry 'em down to Chattanooga or Gatlinburg and sell 'em to the general store. In all my days, I ain't never met a woman who can ask as many questions as you do, 'cept maybe Edna."

"Walton?" I lifted my hand into the air and motioned him toward me.

"Don't ask me. I ain't done ponderin what I need to tell you."

My arm dropped to my side. "Tomato squash!"

I'd only known the man a few days and he could already read my mind. Momma used to tell me that curiosity kilt the cat. I reckon I'd always been the curious sort. All them times Gerald set studyin his reader he'd drug home from school made me wanna know what the letters meant. I'd laid in the loft and looked over, listenin as he'd sound out words.

Then there was the times I wanted to go into town with Poppy and see what town looked like, what kind of people lived there. I wanted to hold a nickel just to know what it felt like. Poppy talked about the livery and how the blacksmith forged the horseshoes for his team. I wanted to smell the hot iron, feel the heat the bellows shoved out into the stable.

All I'd ever known was the sound of the river and a view of the steep summit by our cabin. Beautiful as they both was, I'd wanted to see more.

So I suppose Momma was right. I was a curious sort and my belly ached to know more about the world. But today was not the day I'd get my answers and I was growin impatient.

I walked them rows, measurin and plantin, and before I knew it, I'd run them ten rows of beans, strung 'em off with twine, and set the tomato plants Edna carried to the edge of the garden. Walton had done covered the most of my work with hay in case winter won the battle over spring.

Time passes in a minute when a body is busy, and as I finished coverin the lettuce with cheesecloth, I realized the sun had done passed overhead and worked its way to the other side of the mountain.

"Lochiel! You ain't no slave, honey, come on down for supper." Edna waved from the porch. "Come on, child. Work is done for the day."

I looked around and Walton was nowhere in sight. To beat it all, I wasn't rightly sure when he finished his plowin and strewin hay. I'd been lost in thought while I worked, thinkin through the last few days. I clapped my hands together, sendin dust flyin, and waved to Edna. Though the sun had started to warm the earth, there was still a bite in the air. Spring hadn't come yet, but it had dried enough to make dust. I needed to wash up.

"Miss Edna—"

She pointed toward a bucket and a rag by the clothesline. *Lord have mercy. I'm stayin with a family who knows what you need before you utter a word. Plumb scary.*

The pouches of seeds weren't empty, so I carried them into the barn. I knew enough to hang them on a high nail so the mice didn't help theirselves.

"Much obliged, Lochiel."

I gasped, whirlin around. "You scared the tarnation outa me."

He reared back and laughed. "You're a might jumpy."

"Reckon, Walton? My brother nearly kilt me with a rock, then come to hunt me down with his dogs. You reckon I'm jumpy?"

"Well, despite your bein jumpier than a frog on a hot rock, I'm still obliged. Thank you for settin them seeds. You can see Miss Edna can't really do the work these days."

"I see she has that limp. How'd she get hurt?"

"Ah, age is some of it. But she took a nasty fall down by the river. I reckon she'd have died had it not been for her people." Walton took a burlap cover from a hook on the wall and settled it over the back of one of his mares, pullin it snug.

"Her people?"

"The Melungeons have a camp just over Mulls Mountain there." Walton pointed over his shoulder at the mountain. "They share a track of land with the Cherokee."

I pulled the other burlap cover from the wall, and Walton nodded at me.

"They're good to check on her a few times," he continued. "That's the good thing about these people. They're a mixed sort, but despite folks tryin to make them out bad, they ain't." Walton took out his handkerchief and wiped his hands. "Our people care about one another. They work together, mind their own business and take care of their own. Even the ones is only half. Like me." He stuffed his handkerchief deep in his pocket.

"Anyway, two of the hunters found her and got her back to the cabin. I'm guessin she broke that hip when she tagged that rock at the edge of the river."

"How did she manage by herself?" I rubbed the side of the other mare so I wouldn't startle her. She swung her head, gently nudgin me.

"They sent a couple of the women over to help her. By the time I got word she was hurt, she'd done healed as best she was gonna heal when you have work to do and a life to live."

I tossed the burlap cover over the horse's back and tied it under her belly. "Edna's a good woman. Kind."

"She is that. Though I worry about her every once in a while. She takes care of herself and anyone else who wanders up her lane."

"Miss Edna goes out on her porch every mornin to watch the sun rise."

"Yep. I can't remember a time when she didn't. I ain't rightly sure where she learned about the good Lord, but when she did, everthing about her changed. The mornin is her time to be grateful."

"There ya go, girl. That'll keep the chill offa you tonight." The horse snorted and pressed her nose against my shoulder. "Good day's work. Good girl." He rubbed his hand down her back and patted her rump.

Me and Walton headed toward the house, and I headed to wash up for supper. The smell of Edna's bacon and fried potatoes had done seeped outa the cabin and made my stomach growl before I made it to the porch.

A cool breeze bit at my face as I splashed water over my mark. There it was again. For a short time, I'd almost forgotten. I saw it in my reflection in the water.

"Lookie there, quick." Edna appeared at my side and pulled my hand from my face, placin a rag in my palm. She pointed to the silhouette of an eagle soarin against the darkenin sky.

"Look a yonder at that eagle. This here is why I'm grateful. The good Lord feeds my soul. He mounts me up on wings like that there eagle, and He sets me to soar through the mornin on the breath of the day." She sighed. "Ain't it beautiful?"

I'd never heard such pretty words. Never seen a soul who lived every word she uttered. If I could have one wish—outside of knowin who I am—it would be to be like her. Kind. Grateful. And joyful. But the Devil in me would never allow that.

Thirteen

I SIPPED A cup of hot coffee and watched Edna as she greeted the day. It was the same every mornin, now goin on a month. I was home here—welcome. And though I wasn't quite comfortable talkin out loud to the good Lord, I found a peace in listenin to Edna say her mind.

"Red sky this mornin. You know what that means, don't you?"

"Yes, ma'am. Rain."

"Good possibility. So we best get on the stick. I have a place to show you." Edna grabbed her walkin stick and a basket filled with jars.

I rushed to her side and slid the basket from her arm to mine. "You let me haul them jars."

Edna stepped slowly off the porch and wiggled her finger for me to follow. She pointed to a path into the dense woods. "We'll walk that way about ten minutes." She seemed to be favorin her walkin stick a bit heavier than usual.

We ducked under a wall of grape vines hangin thick from two giant elm trees. The strings of vines had tangled together, makin it hard to sift through.

"Another year or two and you can cut them vines loose from the ground and swing on what's left hangin from the trees." I wrapped a young strand around my hand and yanked them to the ground.

"Where'd you get all these jars?" I pulled one from the basket and gently rolled the preserves inside.

"Careful. Don't you bust my paraffin seal. It'll spoil the preserves." Edna snatched the jar from my fingers and gingerly placed it back in the basket.

Before this, I'd never seen but one or two ever. Momma had one that

Poppy brought her some jelly in once. Momma would never let us touch it. "Breaks too easy," she'd say.

"There's somethin to be said for a son who's a peddler." Edna turned to me and put on a sneaky grin. "Walt brings me one or two jars every here and there. Makes me a nice way to bring in a few coins. Down in the town, the folks that crawl off the train from the big cities call canned goods a treat. Makes me a nickel or so."

"I ain't never seen a train. I heard Gerald talk about one that run through Chattanooga."

I hadn't much more than got his name off my tongue before my stomach started to turn. Love and hate havin a fistfight in my gut. Thinkin about Gerald stirred up the Devil in me for sure. I swung the basket of jars from one arm to the other a might hard and the jars rattled. "I'm sorry!" I quickly checked the basket. "Nothin broke."

Edna pushed ahead and our talk hushed for a while. Though the trees along the path hung heavy with vines shadin the sun, tiny purple crocus blooms peered from the underbrush. The scent of the damp forest filled my senses with a woody freshness. Black and brown wooly worms inched their way up tree trunks in search of the perfect place to wrap themselves in a warm cocoon. Their day would soon come when they'd break free as beautiful butterflies, wings spotted with drips of color. Havin wings to fly sounded mighty fine to me. Flyin on the air, so free.

"I reckon Walton ain't told you no more, has he?"

No *more*? Walton hadn't told me much of anything, but I knew that he was thinkin on it. Almost like he was gettin up his courage. "No, ma'am. Not knowin is killin me."

"I'm gonna give you some thoughts. And you need to know these is long, hard, mulled-over thoughts. We ain't tellin you everthing for a reason. And hard as it is, you have to trust that me and Walt is just protectin you. You understand?"

"I suppose I do, as best as I can. And I'm tryin to be patient. You and Walton have been so kind."

Edna stopped.

"There is one thing you need to wrap your finger around. Pure and simple. People choose to be the way they are. If you choose to be mean as a rattler, then you are. If you choose to be sweeter than honey, then you will be. A body chooses the path they walk. Do you understand me?"

"Yes, ma'am."

"Good. Then you start right now by tellin me what you choose to be. Everbody knows their choices. What's yours, Lochiel?"

Her question took me back. I wasn't sure how to act, how to answer.

"I'm waitin. What ways do you choose?"

"Miss Edna, are you askin me to choose if I'm gonna be kind or mean?"

"Indeed. That's exactly what I'm askin. You got a family who raised you. Ain't rightly sure they loved you, but they get credit for raisin you. And they ain't been all that bad all the time, 'cause you know manners, and cookin, and such. They took time to teach you. They didn't whip you 'til you was black and blue, but they didn't take the time to love you either." She sighed deeply. "There's times that's worse than a beatin." She said the last part soft, like she was sad.

"Momma and Poppy give me what I needed." Didn't Momma tell her that over and over? *We give you all you need, Lochiel. Just be grateful you're alive.*

Edna shoved her shoulder against a branch and pushed it to one side. "Well, that right there is where you need to cypher out the difference. Givin a person what they need and lovin a body, them's different things."

She was right. There was a difference. A real difference. This was just the first time a body had made an effort to show me.

"I know Gerald has never been good to me. It was always his aim to get me in trouble."

"What do you choose now? Don't matter what was in the past. What do you choose to be now? Angry? Bitter? Or will you be better than that?"

I wallowed that round in my head. We hiked up the steep trail windin back and forth across the side of the hill. Jonquils popped their yellow heads through the still, cold earth. The first real signs of spring. In the lower valley, thunder rumbled.

"You best step it up, elseways we'll end up caught in the rain." Edna's pace took to speedin up.

A minute or two later we stepped into a clearing with a small shack, one side covered in kudzu. We hightailed it toward the buildin.

I gazed across the field and realized we were at the summit of this mountain. To one side the sky was all there was to touch. To the other side, another mountain. Another summit to reach and it was just as beautiful as this one. "Ain't this place somethin? It's like the mountains cradle it like a newborn. Look at that sky. I swear, I believe I could reach up and touch them clouds."

Edna didn't respond, starin out like she was lost in her musings.

I glanced back at the shack, frowning.

"Your birth momma was a nice woman. She was kind . . . but her heart grew cold and hard when you was took away. She changed. Before you was born, when I knew her, she wanted a youngin so bad. Her body just kept spittin them babies out before their time. It was like they was poison to her. Then they was too little to live more than a few hours."

Just like Momma Ogle. "If she wanted a baby so bad, why would she toss one out to die? Was that payment for her sin?"

Edna stopped again. She turned and pointed her finger at my face. "I done told you once and I want you to take this in. Are you listenin to me?"

I nodded. Hearin wasn't a problem for me. I was used to listenin real good.

"Your momma never throwed you out to die. And since you got no sense in what is sin and what ain't, then your right to judge a woman you don't know means nothin. We clear?"

Edna meant business and her scoldin proved to me I needed to be a better judge over my words. I didn't mean to rile her.

"I just told you every baby she had, her body spit it out like poison. Why in heaven's name would a woman who wanted a child so bad, toss the only one her body managed to birth out to die? Think, girl. Think."

Edna grumbled under her breath. I wasn't sure if she was maybe talkin to her good Lord or if she was growlin about me.

She could be right. If my momma really wanted a baby so bad, then maybe she wouldn't throw a youngin away like an old rag. Even one marked by the Devil. But if that were true, I'd been blind as a bat.

"So, what happened?"

"Here we are." Edna clicked her walkin stick on the one step that led into the shack. "Least if it commences to rain, we got a roof over our heads." She patted my shoulder. "Let's go. I want you to see this."

I pulled the rope to the inside latch and pressed against the door. The hinges creaked and cried like they was bein punished. Edna made her way up the step, her stick givin her the strength that bad hip needed to steady herself.

She turned a right proud grin. "Watch your step."

"Well, ain't you just sneaky? This your little home away from home?" I set the basket of preserves on the table.

Edna slipped her hand into her apron and drew out two pieces of flint. She cracked them together once, twice, three times before she got enough spark to light a lamp.

"There's three more lamps. Gather them here." She motioned with her arm. "Don't just stand there. Get the lamps."

I jumped and made my way around the poorly lit shack, collectin the lamps.

"Reckon there's still oil in them?"

"Lordy, yes," Edna said. "I keep them filled."

It didn't surprise me. She seemed to always be one step ahead.

"What is this place?"

Still no answer. She was hidin somethin, for sure.

Edna walked the room, rubbin her hand over the small, hay-filled bed, then along the edge of a tiny table. She hooked the toe of her shoe around the stool and pulled it toward her. The legs scraped the floor, squallin like a cow givin birth.

"Do you feel anything special about this place?"

I wasn't right sure what she was gettin at. It was like she had sweet memories here, but what did that have to do with me?

I turned slowly, takin in every inch of the room. Edna wanted me to find somethin, but what was it? If I did find it, how would I know what it meant?

To one side of the room stood a wash basin and a small shelf. The tiny bed dipped in the middle like it needed to be fluffed. A quilt lay folded neatly on the edge. Across the room, a pantry held a few cups and plates.

Over the fireplace, a cast iron kettle hung with a long-handled wooden spoon restin inside. A table and two stools sat by the window.

I squinted, lookin at every detail of the room, but nothin—not one thing—seemed familiar.

Edna had finished lighting the lamps. "Anything draw you toward it?" She waved her hand around the room.

I came to a standstill beside the table. "I'm sorry. There ain't a thing in this room that means one iota to me."

She dropped her head, waggin it from side to side, and made little clucking sounds.

"What's the matter, Miss Edna? What is it you think I should remember from this place?"

Edna sat and rested her elbow on the table, her wrinkled face turned up to see me. "I was hopin somethin might stir in your heart."

"I don't understand. What am I missin? Just tell me and I'll look real close and see if it jars a memory."

Her nails clicked against the table as she pondered my question. Then she reached for my hand.

I cupped hers in mine. "Just tell me, Miss Edna."

"An old lady could only hope. That's all I can say."

"Hope for what?" I was startin to feel a might cranky that she wouldn't just come out with it.

"I brung you here for two reasons. First, it's hid away. Safe. Ain't hardly a soul knows this place is here. There was a time when a road made its way past the cabin, workin its way down the mountain. It's still there but grass covers the deep furrows of the wagon wheels. It just ain't used no more."

I grasped Edna's hand tighter. "You ain't makin no sense. What's on your mind?"

"You have your momma's eyes. Them golden eyes." She let out a sigh. "Lochiel, this is where you was born. This here is your home."

"POPPY, DON'T GO. *Don't make me stay here.*" It seemed that was all the youngin did. *Fuss and cry. That's how I found her and years later it was the same.*

Poppy tightened the knot at her waist and then took her by the shoulders. "Stop your squallin. We'll be back tomorrow. You can git to the outhouse and that's the only time you set foot off this porch. You understand?"

Lochiel snuffed and nodded.

"You hear anyone—the slightest sound—you hide inside, you hear? If anyone's to see you, they're more'n likely to shoot you dead."

Little devil. If only someone would, we could be done with her. I could tell Poppy's patience was growin slim and I know I was done tired of listenin to her beller.

"Here, Momma, let me help you up on the wagon." She smacked my hand away. "Momma, I'm just tryin—"

"Tryin don't accomplish nothin. Don't touch me. I can manage." She lifted her foot onto the stepboard and pulled herself onto the bench.

"I'm ready, Lloyd. Let's go. Leave her be." Momma pulled her shawl tight around her shoulders. "Lest you wanna leave Gerald here to watch her."

I piped up. "No. I ain't stayin back. She ain't my job."

Momma wheeled around. "You're the one that dragged the little animal home."

Poppy lifted his foot over the footboard and crawled up. "The child ain't an animal. You hear?" He snipped at Momma. He pulled the reins from the brake and slapped the horse on the rear. The wagon jolted and bumped over a rock.

I stood watchin as the wagon pulled away. *For you. I dragged her home for you, Momma. Not a day went by I didn't wish I could take her back.*

"Gerald, come on!" Poppy shouted.

"I'm comin. I'll catch up." I saw Poppy shrug and press his hat tight on his head.

Lochiel was hunched over on the top step. I walked to her and pulled her up by the arm. Takin hold of the rope, I worked the knot loose enough that the rope slipped to her hips. "There. Now if you've a mind to you can slip on outa that rope." And wander off into the woods. And if I was to get real lucky, get ate by a bear.

She just looked at me with them golden eyes wide. I patted her cheek real hard. Then I took off runnin and jumped onto the back of the wagon.

Fourteen

There was no words that come to mind. Nothin I could think even come close to what feelins started to boil inside my gut. I know Momma Ogle used to say I wasn't always the straightest stick in the woodpile, but a few of them hints from Edna and Walton started to make their way into my head.

It ain't for you to worry about . . . when the time is right . . . you have your momma's eyes . . . I knew your momma.

And now this? This is where you was born.

How was I supposed to get aholt of that?

My knees grew weak and for a minute I swayed like a tree in a hard spring wind. I sat straight to the floor and buried my face in my hands.

There was nothin to cry over. I was just put back. I couldn't move past the rocks bein thrown at my past. If this was true, Momma and Poppy had lied to me and I hadn't seen it. Reckon I never knew any different. Reckon they'd thought I'd be too stupid to see the truth, and they'd been right.

"Lochiel, honey. You alright?" Edna pulled me close to her knees. Her tender fingers gently scratched my back.

I couldn't find a word one.

"That's why Walt and me, we're givin you just a bite at a time."

I crawled to my feet and walked about the tiny shack. I took aholt of a cup and held it, runnin my fingers around its shape—tryin my best to force a memory.

But there was nothin. I stood at the window and looked out at the unfamiliar view.

The Devil in me had been held mostly at bay, but now he was hankerin to lash out. And Edna was the only person around. "I got no memory of this place. How could you expect me to?"

"Well, it wasn't no matter of expectin, it was more a matter of hopin. I know this is a might to take in. And I know you still got questions. But what you gotta get hold of is, a body can't reshape their life in a day." Edna stood and came close to me. She put her hand out to touch my sleeve, looked into my face, and pulled her hand back. "When I find a piece of fabric I want to put in a quilt, it takes me time to figure how it's gonna fit. I have to trim at it, fold it, twist it, 'til I find just how it lays best. Sometimes I cut a piece and, if I ain't careful, I cut it wrong. That's when I have to do some figurin. Sort out just how to remake the piece so it works in the midst of all the other pieces. That's what you're fightin with right now."

I was fightin alright—fightin with the Devil inside me. The Devil was breathin hot down my neck and whisperin in my head. *What does this old woman know? Why's she tryin to mix you up inside? Why did Momma and Poppy lie to you? Why does Gerald hate you? What else ain't they told you?*

I struggled back to snuff out that voice. I didn't want to be mad at the people that raised a child with the mark of the Devil. There was credit to be give to them for what they did for me. Momma never let me forget that. She never stopped remindin me what was give to me.

But at the same time, my heart ached.

"Edna, look out over the mountain. Them fluffy clouds has turned dark. That's how I feel. Like my insides has turned dark."

The thunder rumbled across the gap, echoin through the valley.

Edna blew the dust from a pantry shelf. Bits of dirt floated in the softenin sun.

"There's one thing I've learned in this ole life. And I told you this before. Pure and simple, I make a choice every mornin when I step out on my porch. Every day, I present to the good Lord what I choose to be. This is why I ask you, what do you choose?"

How could I choose what to be when the rocks crumblin my past hit me square between the eyes?

And the truth was—I didn't know.

Edna lined the jars from her basket on the pantry shelf. She straightened each one in a perfect line.

"Ain't them jars pretty? I mean some is colored with red jam. Some with blue from blueberries. Some is empty and clear. My favorites is the ones that is clear. I figure that's what I choose for my life. I wanna be clear so folks can see what's put inside my heart. It's important folks see who we are."

This woman had done give me more than I could chew on for one day. Between the walk to the shack and the news she'd give me, I felt like I'd been run down by a team of horses.

"Don't you s'pose we ought to head back down to the farm before this rain hits?"

"Sounds 'bout right. Leastways for me anyhoo." Edna commenced to pull other items from the basket that I thought held only jars. "Now, here's some bread and some apple butter. There's a slice of fatback here. You can just warm that over the fire." She turned to me.

"Oh, and you'll need these." Edna placed the flint rocks in my hand.

"Wait a minute. What do you mean, I'll need these?"

"Well, a person can't build a fire without somethin to start the flame with. And there's dry kindlin in the wood crate over yonder. There's shavins too. So, you can start a fire easy."

She stepped out of the shack and down its one step.

I followed on her heels. "Are you leavin me here? By myself?"

"Gotta fit them quilt pieces together. Start to shape a new life."

"But—but you can't just leave me here." Now it was my turn to grab at her sleeve. "What if Gerald comes? I got no way to protect myself."

Edna patted my hand. "I'm just a short walk away. And Walton will be by. Child, we won't leave you to fend for yourself. But we will leave you to fit the pieces."

"But—I—"

"There ain't no buts. You stay here today and tonight. Then you come back down the trail to the house in the mornin after the sun comes up. I'll get you breakfast. But today—tonight—you need some time to yourself."

Edna kissed my cheek and pulled her shawl over her head.

"Gotta beat the rain." She took a few steps and turned. Her smile spoke louder than any words. It was almost like *she* had me home. Almost like I was *her* long-lost child.

I sat down hard on the step of the shack.

What would I do?

All my nineteen years, all I'd ever done was work to please other people. Maybe there was more to life than waitin hand and foot on other folks, workin to prove my gratitude for my food, and for a roof over my head, and for my very life. And that work didn't have no meanin, 'cause I'd just have to do it over and over. It was never enough. I always had to show more gratitude, and more, and more.

A soft mist began to fall. My dress stuck to my skin, but I had no desire to up and hightail it inside. I just sat there on the step, feelin the rain drip from the sky.

Thunder rumbled across the ridge and the sky grew darker. The rain started to fall hard and I was gettin doused. I pushed open the door and crawled inside. Sprawlin out on my back, I stared at the thatched ceilin, then took in a deep breath and let it out real slow. My body relaxed in the yellow glow of the lamplight.

Here, in this little shack, the work I'd do would have meanin. I'd be doin it for myself.

This is right nice. I may be a bit scared, but there ain't no rope tied around my waist. Ain't nobody to squall at me to get movin.

A smile slowly turned up the corners of my lips.

I rolled to my knees and stood. The wood box was filled with plenty of kindlin and logs. Gatherin what I needed to build a fire, I searched for the flint Edna had left me. I took a wad of the shavins and struck the flint. In minutes, a nice flame filled the fireplace.

I scoured the shelves to see what they held. Found a bit of coffee and hung the pot over the fire. I planted myself back on the floor close to the fire. It reminded me of Momma and Poppy and the loft. There was nothin nicer than bein close to the warm rocks of the fireplace.

I poured a bit of coffee into a tin cup and blew across it. Just then the door flew open, and before I could get to my feet, that blessed ole puppy of Edna's was all over me.

"Otis! You scared the tar outa me." His tongue lickin was as relentless as his tail slappin at my back. I tried to push him to one side, but he kept on crawlin up my chest and slobberin all over me.

"Fool dog. Get down." Otis pushed me to my back, and despite how I tried to escape his attempts to show me love, I failed. It was the sweetest feelin, that puppy lickin all over my face.

Sweet, in that the little scutter didn't care who I was. He lapped at my skin despite the mark that marred me. Whether it was plumb stupidity, or genuine love, Otis didn't seem to care. To him, I was a soul—a soul he could love. A soul that could love back. It seemed queer—a puppy teachin me how to love and be loved. I liked the feelin.

I found myself laughin, rollin and rough housin with that darned puppy. Real laughter. Hard laughter. The kind that makes your sides hurt. It was a good thing. Real good. Like I was breathin after holdin my breath my whole life.

I stoked the fire, twisted the wood latch on the door, and watched out the window as the sun dropped behind the peak. Otis followed every step I made in the shack.

"Here you go, buddy. Take a load off." I folded a blanket and placed it next to the bed. The puppy made three or four circles and laid down. Me, well, I enjoyed myself one last cup of coffee and then snuggled into the tiny bed.

Rain pelted the roof and my thoughts drifted. One second I was scared, the next . . . overjoyed. My heart racin the same either way. I had no idea what the night would hold or what the mornin would bring. But for now, I gazed into the flames of the fire, warm.

Free.

Fifteen

The sun seeped through the shutter, warmin my back. I rolled over and rubbed my eyes.

"Otis. Here boy." I slapped the side of the bed.

The puppy leaped to his feet. His front paws clawed at the covers.

"I call you to pet you. Not to share my bed." He whined and I rested my hand under his haunches and nudged him up. "Oh, alright. Just for a minute. But don't you be gettin used to layin on my bed. Your place is on the floor."

I scrubbed his ears with my fingers. "Truth be known, a dog's place is outside."

I swung my head from side to side tryin to stay out of reach of the puppy's tongue. Mid-lick, Otis stopped dead still. His ears perked and he bolted off the bed, barkin at the door.

"What's got your hackles up?" I cracked open the shutter. "There ain't nothin out there."

Otis scratched at the door, whining.

Maybe he just had to do his business. I twisted the latch and opened the door. Otis tore around me like a madman, howlin and barkin.

"Crazy dog." I took the bellows that hung from the fireplace and pumped the coals. A small flame flickered, enough to restart the fire. The hook holdin the coffee pot squeaked as I pulled it over the flame. Otis kept up his ruckus and, after a few minutes, it started to grate on my nerves.

"Otis!" I hollered as I walked out on the step. The dark clouds had passed and a sky as clear as the river held a crisp, cool breeze. "Otis! Get over here." I felt my skin crawl. Was Gerald out there waitin for just the right time to pounce? Fear dug deep into my soul.

The pup ignored me, so I pulled on my boots and walked toward the edge of the woods. His butt stuck straight up in the air and his whinin kept up. I took him by the nape of the neck and lifted him out of the weeds.

"Lordy, lordy. Oh, lordy." A child lay face down.

This little feller was soakin wet. I turned him over. His face was muddy, his hair matted to his head, and blood trickled down his neck. I looked up the bank he'd come down but there was not a soul in sight—nothin but a pony with no saddle. Only reins and a blanket. I brushed the clay from the boy's mouth and nose. He was cold as the river in winter.

All the sudden the hair on the back of my neck stood on end. I looked around for another person. Was this another of Gerald's tricks? Usin a child to find me out, same as last time? I didn't see anyone, but that didn't give me any comfort.

"Hey there, little one." My voice trembled. I gently leaned my face against his nose and caught a trace of warm air.

"Thank goodness you ain't dead." I slipped my arms under the youngin and lifted him from the mud and weeds. "Let's get you inside."

The sound of Walton's team rattled up the old road. His timing couldn't have been better. Walton would know what to do.

I tugged the child against my chest.

Walton's wagon made the turn in the old road and I went to hollerin. "Walton, help me. Quick. Help me."

He stood in the wagon and slapped the reins against the horses. "Hup there, team. Hup."

I begin to run toward the shack, that youngin bouncin in my arms. Walton was out of the wagon before it stopped.

"What in tarnation?"

"I don't know. Otis kept barkin and when I let him out, he run to that stand of weeds." I swung my head toward the stand of grass. "I thought he had a varmint pinned, but when I got close I found this youngin."

"Give him here. You get some water from the well. And git that small black box off the back of the wagon."

Walton took the boy from my arms and rushed inside the shack. I stood there, starin. Stunned. Blood dripped down my arm and off my elbow. A dark red spot stained my dress.

"Lochiel, get that box!" Walton squalled.

I jumped. My heart pounded hard inside my chest as I pumped a bucket of water from the well. I set it on the step of the shack, then hurried to the wagon for the black wooden box. My head went to spinnin and my stomach turned. It was just a few seconds before I started to vomit.

Walton grabbed the bucket of water from the step.

"Now ain't the time for you to get weak-stomached," he said. "Buck up. Git me that box."

My knees kept bucklin on me, but I managed to catch enough of a breath to help me straighten up.

This was just a little youngin. I snagged the box off the back of the wagon and headed to the shack.

"Here."

"Open it. Get them bandages out." Walton stoked the fire and hung the bucket of water to warm. "We need to warm this little feller up. There's a few more blankets under that cover on the wagon. And keep an eye out for Edna. She's comin up the path with biscuits and gravy."

That was just like Edna, bringin me breakfast when I was s'posed to make my way to her cabin to eat. I reckon she worried I wasn't eatin.

I rushed back to Walton's wagon and threw the tarp up. It was well stocked, filled with all sorts of goods. Everthing a body needed to survive in these mountains. I pulled two quilts out from the stack and broke into a run back to the shack.

It wasn't long 'til the bucket of water had warmed. Walton and I washed up the boy. We hung his head over the edge of the bed and ladled water over the gash on his head, flushin out the dirt and leaves. The child hardly moved.

"Reckon he's gonna live?"

"Who's to say? We do the best we can to warm him up and clean that wound. Do you see Edna yet?"

I peered out the window. Down the path, Rufus was barkin and jumpin around. Edna couldn't be far behind.

Walton dried the boy's face. Now that it was cleaned up some, the boy's hair twisted into curls all around his face. Then Walton wrapped him tight in a quilt. "Hang that other quilt in front of the fire. Warm it up."

As I did it, I realized that it was one of the blankets I'd used up on the mountain. Seems it'd been used to rescue more than one lost soul.

The door opened with a creak and Otis dashed out. "Well, I reckon I thought *somebody* would help me up the path—" Edna caught sight of the child. "My lands, what on earth?"

"Otis found this boy in the weeds."

Walton dropped a bloody rag onto the floor. "Child's got a nasty gash on the back of his head too."

"Oh, lordy. Youngin ain't conscious, is he?" Edna run her fingers through his hair, clearin the strands from the cut.

"He was out when I got to him."

"Lift that youngin up and let me wrap his head. We need to stop that bleedin."

Walton held the boy's head while Edna tore strips of fabric. All I could do was pick up the wad of red rags from the floor.

Edna gently wrapped the wound. Her compassion ran deep and was as natural as the flow of the stream. She didn't make no mind over who a person was, just that their needs was met and they was loved. Her tenderness pricked my soul.

Edna kept up a gentle chatter. "Poor child. He's all of maybe five or six. How did he wind up here? Give me that extra shirt you got on, Walt."

Walton didn't hesitate. Without takin time to unbutton his shirt, he pulled it over his head and handed it to her.

How did the child wind up here? What kind of evil had I conjured up now? How could this boy have gotten here unless it was because of me? His head was injured just like mine was. He was left for dead, just like I was. Tears sprung to my eyes. "I'm sorry—"

"Lochiel, look at me." Edna took my shoulders. "This boy bein here ain't your doin. Your doin stands on how you saved him. Now, you stop bein afraid. Just open up your heart. It's that easy." She pulled me toward her and kissed my cheek. "Now, you pull this shirt over that child's head and let's get him warmed up."

I slowly walked to the bed. Walton sat the youngin up and loosened the quilt. His little eyes was swelled like grapes. Edna took my hand and pressed it against the boy's bluish face. "Let his little head rest in your palm and pull his arms through the sleeves with the other hand." Walton's shirt swallowed the youngin up but it was dry and warm. For now, it would do.

I managed to get him situated into the shirt and, without a second thought, scooped him into my arms and walked to the pine rocker. His head bobbled like his neck was broke.

"Lochiel," Edna whispered, "steady his head."

Walton pulled the rocker to the fireplace, and I slipped around the edge and sat down. The child's legs dropped over my knees. He was so small, so sweet. I pulled his head under my chin and rocked him. Edna wrapped the warmed blanket around us.

Chills climbed my arms, the kind of chills that come when you're snuggled in real good. It don't get much better on a brisk wet mornin than to wrap up in a warm quilt.

I found myself hummin as I rocked. Edna warmed her gravy and biscuits while Walton got fresh coffee brewin. Otis and Rufus whined at the door until Walton took pity and let 'em in.

Edna looked to Walton. "You've been around these hills more'n once. Where do you reckon this child come from?"

"It's hard to say." Walton poured a cup of coffee. The scent twirled around the cabin, teasin my taste buds. "I'll head up the mountain to the settlement in a bit. The boy is one of *ours,* Mother."

Edna smiled. "That creamy skin gives him away. And them soft curls. He's one of us, for sure."

Walton had said his momma was mixed blood. And now that I saw this boy, I understood what he'd meant by bein a half-breed.

Nobody knew better than me what it was like to be different. I touched the mark on my face. Livin with Walton and Edna, I could almost forget it was there.

"There was a pony not far from him," I said.

"We got no way of knowin if he was hurt before he got on the pony, or if he got hurt in fallin off it. I reckon at this point it don't rightly matter. Fact is the child is here and he's hurt. It's our job to care for him."

I hugged that little boy closer and, in an instant, my heart opened up. It didn't matter the color of his skin or the softness of the curls on his head. All that mattered was this sweet boy needed to be loved. Needed to be cared for.

I'd been given the task—a task to take real serious.

Sixteen

WALTON MADE HIS way up and down the mountain twice. He didn't have no luck neither time searchin for the boy's family, and it wasn't settin right with me that nobody missed him. How could a youngin—one of *them* youngins . . .

I caught myself settin that child apart from other folks like Momma and Poppy woulda done. They didn't have much good to say about folks that was different. I dampened a rag and laid it across his forehead. How could I, bein marked, think bad of a child who had no choice who his momma and poppa were? I was ashamed.

Edna wasn't in any shape, with that hip of hers, to keep trekkin that path from her cabin to the shack. But she did. Three times a day. She was up with the sun and peckin on my door before the cock crowed. Poor thing was back and forth carryin goods for me to use to care for the boy.

This mornin was no different. She grunted as she hoisted herself up the step into the shack.

"Edna, I can go to your cabin and carry them baskets up here."

"Don't be foolish. You was the one led to this child. It's you that was meant to meet his needs. Has he roused at all?"

"He come around for a spell. I was able to get a bite of bread down him. But just a little. He hasn't said a word. Seems that fall he took knocked him senseless."

"Well, we'll just keep prayin the good Lord sees it in His will to restore the boy."

I followed Edna out of the shack. She was somethin to behold. Her believin the good would always happen—no matter what.

Edna stopped and lifted her hand to the sky. "Well, Sir, I believe Your

Word when You say all things work together for the good to them that
love You. And, well, I love You, Lord. In the meantime, I won't hassle You
with things You done already know, but I'll just ask two things. First, that
Walt can find this boy's momma. No child should be ripped away from
its momma. And second, that You hand down some of that healin you
have. Amen."

She brought her hand to her chest and tapped at her heart.

No child should be ripped away from its momma. Them words stuck
deep in my chest. Was she really talkin about me?

All the questions I'd been pushin down in my head bubbled out like a
new spring seepin outa the ground. They burned. Burned so bad my soul
hurt. Now was as good a time as any to get my curiosity put to rest.

"Miss Edna, don't go yet. I got too many questions and I been good not
to keep askin you or Walton over and over. You told me to just ponder my
questions and when the time was right, I'd know. Well, I've done everthin
you've asked of me. Don't you think it's time I get my answers?"

Edna stopped short, rested her palm against her hip, and shook her
head from side to side.

"Lordy, lordy. Give me the words." She turned and twisted me toward
a set of saw horses Walton had left by the shack. I picked up a plank and
laid it across them. Edna rested one hip on the board.

"Alright. Ask your derned old questions." She give me a stare that
burned right through me.

"What's you and Walton get out of helpin me? I don't mean that to
sound ungrateful 'cause I'm more than beholden. But for the life of me, I
can't understand why y'all would just help me outa the blue. It don't make
no sense."

Edna traced a circle on the plank with her finger. She looked to be
thinkin hard. Pickin her words.

"There ain't no easy way to put this. I reckon whatever I say, you're
gonna get your hackles up. Might as well raise 'em all at once." She took
in a deep breath and rolled her head. The bones popped and cracked.

"The truth is, *we* are your family." Edna's eyes drew a blank expression.
It was like she was free by tellin the truth but she stood waitin for me to
lash out. "There! Now you know."

The leg I'd propped on the plank shifted and slipped off. I stumbled tryin to gain my balance. It was like somebody covered my mouth and nose and sucked the air outa my lungs. I couldn't breathe.

"You're my *fam-i-ly*?" The words hissed out of my mouth.

"Yes. I reckon you would find out soon enough."

"But—but—" I couldn't find the words. "What kind of family?"

"Well, that's a right confusin question, but I reckon you deserve to have it answered. I'm your granny."

"My *granny*?"

Once Poppy brought Granny Ogle up to help Momma when she was tryin to give birth. It was the only time I ever laid eyes on her. And I didn't speak to her. I wasn't allowed. "Stay in the loft," Poppy'd said. "Keep to yourself. You hear?" When Momma couldn't have that youngin like she oughta, she went to screamin. It'd been a hideous scream. Painful like none I'd ever heard.

Granny Ogle called me down from the loft to help Momma push that infant out.

"Don't sit up there like a vulture on a limb. Get down here and help me." When she saw my mark, she went to hollerin at Momma. "It's no wonder you can't birth no baby. You got a child marked by the Devil. She's suckin the souls outa them."

Granny run from the cabin, leavin Momma squawlin in pain. Long time after, I heard Poppy tell Momma that she took down the mountain swearin she'd never be back. And that she'd never speak of me again so as not to have her tongue marked by the Devil. "That's somethin to be grateful for, then," Momma had answered. Wasn't a day later that Granny Ogle died. Poppy said her heart give out. I wonder if it was me that killed her.

I didn't know nothin 'bout bringin a baby into the world, but I stood there at Momma's feet. When that youngin came out, I caught it in a blanket. It was blue, and its life cord was wrapped tight around its neck like a snake squeezin a mouse.

Poppy grabbed the infant and untangled it, but despite his best efforts, the child never took a breath. Momma screamed again, only this time it was the scream of a broken heart.

Grief. Hurt. She'd lifted her hand and pointed at me. "You killed my baby."

"Child. Take a breath." Edna patted my back.

Edna's words crashed down on me like a mudslide. Squashin the breath right outa me. And the feelins. And the words. There was no sortin through to find the right ones to let escape so I just stood there.

"Lochiel! Breathe." Edna pulled me close. Her nails gently scratched my back.

I gasped a breath.

"Walt is your daddy."

And that done knocked it outa me again.

Edna squeezed my hands, refusin to let go. "Walt's been lookin for you since you was took. But in these parts people with a mark is either hid away or killed. Walt never wanted to believe you was dead. He just kept sellin his goods over three mountains, keepin an eye out for you."

She was talkin real fast.

"Every time he'd hear a story about a marked child, off he'd go again. Hopin he'd find you. Tales as tall as they is long, and hardly any truth in 'em. Hurtin his heart over and over. And when he did finally find you—"

"I was nearly dead." I'd finally caught a breath and found some words.

"Yes." Edna smiled. "But you ain't, now are you?"

I'd had more surprises in one year than a body oughta have in a lifetime. Her smile triggered the Devil in me for sure. I was strugglin between grabbin the old lady's neck and shakin her silly, or runnin down the side of the mountain and never lookin back.

"When Walt run up on you, he knew he'd found his daughter. That mark wasn't somethin everbody held. He sold goods to the Ogles, knew the three of 'em. Knew Gerald's meanness." I shook my head from side to side.

"Then why didn't he—?"

"He'd never seen you until he saw your brawl. He was comin to trade goods that day."

"But, if he saw, then—?"

"He didn't see the mark right away." Edna paced, limpin on that bad hip. "He was still on the other side of the river. He saw the ruckus but didn't realize what Gerald was gonna do 'til it was too late. When Gerald hauled you up the mountain, Walt watched and followed. Then he saw." Edna brushed her fingers through her hair, catchin tangles around her knuckles. She stared at the floor as though she might have made a grave mistake.

"The good Lord finally gave him a chance to save you." Edna gripped my arm and looked into my face, tears wellin in her eyes.

"You seem to know this story pretty good." I had half a mind that she was makin it up.

"Oh, honey. Walt's rehashed parts of this story nearly every night since he's been here. He's wanted to tell you, but it was too much to take in, Lochiel. We couldn't just tell you like it was. You was hurt bad. Scared. You was, and still is, bein stalked like a wild boar. We wanted to give you time to take in everthin. It's easier to eat a pig a rump roast at a time."

I clutched my arms tight to my belly and bent over, rockin to and fro. "My stomach's a turnin."

"You're just beside yourself. Breathe slow. I told you this would be hard to take in."

Walton's team rounded the bend in the old grown-up road. The wagon's wheels squeaked and popped as he brought it to a halt.

"Mornin, ladies." Walton flashed a smile as he pulled the brake tight on the wagon. It didn't take long for him to see somethin was wrong. He climbed down from the seat and walked toward us. His gait slowed the closer he come.

"Walton. She knows."

My rockin came to an abrupt halt and I snugged my arms even tighter. He stopped midway to me. His head hung as he shoved his hands deep into his trouser pockets.

I glanced at Edna. Her lips moved gently as she whispered words to the Almighty. It was right awkward. But the more I looked at her, the more I realized her heart was pure. She cared for me. And she'd cared for me from the very first time she laid eyes on me. She cared for me when she stitched up my head and when she lifted her hands to pray. It seemed right to believe her. She didn't have no reason to lie that I could figure.

She maybe even loved me. I used to think Momma loved me, until she told me I'd killed her baby. Couldn't no one love the Devil's daughter if she killed a baby in the womb. From then, I knew Momma couldn't love me, but that wasn't her fault. Poppy still loved me best he could. I made it hard for him by fussin with Gerald, but he still took care of me, told me things, helped me understand things, like why people was scared of me. But gradual-like, his love seemed to wear thin and be harder to conjure up. He'd sooner walk past me than look at me too.

But Edna's love could be felt in her touch. The way she'd scratch my back gingerly with her nails, or take my face in her hands, even touchin my mark with gentleness, the way she'd squeeze my shoulder, or press her fingers tenderly into my palm.

I reckon what she was doin was showin me her love. Lettin me see it before she up and told me she was my granny. Them emotions I couldn't cypher was beginnin to clear and the Devil in me was stirrin my anger to the top. That's what was makin my insides roil. I got up and started to pace. I had some thinkin to do and these people were confusin me.

Edna was still talkin to her good Lord and didn't seemed to notice I'd moved.

Walton slumped off to the shack, opened the door, poked his head inside, then let it close again, real easy. The boy must still be sleepin. When he turned, his face looked all twisted. He pushed his shoulder against the side of the shack. Was he angry that Edna told me? Now he was turnin his back on me? The anger in me struggled harder, and some fear too. Would Walton want me gone now? Why hadn't he just told me right off that he was my daddy and had come lookin for me? If he loved me, his love sure looked different from Edna's. He didn't touch me except when he was rescuin me from one thing or another. And he'd even taken some time to teach me letters. Other than that he just pretty much went about his business.

As I paced, my feet started to feel weighted down with rocks. Each step got harder and slower. I looked at Walton again, his shoulders was shakin, and a strangled noise come from him. He was cryin. And it stirred up the anger in me. What was he cryin about? He wasn't the one who'd just learned about more lies. He'd been keepin purt near as many secrets as the Ogles ever had. My hands itched to do some hittin and hurtin, and I curled them into fists so tight that my nails bit into my palms.

Edna's arms came at me from behind. I whirled and ended up locked in one of her gentle hugs, my arms pinned to my sides. "We was just tryin to protect you. Feed you little bits of news at a time. We ain't never give up hope you was alive." Then she released me, turned, and went into the shack.

Her touch always seemed to help the Devil in me simmer down.

I looked at Walton's back. This man saved me from dyin on the mountain. Saved me from Gerald. I reckoned that was love enough. Though I wasn't one to know what love really is. This was my chance to be angry. To hate. It would have been an easy choice too, but I didn't want to be like Gerald. I wanted to be like Edna. Lovin and forgivin. I managed to lift one foot in front of the other and walk toward Walton. He musta sensed me comin 'cause he slowly turned to face me, his eyes red. Streaks of salty water lined his shadow of a beard.

"I'm sorry," he uttered. He pulled a handkerchief from his pocket and swiped at his nose.

That made me curious. "What are you sorry about?"

"Sorry I wasn't there when you was born. Sorry I couldn't stop you from bein took. Sorry it took me so long to find you."

And, to my surprise, I wasn't angry. The Devil in me didn't rear. I felt relief. There was still questions—a blue million questions. But for this moment, this time, they could wait. I nodded at him, lettin him know I accepted his words as truth.

In a swift motion, he yanked me against his chest. His hand cupped my head and he kissed my hair.

I could have sworn a tender breeze blew past at just that moment, whisperin *welcome home*.

SEVENTEEN

THE REST OF the day was outa sorts. None of us had any mind what to say, but we kept at it. The air was cleared, but we was all left in an awkward way. It was best to focus on the boy. Although I wondered about my mother, I didn't ask. I had more than I could take in for one day. It was a relief when Walton took Edna back to her cabin. I needed more time to sort through everthing. And some time to think about nothin at all.

It bothered me that this youngin couldn't wake up. I could rouse him, but his eyes was heavy and he'd drop right back off. Before turnin in for the night, I warmed some broth over the fire and spooned a few drops into his mouth. His lips was cracked and his cheeks red. Dark circles lined his eyes and his tongue looked dry and rough. Edna had said a few words to her good Lord before she left, askin if he'd consider givin that boy his life back. As I snuffed out the lantern, I wondered how Edna knew when the Lord was listenin, and hoped for the boy's sake that He was.

The next mornin, I was warmin that bit of broth once more, when the latch on the door popped and Edna eased in.

"How's the child?" She placed her hands on my shoulders and gently rubbed. I grasped her fingers.

"He ain't good. The boy's dry as a bowl of dust."

Edna run the back of her fingers along the boy's neck. "He's hot. The boy's feverish."

"Feverish? I didn't know." I jumped to my feet.

Edna lifted his eyelids. "Lord have mercy. The boy's eyes are rolled plumb up in his head. We need to get him cooled down."

"Where's Walt?"

"He makin another trip up the mountain to hunt for the boy's momma."

Edna went to unbuttonin the youngin's shirt. "Help me get him down to the stream."

I picked the boy up and straddled his legs around my waist. "Come on, little feller. You ain't gonna like this cold water, but Edna knows what's best."

His head fell against my neck.

He was heavy, but I limped him down to the shallow side of the creek. Edna stepped into the water, perchin on a rock that jutted from the bank.

"Lay him here." She pressed her skirt into the water and formed a sling. I laid him in her lap and began to dip palms of water over his chest. Edna soaked her hands and gently rubbed his face and neck.

"Come on, little'n. Ole Miss Edna can't help you if you don't help her first."

"This ain't lookin good, Edna. The youngin is burnin up, but his skin is already turnin that pasty grey. I ain't sure how to help him."

"A fever's a lot like a demon. When a body tries to draw it out, it fights like the Devil to hang on."

I stared at her. Still. Quiet. *Devil's daughter.* The taunt echoed in my mind. *Does she think of me as a demon?* Her words cut deeper than a blade. I slid my hand down my cheek, rubbin the raised reddish mark.

"Fever messes with your head. It makes you hotter than hades and makes you shake like you're barefoot in a winter storm. It ain't purty. But you fight the demon's heat. Always fight the heat."

Edna kept right on dousin handfuls of cold water over the boy's neck. His lips went to quiverin and his teeth clanked together.

"I reckon he's had enough." I lifted the boy out of the water.

"It'll have to do for now." Edna glanced at the sun. "We got us a purty day today. Ain't nothin more healin than spring's first sun. It draws what ails you clean out. Take the child back to the shack. I'm soaked to the bone. It's best I head down the path to the cabin and hang out this skirt. This icy water is hard on old bones."

"I got that extra skirt you brought me back at the shack. And the fire is stoked. You can stay here."

Edna let out a laugh. "Child, I'm used to old bones and wet clothes.

I'll be fine. You get that boy back to the shack. Change his shirt and wrap him in a quilt. He's most important. I'll be back when I can. Bring some herbs that may help with that fever."

Edna took my arm and pulled herself out of the creek. She brushed her hand over the boy's face once more, closed her eyes, and spoke. "Lord, this is Your child. We've done all we can do."

She twisted her skirt tail and wrung out the water. "Get that boy back to the shack. I'll be fine. Go . . . go!"

I headed across the field. Edna was right. The mornin sun felt like a sweet balm on my face. It come to mind how warmth, a flame, was two-sided. It could make a heat that saved a life or be the thing that sucked the soul outa someone as innocent as this little boy.

His feet banged against my legs as I carried him. My heart raced with fear. *Don't you die, child. Please don't you die. I'm not a demon that sucks the life from you. I promise.*

I tried not to think about myself. For the time I'd been with Edna and Walton, I'd mostly rested from thinkin on my mark. Now, here it was again. Raisin its ugly head, hauntin me. Drivin me to think this boy could die because I was a child of the Devil.

Lochiel, you ain't no devil. I practiced Edna's words in my head. *Stop tellin yourself you are.*

The plank still lay across the sawhorses by the house. I gently laid the boy on the wood. The pony stood a little ways off, munchin on the feed Walt had coaxed him with.

A ray of sunshine brightened that side of the shack. Maybe it would warm the chill off the youngin. I tucked his hands under his backside to keep him from fallin and run into the shack for a quilt. When I pulled the quilt off the bed, a cloth rabbit dropped to the floor.

I knelt, starin at the stuffed toy. It wasn't much. Stained cheesecloth stuffed with down. Two x's stitched for eyes and a button nose. I poked at the toy. It was soft to the touch. I'd never had a toy. I guessed it come from Walton's goods. My fingers traced the button.

"Ain't you just the sweetest?" I pulled the rabbit close and hugged it. "We'll wrap you up with that boy. You oughta make him feel better."

I stepped out of the shack and froze.

A woman stood next to the boy. Long black hair, tight curls, deep-colored skin. She was kissin his head and sobbin.

I pulled my shawl around my head and draped it over my cheek. Movin slow-like, I eased toward her.

"Land sakes. Are you this boy's momma?"

I gave her a start. She pulled the youngin into her arms. "Stay away. Don't you take no nuther step." Her face and arms were bruised black and purple and her nose looked swelled from a punch.

I stopped and held out my hand. "I ain't gonna hurt you. What's your name?" I inched to the end of the plank.

The woman didn't answer.

"Otis, my puppy, found this youngin over there in the weeds. Me and my family . . . " I hesitated when the words came out. *My family.* They was my family, Edna and Walton. It felt strange sayin so. Strange, but oddly good.

"Like I was sayin," I continued, "my puppy found the boy. We took him and cleaned him up. He's got a nasty gash on the back of his head and now he's courtin a fever."

A soft breeze caught the edge of my scarf. Without a thought, I grabbed it and snugged it tight around my face.

"Come on, tell me your name. I got some hot soup in the shack. If you're hungry."

The woman eyed me, most likely tryin to decide if I was friend or foe. After she stared a hole through me, she spoke.

"Rita. My name is Rita. This here is Joshua." She squeezed the boy tight to her chest.

"There, that wasn't so hard, was it?" I stepped away from the plank. "Why don't you come in and let me clean up your eye? Let me help you."

"Why was my boy laid out on a board?" Her voice was shrill and her eyes darted to and fro like she was lookin to run.

"The boy's fever was terrible. I took him down to the creek to try and break the fever. When I got back, I laid him in the sun to knock the chill." I pointed toward the sun. "It was real warm right here. I thought it would dry him out some. I just went in long enough to get a quilt."

I held out the blanket. "Please, come inside. Let me help you."

Rita kept eyein me. I could understand her thinkin things through. I was doin the same just a few weeks ago with Walt. It looked like somebody had beat her like a rug.

"I ain't gonna hurt you, ma'am, but that boy is sick. Real sick. At least let me help Joshua." My voice raised a notch with every word.

She stood holdin her son tight. I could see she didn't know what to do. I inched toward her, hand extended.

"Please, Rita." This time I whispered. Each step I took was like tryin to ease up on a deer. A body just waited for it to bolt. In my own pain, Edna had whispered kindly, but stern.

"Listen to me. Joshua needs to get warmed up. We need to get rid of that fever. Come now, Rita. Come on."

She slowly touched my hand and I closed my fingers around hers and draped the quilt around Joshua. Rita's legs give way, but I caught her before she fell. It took a few minutes, but I managed to get them both into the shack. We wrapped Joshua tight in a blanket and propped him in the bed. Once he was snuggled in, I turned my attention to the woman.

Walton's black box still sat by the bed. I poured a bowl of water and gently blotted away the blood from her face.

"Miss Rita, I'm so sorry for your bruises." She grimaced as I dabbed at the cut over her eye. "You wanna tell me how this happened?"

She stared at the floor. I could see she held to a secret.

"Did someone do this to you?" I rubbed some of Edna's root salve over the cut, then wrapped it with a piece of cloth.

She nodded. "A man," she whispered.

"You ever seen this man before?"

She didn't answer right off. "No. Uh . . . yeah. Kinda." Her eyes shifted to the floor and I knew she was lyin. "He was with two other men. Lookin for a girl."

My stomach turned, and I swallowed hard to keep the bile down. "Did they think you was the girl?"

"No, but they said she was one of us. One of our kind, and if I didn't tell him where we hid away strays, he'd hurt Joshua."

Her story seemed forced. I couldn't put my finger on what didn't set right except that she was hidin a lie maybe, or leastways part of one.

The nightmare I thought was ended had just snuck back in. My hands shook while I poured Rita a bowl of soup.

"He grabbed me and Joshua run at him." Her voice quivered. "He slung his shotgun at Joshua. Then fixed on showin me what a man he was by liftin his fist on me." She buried her face in her hands and cried. "My poor boy. He tried to help me." Her tears were real.

She peeked over at the boy. "He looks bad. He must have got lost after he fell down the hill."

"He fell down a hill?"

Rita squirmed in her seat.

I knew somethin wasn't right but like Edna preached, I chose to think otherwise. Now wasn't the time to prowl for a better answer. "I'm doin all I can to help the little feller."

"I'm much obliged for your help." She took the bowl in both hands and raised it to her lips but then set it back to the table with a sob.

"Don't you worry none. Why don't you crawl up there beside Joshua and rest? You've been through a lot. I'll go outside and let you sleep."

Rita nodded. She crawled on the bed with Joshua.

I covered her and stoked the fire. Despite the warm spring sun, the shack still carried a chill.

"You rest now."

I slipped outside and headed to the field. Fear was climbin up me like a squirrel in a tree. There was no doubt, the man who did the beatin was Gerald. I knew his mean side was nasty, but always figured that was just the way of brothers. Despite what he did to me, I never guessed he'd be brutal to an innocent woman. Gerald had turned evil—I'd said it a hundred times before. Like a mad dog with a bone he had no intentions of turnin lose, Gerald wanted me dead. I just happened to be that bone.

Out of this whole blessed mountain, how did this boy happen to my doorstep? Edna said the boy bein here weren't my doin. But seemed like maybe it was.

Eighteen

I MUST HAVE set out in the field for some time.

All I could think about was what Gerald had done to that woman and her son.

Seemed like no matter what I tried, I couldn't shake knowin that what happened was my fault. The knowin sat like a rock on my chest that I couldn't wriggle out from under. He'd always been right nasty to me, but it was my diggin back at him that turned him to pure evil. If I'd not given in to the Devil, not let him get under my skin, none of this woulda happened. That little boy and his momma wouldn't have got hurt. I sat and fretted over it until I was thinkin back in circles over thoughts I'd already had.

I had to do right by them. *I better see if Rita is ready for that soup now.*

The pony seemed to have wandered off, but he'd likely not mosey far. Walton could find him.

"Rita? You awake?" The sun had passed to the back of the shack, and the room had grown a little darker. "Rita?"

Joshua lay on the bed, arms tucked tight around the cloth rabbit. Rita was gone. She'd slipped out without me seein her. This was one of them times I wish I'd had the wherewithal to kick my own rear. I shoulda kept an eye on her.

"Aiiii law." It felt like somebody had took a branch to me. She must've taken the pony.

It befuddled me why Rita would leave without her son, but there was nothin I could do about that now. I pressed the back of my hand against the child's jaw. His teeth still clanged together.

"You're still fightin that fever."

I rolled Joshua into my arms and carried him outside. The sun still hung to one end of that plank, so I gently placed the boy there, hopin the warmth would draw out some of the fever.

"It would sure be nice if Edna was here. She'd know what to do to help you, Joshua."

I snugged the blanket around him. He bore the resemblance of a fly wrapped in the webbin of a spider. I felt so bad for the little feller. Worse too, I felt the guilt of what my brother had done.

What if I'd never done this or that? What if I really was cursed and bringin sorrow down on others? What if I'd never be able to escape the Devil eatin at my insides? "I'm sorry, Joshua. I'm so sorry." All them *what ifs* pulled at me, makin tears run down my face.

I didn't know much about the good Lord, other than what I saw from Edna and Walton. I'd listened to them pray to . . . what? Nothingness.

I couldn't see this God they lifted their hands to, but I guess what I could see was this kindness, this special kind of love that Edna held in her heart. It made her right happy and for that reason, I figured there must be somethin to it.

I touched Joshua's soft hair then got down on my knees, restin my head next to his limp body.

My mind turned to the good Lord. *"Well, Sir, I ain't right sure what to say other than this youngin is past what I can do to help him. And now it looks like his momma has tucked tail and run. I don't understand how Edna and Walton can be so quick to speak for You, sayin You'll handle this mess and it'll be done right. If that's so, why ain't this boy any better? Would You really let a sweet child die at the hand of Gerald?"*

"For I know the thoughts that I think toward you, saith the Lord, thoughts of peace, and not of evil, to give you an expected end."

I scrambled to my feet. "Didn't hear you and the team."

"Seems I'm gettin fairly good at that. I see you found your way to your knees. When a body bends at the knees, it ain't an odd thing to hear the good Lord speak to their heart."

I dried my eyes. "A body can kneel when they's tired, can't they?"

Walton crossed his arms. "I reckon so. But they can pray too. Just sayin." He smiled and nudged me.

"Where you been anyway?"

"I made my way back up the mountain, lookin."

"The child has a ragin fever. Me and Miss Edna tried to cool him down in the stream, but it doesn't seem to have helped none." I gently patted Joshua's chest. He looked so innocent, he didn't deserve what Gerald had done.

"Well, luck ain't on my side. I didn't find the youngin's family. But I did get wind of some news."

"What news?" I stared into Walton's eyes. I wondered if my momma's eyes was like his, like mine. Golden.

He picked up Joshua and sat on the plank, rockin the youngin while he talked. "Well, seems Gerald threatened a woman—"

I butted in. "A child run at him and Gerald hit him. Knocked him down. Beat up his momma. The boy climbed on his pony and took off."

Walton furrowed his brow. "How'd you know?"

"Gerald was right about one thing he said years ago. Trouble follows me. And it has. A woman showed up here huntin her boy and said his name's Joshua. She was beat black and blue. But now she's run off again." I fiddled with my shawl. "She didn't say where she come from or how long she'd be travelin. Somethin don't fit though. I can't put my finger on it but I got a notion his momma was lyin."

Walton brushed his knuckles across the boy's cheek. "Well, I've found when your gut presses at you, it's probably right in some fashion. It'll come to you."

"This is my fault, Walton. Gerald did this to them on account of me."

"Now, don't go blamin yourself for Gerald's actions. I believe, without a doubt, ole Gerald is like a crock of fermentin kraut. He gets sourer and sourer and the fumes just keep buildin. He's done popped and there ain't no controllin what the man does now. When your life is fueled by hate, the only thing you see is what you think you want. And seems pretty certain he wants you dead."

"And all because I clawed a bit of skin from his face."

"Aw, come on, Lochiel. Do you really think scratchin back at Gerald is what caused all this?"

Walton stood with the boy and walked toward the shack. "I done told you. A man like Gerald is just waitin to blow. Your strike set in motion the animal inside him. The one that's been clawin to get out since he was a kid hisself."

"But if I had've—"

"What? If you had've what? Cowered down like a whipped dog and walked away? Gerald would've still made the same choices. He'd lash out sooner or later come hell or high water. Meanness does that. It seeps out no matter how hard we try to plug the holes. You think you're like him, but you ain't."

I followed Walton into the shack. His words put me to thinkin. *The animal inside him.* What would've put that animal inside Gerald? It didn't seem right to think of Gerald that way. But what coulda made Gerald so angry that he wanted me dead if it weren't nothin I'd done? Oh, why'd Poppy take me anyway, if he didn't really want me neither? Gerald was huntin me, and Poppy didn't seem to be lookin for me none.

I couldn't answer the questions my head kept spittin out. And the harder I tried, the more questions popped up.

What kept comin to mind was Momma havin them babies and them dyin before they could get a good first breath. Poppy told me of two he'd buried before I come along. But it was the dead baby I'd helped her birth that she blamed me for. She had Gerald—wasn't that enough?

I just didn't know what to think anymore. I'd been called the Devil's daughter for so long that I'd figured it must be true. I'd certainly never wished her baby dead. I never laid a hand on Momma, never hugged her, or kissed her good night. Never asked her a question one about her dead babies or the one she was carryin. How could I have hurt that baby without even knowin I wished it evil? The times I had tried to summon the Devil in me, it'd never work. Just left me feelin angry.

I'd watched Momma sway in her rocker, wrappin her arms around her belly while she hummed. I saw Gerald kick at Momma. Swear. And when that baby was born dead, I remember him laughin while Momma laid flat out on the mound of dirt coverin the dead child.

For the months after that child died, Momma'd cursed me. She swore it was the mark of the Devil on me that took that baby. That's when Satan come to claim his own, she'd say. And I somehow traded that baby's soul for mine. Through all that, I'd still loved Momma and Poppy. I'd still loved Gerald even when he was a devil.

One thing sorta stuck in my craw. Maybe it was somethin, maybe not. But it seemed Gerald got worse toward me after we buried that baby. Every time he looked at me, he bore a hatred I'd never seen before that. Somehow things had to tie together. Somehow, I had to remember.

I started fryin some pork in a skillet while Walton tended to Joshua. I'd already mixed up some biscuits and the water and flour was ready to stir into the grease for gravy. The shack was smellin right nice, and I hoped the scent of good home cookin would rouse the boy.

It was comin clear to me how strange love is. How, despite Gerald's meanness and Momma's blamin, I cared anyway.

"Walton?"

"Hmm?" He whispered as he dabbed a cool rag on the child's face.

"A while back, Edna told me people choose who they plan to be. Do you believe that?"

He gently swiped the boy's chin and then wet his lips with a dab of water. Layin the rag to one side, Walton walked next to me. He placed his finger under my chin and lifted my head.

"Lochiel, I do believe our choices is what makes us. You can be raised meaner than a snake, but make the choice to be good. I believe sometimes, even if we don't know nothin else, there's somethin the good Lord puts deep inside us that roots its way up, urgin us to be better. Why d'you ask?"

"I was thinkin about Gerald. I was thinkin for all the times when we was youngins that he was terrible to me, I still wanted to please him, for him to be happy. And Momma, when her baby died and she blamed me, I still wanted to care for her. I didn't know no other people. But I didn't want to be like them. I wanted to care anyway."

Walton pulled my hair behind my back and kissed my head. "That makes me right proud, Lochiel. Right proud."

I pulled the shutter open. Night was still comin early this time of year.

"Where do you reckon Edna is? She was just goin home to change her skirt from bein in the stream with Joshua."

"I ain't been down to the house since I left at dawn."

"It ain't like her to say one thing and do another. And she was right worried about this little boy. She mentioned she had some herbs that might help beat his fever."

Walton ducked through the door and paced a few steps before he called me out.

"Lochiel, when did Edna go to the house?"

"Early. Long before dinner. She was soakin wet from sittin in the stream. All she said was that cold water was hard on her old bones. She was gonna hang her skirt and bring the herbs. I'd thought she'd have been here long before now."

Early spring on the mountain would warm you in the day and freeze you at night, and it was turnin chilly. A cold breeze whipped up from the valley and against the darkenin sky a hawk circled. I pulled my shawl tight around my arms.

"I'm gonna check on her." Walton pulled his revolver from under his coat. He emptied a few extra bullets from a small cloth bag stowed in his pocket, and popped them in the cylinder.

"You're takin your gun?"

He walked to the back of his wagon and opened a wooden chest, pullin out a second gun. Walton spun the cylinder and checked to see it was loaded, then he tucked it in the waist of his trousers.

"You're scarin me. Do you think somethin is wrong?"

"With Gerald runnin the mountain, anything is possible." He un-hitched a horse and threw his leg over its back.

"Walton, you don't have reins."

"Don't need 'em." He wrapped the fingers of one hand through the mane of the horse and kicked its side. "Stay inside. Slide somethin in front of the door."

The shack wasn't an easy place to find, tucked into a clearing in the crevice of the mountain. But the footpath, steep as it was, was still the fastest way to Edna's. Walton leaned to dodge the overhang of vines and guided his horse down the small dark path into the deep woods.

I wrapped my arms around myself and watched as he bolted into the darkness. This was my father and, though I hardly knew him, I cared for him. Probably loved him, but I was still gettin the meanin of that worked out.

I pulled the latch rope, and just as I pushed open the door, a gunshot echoed up the ridge.

Nineteen

My heart sank. The sound of the gunshot rung in my head.

"Lordy, lordy." I slammed the shack door, twisted the latch, and slid the heavy pine table in front. I pushed the window shutter closed and dropped the wood plank across it, settin it in the rope loops on either side.

When Momma and Poppy would leave me at the homestead and go down the mountain, Poppy would tell me, "Anytime you feel like you're in danger or scared, stoke the fire. Heat up that chimney. Ain't a soul gonna come down a hot chimney into a flamin fire."

I threw two logs on the fire and fanned the flames. I grabbed the lamps and lit them despite the bright glow from the fireplace. My heart raced like a fox chasin a squirrel.

What if Edna was dead? Or Walton was shot?

I pressed my face into my palms. "Law. Law. Lordy mercy, help me. What else can happen?"

Joshua began to rouse. He rolled to his side and worked his arms out of his quilt cocoon.

"Momma?" His voice was weak. I rushed to his side, quickly drawin my scarf around my face.

"Hey there, little youngin. Welcome back. How you feelin?" I stroked his chubby hand.

"Who are you? Where's Momma?"

I pulled the cloth rabbit to his chest and loosened the quilt around him. "Oh, I'm a friend. Your momma left earlier. I'm sure she'll be back soon."

"I don't know you." He pulled the covers to his chin.

"No, honey, you don't. But I found you out in the weeds at the foot of the bluff. You was hurt real bad. Then you took on a fever."

I dipped a cup from the cupboard into a bucket and drew a cold drink.

"Here you go. Take a sip." I tilted his head forward so he could drink. With every move I made, his eyes trailed me. "You ain't told me your name."

I smiled. "Well, does that matter?"

"Well, what do I call you?"

I was torn. I wanted to tell the boy my name, but if I did and Gerald ever run across him again . . .

"You hungry? You ain't hardly eat a bite in two days. You have to be plenty hungry. I got supper ready. Just have to stir in the fixins for the gravy."

I wrapped my skirt around my hand and pulled the hot skillet off the grate. The flour water sizzled as I poured it into the pan. It only took a few minutes for the thick gravy bubbles to rise. I had to work harder to set aside my worries for Walt and Edna.

"I hope you like pork. I'm gonna make you a little plate. Since you ain't had much on your stomach, we'll go easy. Start with a few bites." I cut a slice of pork into small pieces and dipped a ladle of gravy over the meat. "It ain't much. But it'll fill your belly. Eat slow."

I pulled a stool up to his bed and set the plate in front of him. Steam twirled off the hot gravy. He stuck his finger in the food and licked it clean.

"That ain't bad." He pulled off a bite of biscuit and sopped it through the gravy.

"I'm glad to see you eat. You scared me earlier. I thought you was gonna meet your maker." *Meet your maker.* That was a phrase that Walton liked to use. I hoped he wasn't doin that very thing.

Joshua ate a few bites then rolled to his side. "My head hurts." A drip of blood seeped from under his bandage.

"I reckon it does. You got yourself a nasty cut. Do you remember what happened? How you got that gash?"

The boy grew still. He wrapped his arm around the rabbit and nodded. "I 'member."

I sat next to him on the bed. "It's alright now. I didn't mean to upset you. You don't have to tell me about it. Just rest."

Joshua had the prettiest eyes. Deep brown and tender. It was like he could speak with them. He was a sweet boy, and it cut me to the quick to see this little feller scared and hurt all because of me.

"I'll be right here. Don't you worry yourself." I started to give the youngin my name. But I stopped. Did I really want the boy to know?

"Ma'am. Can I ask you a question?"

"You sure can. You can ask me anything." It never occurred to me what might come from his lips.

"Why you got that scarf wrapped around your face?" Joshua's finger lifted toward my scarf.

I felt the color drain from my face. I've never been one to lie, but I felt the hankerin to make up some gosh awful story. Instead, I stared into them deep brown eyes.

My hand eased toward my face.

Edna had told me over and over the last few days a mark was just a mark. It wasn't what made the person. I'd hid behind a scarf most of my life. It was enough to have Gerald and Momma remind me about the purplish red mark that covered my cheek. It was just easier to cover it. There was less snide words. As Momma would say, "Outa sight, outa mind."

And I tried to do that for the most part. Keep my cheek covered and stay outa sight. Momma was right. When I was outa sight, there was nobody to rag over me. No one to torment me.

My courage began to rise. I slipped my fingers under the scarf and loosened it from my face. "I got this mark on my face. It tends to scare folks, so I just keep it covered."

"You ain't scary." Joshua smiled. "You got purty skin. And your eyes look like the sun settin over the mountains."

"Well, that's right nice of you, Joshua. You keep sayin words like that and when you get ready to find you a wife, you'll lull her right into your arms." I smiled back at him. "I don't think I'm scary either, but then I reckon I ain't most folks, am I?"

"You was nice to me."

This little boy warmed my heart. I wondered what it would be like to be a momma. To carry a youngin, birth it, and raise it. How sweet it must be to rock a wee one to sleep. I cocked my head to one side and sighed.

The child tugged at my scarf and it dropped around my neck. His tiny hand gently touched my face.

"That ain't so bad," he said.

Kinder words couldn't have been spoken to me. This little child, in all his innocence, looked past the horrible mark to see only my heart. And it felt real nice.

A second gunshot popped and I jumped clean off the edge of the bed. *Walton? Edna?* I had no way of knowin if Edna had unloaded both barrels on her shotgun or worse, if one was a shot from the enemy.

"Joshua, you stay right here on this bed. I'm gonna check and see if my family is headed back. You stay there. You hear me?"

"Yes, ma'am."

I worked my way to the door and pushed the table away. The hinges creaked as I pulled open the heavy wood door. I stepped outside and the wind that cut across the field drew a chill. The sky was clear. Not a cloud anywhere.

As my eyes grew used to the darkness that had settled over the cove, stars appeared, clear and bright, offerin up enough light to see the dark outline of the trees. I loved that about bein up here. High on the summit, tucked away in a crevice of the mountain, the beauty of the night sky. Peaceful. Despite the fact of the danger that might be lurkin, the mountain has a way of soothin a person's fear. I took in a deep breath and stepped into the night, squintin as my eyes grew used to the soft shadows. The sound of my heart banged in my head. *How could I hear a body sneakin up on me if all I heard was my heartbeat?*

I eased across the field toward the footpath, tryin to think about the beauty of the night instead of the horrors it might hold.

Poppy used to tell me that every star that shined was a soul that had left its body. I just figured they was made by someone bigger. Now I understood. Edna was right. The good Lord must be purty handy.

Along the ridge, the wolf called to the moon. His cry, eerie but somewhat peaceful. It was like he was standin watch and as long as he bayed at the sky, there was nothin comin up the path to give him a start, and that was good for me.

I'd no sooner thought I was safe when I heard the steps of horses. My heart sank. *Was it Gerald?* Had he found me and come to kill me?

I run to Walton's backboard, tripped over stones and fell to my knees. Though the stars lit the sky, I still couldn't see good through the blackness of the night. I crawled until I could pull Walt's extra shotgun from under the rig's seat. I'd never even cocked a shotgun, much less fired one. I wrapped my hand around the butt of the shotgun. *Lord have mercy. Help me figure this thang out.*

In one swift motion, I raised the gun to my shoulder and shouted, "You stop right there! Stop or I'll have you pushin up flowers by mornin." I'd seen Poppy pull back the hammer on his shotgun, so I did the same, hopin I didn't have to pull the trigger. Hopin if I did the thing was loaded.

The footsteps stopped.

"Lochiel, honey. Come help me."

"Edna? That you?"

"Yea, baby, it's me. Me and Walt. Come on. Put that gosh derned thang down."

I dropped the shotgun to my side, headin toward the sound of Edna's voice. Walton reached up and lifted Edna off the horse, then eased the shotgun from my hand.

"Are y'all alright? I've been worried out of my gourd. And where did you get another horse?"

I wrapped my arm around Edna and helped her get her footing.

"Well, ole Edna here is a pretty darned good shot. Seems your brother sent a few men up to check her out again. Edna's the best at landin a shot just in front of a horse's feet." Walton took to chucklin. "She'll force a horse to rear and bolt every time, droppin its rider flat on his back." He squeezed Edna in a bear hug. "Reckon you snagged you a new horse when that boy up and took to runnin without his horse."

"I told them scutters there wasn't no young girl at my cabin. And that was the truth. You wasn't at my cabin. You was up here." She busted into a belly laugh.

"When they wouldn't leave, Edna showed them what buckshot was."

"You shot them?"

"Oh, honey, I don't shoot people unless my life is hangin on the fringe. But I got close enough that them two boys knew I meant business."

I opened the shack door and there sat Joshua, arms curled around his knees.

"Lord have mercy. He ain't dead." Edna hobbled to the boy's side. She pulled up the edge of his bandage and checked his wound.

"Well, would you look at that?" Walton rested his hands on his hips. "I reckon the good Lord heard your cries today, Mother."

"I reckon He did." She brushed her fingers through Joshua's hair. "Praise be."

Edna wasn't the only one who had cried out to the good Lord today. I guessed He heard my words too.

POPPY AND MOMMA *was sure their crosses would fend off Lochiel's hexes. But me they left unprotected from the girl. Figured I was the one that brung her home so whatever harm she may bring me had already been had. Like a baby possum trailin after its momma, she followed me everwhere. Each day it took more work to get her to leave me be.*

"Git on back to the house or I'll use you for bait." I pressed my palm into her stomach and shoved. "Go on. Git!"

The loud snap sent chills up my back. Lochiel had stepped on my fishin rod.

"Now you've done it. You broke my rod." I yanked up both pieces of the rod, sendin the girl sprawlin to the ground. Poppy would be madder than a wet hornet 'cause my rod was broke.

"I didn't do nothin. You pushed me," Lochiel whined. "I just wanna watch you fish."

I slammed the pieces of my rod against a rock. "There ain't no fishin now, is there? You belong at the cabin, workin."

Lochiel scrambled over and picked up the rod. "I can fix this."

"No you can't. I said, git away." This time she'd cost us supper and I'd be headed for a whoopin.

I snagged the pieces from her hand and smacked her across the stomach with 'em.

"You're mean!" she squalled.

I drew back and hit her again to make sure each word stuck. "I said, you can't fix this."

She commenced to scream.

Poppy come runnin down toward the river. "What in the Sam Hill is goin on down here?"

Lochiel run at Poppy ready to tattle. I grabbed her and heaved her onto my hip. "Everthin is fine. I was showin Lochiel how to fish and we landed a big carp. Broke the rod. She's just upset we lost the fish."

Poppy shook his head and walked away. When he was outa sight, I dropped her to the ground and slapped her face.

"You better not open your mouth. If you do, I'll feed you to the fish." I shook her by the shoulders. "Not a word, Lochiel. Not a word."

TWENTY

AN EERIE FOG hung in the tiny cove around the shack. I walked across the field, squintin just to see an arm's length in front of me. Walton had set a milk cow loose in the field and it was my job to gather her up and milk her.

"Come on, Bess. Breakfast." Edna had the old girl well trained. At the sound of breakfast, she would moo and meander over. Bess nuzzled next to me. I felt down her side to her belly and patted.

"Be nice if this fog would lift. Don't you think, girl?"

I set down two buckets. One with feed and the other for milk. Bess rammed her nose into the feed and commenced to chomp. I squatted to my knees and felt for her udder. "I don't need no bucketful. Just enough to feed Joshua today. I'd thank you for just the right amount."

I leaned my shoulder on the cow and rested my head against her side. As I pulled on her teats, I could hear her stomach rumble. With each tug the milk splattered in the bottom of the bucket, and as it filled the splat, splat eased into a swish, swish. I caught myself hummin to the rhythm of the squirts.

"Mercy, cow. Your stomach is rollin like you ain't ate in a month. I believe you sound a bit greedy, girl." She swung her head around and shoved me then went back to the business of eatin. What little milk I'd squeezed dumped onto the ground.

"Fool cow."

I'd been with Edna and Walton comin on two months now and things had seemed to quiet down with Gerald. Like Edna always said, "No news from that devil is good news."

Still, every time she mentioned somethin like that, it made me cringe.

My mark still haunted me. No matter how I tried to forget it, it dug at my mind.

Joshua seemed no better and I wondered if this boy wasn't healin because of me. Could it be my fault—this mark on my face—that made Joshua's sickness come and go? One day the boy would be playin in the field, and the next he'd be down with a ragin fever again. Edna fretted over that gash on his head festerin up instead of healin up.

We'd tried everthing to get it to heal, but here we was, days later, and it was still the same raw mess it was when Otis found him. The last few days, the youngin seemed to worsen. Despite what I fed him, he wasn't fillin out at all. He was a bag of bones. Walton had tied his britches up with a long string of twine to keep them on his hips. I hated the thought of it, but the boy was frail. Real frail.

I patted Bess and gathered my buckets. "Thank ya ma'am. Go on now. Git outa the way." She pulled at the feed bucket, lookin for one last snack. "That's all I got. Go on now. Go graze." The lazy animal would rather eat out of a bucket for the little bit than graze the field for the bounty.

I gazed up at the sky. A giant circle hung over the mountain, blurred by the dense fog. When the fog burned off it would be a purty day.

"Woooo. Woooo. That you I hear, Lochiel?"

I turned toward the path. The glow of Edna's lamp barely cut the white mist.

"Mornin, Edna. You're up here early, ain't you?" I blotted the damp fog from my face.

"Lordy, lordy, what a haze. Thicker than soup. But it's a good sign for a hearty spring. It's when we get these in the fall, I dread 'em." Edna slipped one arm through mine and leaned against me. The walk seemed to be tirin her more than usual. "I just wanted to check on Joshua. I brung some clean bandages."

Edna stepped into the shack. "Ooooh. Nice and toasty in here."

"Is it too hot? Am I makin him worse? He just chills so when that fever attacks."

"No, no. You're doin just the right thing." She rolled Joshua to his back and pulled off the wrap around his head. Blood spilled out.

"Oh my. This ain't good. No good at all. I can't see where it's comin from." Edna pulled some strips from her bag and bound the boy's head.

"Why does it keep bleedin like that?"

"I don't know. Them clots are breakin loose and if this keeps up . . . "

"What are you sayin'?"

"I'm sayin if this bleedin don't stop, the child is bound to run out of blood. He'll die."

"Can't you stitch it like you did my cut?"

Edna twisted Joshua's head from side to side. "Gash is wide. I don't reckon there's enough good skin to pull it closed."

I grasped at ideas to fix the child. "What about some of that mash you make? Could we make a paste to fill in the hole?"

Edna pressed her fingers over mine. "I've done everthing I know to do. Waitin is all we have left. We can't make his body accept help."

I sat next to Joshua and tried to spoon-feed some milk into him. "Just yesterday he was sittin outside playin with the dog. He wasn't runnin and turnin flips, but he felt well enough to sit outside and love on Otis. I don't understand how he can be good one day and near death the next."

A peck come at the door, givin us both a start. Edna took over my spot and I peered through the window and spied a young woman.

"Well, I'll be. It's Rita." Walt had been searchin all over the mountainside after she'd run off and hadn't found hide nor hair of her. "Joshua, it's your momma."

"Hustle up and let the poor girl in," Edna urged, wavin the spoon at the door.

I unstuck my feet from the floor and pulled my scarf around my head, coverin my cheek. I pulled open the door. "Rita, where you been? I was worried sick."

"Don't matter. How's my—? Who's that?" She looked warily at Edna, hovered over Joshua.

"That's Miss Edna. She lives down the ridge. She's good with healin."

Edna stood and moved a bit to the side, givin Rita full view of her son.

In a moment, she was kneelin at Joshua's side, touchin him all over, pressin gentle kisses to his hands, layin her cheek on his arm.

"He's not so good." Edna's words were as gentle as she could make them. "Up one day, down the next. Fever, no fever. And now he's took to bleedin again. I was just gettin ready to pray over the boy."

I stepped up. "Edna, let me. Let me pray."

Edna looked a might surprised. "Well now, ain't that just the berries?" She waved her hand toward me. Rita didn't budge as I laid my hand on Joshua's head.

"Lord, I ain't much on speakin prayers. But I reckon I've seen Edna do it enough that I can manage. This here little boy suffers because of the cruelty of another. Help us save this innocent child. Amen."

"That was right nice, Lochiel. I'm guessin the good Lord took note." Edna took my hand and squeezed. "Yes, right nice."

Rita eased up to the boy's head. "He's bleedin bad. You tried pourin cold river water in the hole?"

Edna turned to me. "We ain't tried flushin cold water in it. Lochiel, run out and pump some of that spring water up. It's ice cold."

I grabbed a bowl and run to the pump. *One, two, three.* The rusty pump groaned as I heaved up and down on the handle. *Come on. Any other time you'd shoot water in my face. Seven, eight, nine . . .* Water finally sprayed out of the nozzle.

I filled the bowl and headed back inside. Edna had emptied a bucket and placed it by the bed. We rolled Joshua to his side. His momma held his thin face whilst Edna dipped the icy water into the gash on the boy's head. The clear water turned bright red, but Edna kept ladlin the water on. After a few dips, the red cleared and it seemed we'd managed to stop the bleedin.

"Lord have mercy. Between Rita and the good Lord, we've managed a little more time with this child."

Rita gently blotted Joshua's wound and Edna wound the white cheesecloth tight around his head. "Let's hope we get a few hours outa that."

"I'm glad you came back, Rita. We was so worried." I handed her a cup of warm coffee. "When's the last you ate somethin?"

I buttered a fresh biscuit and laid it on a plate next to her.

"It's been a couple of days. I've been hidin out in that old mine round the mountain. I could hear them dogs howlin and it just scared the water outa me."

"You're safe now. Just eat a bite."

The sound of hooves echoed in the mist. "Whoa there, team. Hooo!"

"There's Walt."

Rita yelped.

"No. He won't hurt nothin, Rita. He's stayin some with Edna." I started to the door.

Walt burst through, nearly knockin me off my feet. His bronzed skin was flushed and sweat run down his hairline. Edna come to her feet.

"What's wrong?" I said.

Walton froze as he took in the sight of Rita.

"Walt, this here's Rita, the boy's mother."

He grabbed a blanket and rolled it tight, then dumped the pan of fresh biscuits into a saddlebag and dropped in his canteen of water. He stuffed the flint from the shelf and the blanket into the other saddlebag. In one swift yank, he snatched me by the arm and run me outside.

Edna followed in a tiff.

"What in the world are you doin?"

Walton untied a horse from the rear of his rig and threw a saddle over its back. "This here is that horse Edna scarfed from her unwanted visitor the other night. Take him."

"You're scarin me, son. What's wrong?" Edna followed on Walt's heels.

He cinched the saddle and adjusted the length of the stirrups, hands and arms flyin.

"We can't talk in front of that woman."

"Why?" I said.

Walton didn't seem inclined to explain. As soon as the saddle was readied, he dragged me and the horse away from the cabin.

"You get on this horse and take up the side of that ridge." Walton pointed over his shoulder to the wooded mountain behind him. "The path is weak, hard to see, but it's there. Get over the ridge and cross the gap to Thunder Mountain. You'll know it when you see it. The mountains rise high on either side. Wind echos off them ridges, soundin like the rumblins of thunder." I shook my head, takin in Walt's instructions.

"There's a small homestead snugged tight in the valley. A man named Silas Dalton lives there. He's a good man. We've talked. He'll be lookin for you."

Walton took my arm and placed it over the horse's neck.

"But I—"

"Give me your foot."

I lifted my foot into his hand, and he heaved me onto the horse. "It's most of a day's ride. Slow goin, but don't you stop. You hear me? Don't you stop for nothin. And you'll be there before nightfall. The path winds. Now go!"

"I ain't goin nowhere 'til you tell me what I'm facin!"

The fog had begun to slowly fade, and the face of the sun barely peeked through. Walton wiped his forehead against his sleeve. He drew back and spit.

"I run across Gerald's posse at the foot of the mountain. He's like a bloodhound, and he aims to find you." The urgency in his voice was strong.

"But we ain't heard nothin from him since his boys come to Edna's."

Edna patted my leg. "You do what Walton says."

"But—Joshua. What about Joshua?"

"We'll get him and his momma home." Walton tied the saddlebags to the horse. "Don't waste no time."

Walton hadn't much more than got them words out of his mouth when we heard a blood curdlin scream.

I whipped the horse around and there was Rita—hands over her mouth—screamin like a banshee. "The Devil's daughter! He was right. He was tellin the truth all along."

In the rush, my scarf had dropped from my head. Fear shot through me like a pellet. Oh Lord have mercy. She'd seen my mark.

Edna rushed to Rita. "What that man said ain't what you think. This here is Lochiel. She's a good soul."

Rita raised her finger and pointed. "Look at that mark. We all know what that mark is." She turned back to the shack.

"Rita, wait!" I nudged the horse toward her and leaned forward, beggin her to understand. "You saw me. You talked to me. I ain't no devil! I helped Joshua and you."

Rita held up her hand. "Don't you come no closer to me. Stay away. My boy is dyin and now I know why." She ran into the shack but I could hear her shriekin, as if the good Lord would hear her better if she spoke real loud. "Lordy mercy. Lord, protect us from this devil."

Edna looked at me helplessly.

Rita ran back out of the shack with Joshua straddled around her waist.

Edna reached out to him, but Rita yanked away. "Rita, honey, the child's head is pourin blood. He ain't in no shape to travel. Put him back on the bed and let's stop that bleedin."

"That's some spell the Devil has cast on my baby. She's the one makin him bleed. She wants his soul. Lord, help my baby." Her wails burned in my ears.

Walton grabbed the reins on the horse and yanked him around. He took hold of my shirt and drew me to his face. "Lochiel! You look at me. Get up that ridge. Don't you stop 'til you find Silas. Remember, Silas Dalton."

"But, Joshua . . . Edna . . . what if—"

"I ain't tellin you again. You just remember, despite it all, you are my child. I will find a way to fix this."

I stared into his eyes. If it was possible, he wore fear and compassion both on his face.

"Walton, I—"

"I love you, girl." He drew back and wacked my horse's hindquarter. The horse reared a bit, then bolted into the fog.

TWENTY-ONE

THE DENSE FOREST couldn't keep the damp spring mist from beneath its foliage. Wet limbs filled with buddin leaves smacked me in the face. The leaves of the past fall covered the trail, makin it slick.

Walton had give me a strong horse, but strength couldn't help with the slippery, wet leaves. The steed would take two steps and slide, groanin and steppin again. Walton was right when he said the path was weak.

I thought the hidden trail from Edna's to the shack was hard. This one climbed the hard side of the mountain—so thin that at times my shoulder would scrape the side of the bank.

I patted the horse. "Come on, boy. Don't you lean to the left. We'll both tumble off this ridge." I tried not to look down.

The mountains are deceptive. Beautiful in one breath, but all the glory, all the beauty of touchin the heavens and kissin the clouds as they pass is dangerous. Even treacherous.

We crested the first ridge and a small clearing came into sight. I shaded my eyes, blockin the sun enough to see the next rise in the mountain. In the distance, I could see the gap openin into sky, and the second mountain Walton described. It looked so far away. He'd said I'd know it when I saw it. I reckoned that must be it. For a minute I wondered if the mountain that laid ahead was Thunder Mountain. I had to trust Walton wouldn't guide me wrong.

"You need a rest, boy." I laid my head against the animal's neck. His heartbeat pounded in my ear.

"I don't reckon we know your name." I slid off the saddle and led the horse to a small spring that bubbled from the ground. "Get yourself a drink. I'm of the mind you deserve it."

The horse sniffed at the water then began to swirl his tongue in the clear puddle.

His wasn't the only heart that was racin. Mine felt it would rip through my chest.

It's funny what fear does to a body. Your mouth dries, heart runs a mile a minute. You shake. Sometimes you lose your water, but for all the times I was afraid as a child, none of that could match up to this.

I ain't right sure that Momma and Poppy would ever know the fear a five-year-old youngin had when left with a rope tied around her waist. Left alone to wonder what banged in the night on the mountains.

I'd been scared witless.

The longer I was away from Poppy and Momma, the more my eyes opened. And though I can't say they ever laid a hand to hurt me, there was more ways of meanness than just layin an ill hand on a soul.

In the weeks I'd been with Edna, I'd felt safer than I had my whole nineteen years. I still wrestled with the fact that Momma and Poppy raised me. I loved them, but hated them in the same breath. And Gerald, there was nothin right or kind about him after Momma lost that baby.

Now here I stood, high above the rest of the world. *Was I close to the door of heaven?* Lookin out over the valley below and seein how them mountains just kept reachin upward, I wondered why I'd been allowed a taste of love only to have it ripped away again.

When I'd ask questions like this, Edna would say things like *faith is the substance of things a body hopes for, the evidence of the things a soul can't see.* I reckon I had faith in Walton, faith that he wouldn't send me runnin like a chicken with its head cut off.

In the short time I'd known him, he'd never outright lied to me. He didn't tell me everthing right off, but I reckon if he had, I wouldn't have believed him anyway.

The horse gnawed at some new grass raisin its stems so I eased to the edge of the mountain and peered over. I didn't know much about the heaven Edna talked about, but if it looked anything like the valley below, it had to be a beautiful place.

The river twisted and turned over the land like someone had dropped their finger into the mud and drew a line for it to follow. The brown limbs of the trees were spittin sprigs of green. And from here, I could see the world below wakin up to spring.

It was a sight I'd never seen from Momma and Poppy's homestead, and one—now that I had tasted it—I didn't think I could live without.

I walked back to the horse. He'd cooled down. No longer did sweat soak his coat.

"I can't just keep callin you horse. So I'm gonna give you the name Sky, since you brought me up this far I can almost touch the sky. So Sky, we got us a ways to go. A few more spots to climb before we hit the summit and bear down on the valley. You ready?" The horse shook his head and snorted. "Glad you approve. We best keep movin."

I'd never been on the back of a horse this big before today. Poppy let me ride a horse around the yard a few times, when I was a youngin. A treat on days when he was feelin restful and kindly. He'd sit on the porch with his feet up and smoke his pipe, watchin that I was careful to keep a slow pace. I mighta been ten the last time. Momma come out and sat by Poppy on the porch. She was feelin poorly and wanted my help with dinner. "She may run off, then what'll we do?" she said, and that was that. After that, Poppy always made excuses why I couldn't ride anymore.

Without Walton to give me a boost, I tried to reach the stirrup with my foot, but found real quick just how fast my backside could hit the ground. Seemed I was learnin a lot the hard way lately. A body learns fast when they get throwed into it. It took a few tries, but finally I hopped, grabbed the saddle horn, and pulled myself up 'til my foot found the stirrup.

"I thank you for standin right still whilst I made a fool of myself tryin to get on your back." Sky flipped his head and huffed. "Let's hope when we start down the mountain it's easier than comin up."

I took the reins and gently kicked Sky. He set out at a walk.

"Reckon Walton said we needed to hurry. Can you pick up the pace?" Sky lumbered onto the trail. I bounced forward in the saddle. "Come on, horse. Go."

Nothin seemed to rush the animal, so I dug my heels into his side. He perked them ears, snorted, and broke into a run. I bounced up and down on that beast for a good while until I figured out how to raise with him. And when I finally come into rhythm with him, I could have sworn the horse whinnied with joy. I managed to pull him to a stop. The balance I'd gained in them few minutes wasn't enough for me to hit that slick path down the other side of the mountain. Sky shook his head and snorted. "Alright, you win. Slow. And hope we make the valley by nightfall."

We had traveled a good mile or so before I picked up the howls of a pack of dogs. *Walton said Gerald hadn't made it this far on the mountain . . .*

The path had narrowed again. The outer ledge, closer than I felt good about. I dropped from the saddle and set about to climb the bank into the woods.

"Come on, Sky. You ain't got me on your back. Come on." I pulled on his reins and the two of us worked our way up the steep bank. The brush was thick and filled with briars grabbin at my arms and snaggin my hair.

Ahead on the path, I spied the carcass of a half-eaten rabbit. A buzzard squawked as it circled overhead.

"I have an idea, Sky. We're gonna borrow that buzzard's supper."

I wrapped the reins around a limb and grabbed the dead animal. I took in a good breath and rubbed it on my arms, legs, and shoes. Then I did the same to Sky. Without hesitatin, I rammed a stick through the rabbit and headed back down the bank, rubbin its body over the path we'd taken.

"Show mercy, Lord. That rabbit's rank. But maybe, just maybe, it'll hide our scent."

I made my way back to Sky and the two of us edged our way through the thicket. At the top of the knoll, I could look across the gap and see the tiny valley at the foot of what I hoped was Thunder Mountain. A small farmhouse sat to one side of a plowed field, and a barn stood at the other. It looked like a friendly place. Rail fencin lined a trail to the homestead. The river wound its way round the side of Thunder Mountain and across the field behind the house.

That has to be it. The Dalton place. Or at least I hoped it was.

I managed my way back onto Sky and we inched our way down the slope toward the valley below. Sky pushed his rear toward the ground and braced hisself with his front legs. The animal was faithful in his efforts to get us down the hill. When the slope leveled, we stopped. The horse's sides heaved.

I put my arms around his neck and squeezed. "Thank you, my friend. Thank you."

The sound of the dogs had faded into the wind and I felt a tinge of relief.

I'd not paid much mind to all that Walton had tied to Sky, but danglin from the back of one saddlebag was a shotgun. Even in his haste to get me away from the shack, he'd managed to offer me some means of protection. I run my hand along the barrel. I'd never liked guns, even though on the mountain they was a necessity. It was the thought of killin somethin—drainin the life out of a soul—that sent chills up my spine. Poppy'd never allowed me to lay hand to one anyway. I slipped off the horse's back.

I slid the gun from the scabbard and popped open the chamber. I'd watched Poppy clean his gun more times than I could count. Two bullets lay seated inside. I plopped to the ground with the shotgun laid across my lap. All them *what ifs* commenced to eat at me. *What if Gerald found me? What if I had to face him down? What if I tried to shoot him and missed? What if? What if?*

As horrible as Gerald was to me, I wasn't sure I could even pull back the hammer and pinch the trigger. But I sure wouldn't want him havin the satisfaction of doin me in. I'd do everthing in my power to keep from havin his face be the last thing I see of this world. I'd sooner throw myself off the mountain.

My thumb rubbed the trigger on the gun as I stared across the gap. How on earth could the world look so beautiful and be so filled with evil?

My mind wandered back to the shack. Rita's screamin and callin me the Devil's daughter. This mark on my face made me a monster. Part of the evil. And whether I wanted to take hold of the fate I'd been dealt or not, Rita's screams was enough to tear a soul apart.

I wasn't sure I wanted to live like that. Always fearful that my scarf might slip. Hidin behind the scent of a dead rabbit. Not another soul had ever laid eyes on me outside of Granny, and that was one time. We never saw her after that and Gerald had taunted me. "The sight of you drove her crazy. That's why she ain't never been back. One look at the Devil's daughter and she went mad."

One look at the Devil's daughter . . .

Tears dripped down my nose and off, findin their restin place on the barrel of the shotgun.

"There ain't a soul on earth aside from Walton and Edna willin to look past this mark and see my heart."

In a second of courage, the tears dried up and I pulled the hammer back on the gun and locked it in place, then turned the weapon to my chest and braced it between my knees. I stretched hard to reach the trigger but my arm wasn't long enough. I rubbed my hand in the leaves until I found a stick.

That ought to do it.

If I put a shell through my own chest, the curse would be gone. Gerald wouldn't get the pleasure of killin me. No one would be saddled with carin for me or protectin me. I could rest from wrestlin the Devil. There was a piece of freedom in that idea. I reached with the stick toward the trigger.

"You need help with that?" The voice boomed from behind me and I let out a yelp worse than a beat dog.

I twisted back to see behind me a stocky man, his hair the color of red maple leaves. A beard hung to his neck, and his eyes was as green as the summer grass.

My heart stopped. "You can kill me if you want to. I'd be better off. Save a lot of folks grief."

The man wrapped his fingers around my gun and yanked it away. "I ain't quite sure why you're feelin so sorry for yourself. Don't think I've seen a purtier sight in ages."

He propped the shotgun under his arm and extended his hand. I eyed him for a minute, then took hold. He pulled me to my feet.

"Name's Dalton. Silas Dalton."

TWENTY-TWO

THE MAN STARED hard at me, but with kind of a smile playin at his lips. "You didn't really plan on pullin that trigger, did you?"

"I—well—I'd got right brave. I thought—"

Dalton. Silas Dalton. This was the very man Walton sent me to find. Of all the creatures on the mountain, this is the one I end up crossin paths with. I shook my head. Now that my courage had been snatched from me, I felt tears comin on again. I wasn't sure if I wanted to hug this bear of a man or run.

I dropped my gaze to the ground. "You got no idea . . ."

"You must be Lochiel." He craned his neck to look under my scarf at my mark. "Yep, you're just who Walton said you was."

"He tell you that you'd know me by my mark?" I snapped.

"That and the fact you'd likely be a woman alone. It's a mighty fine day." He released the hammer and shoved my shotgun into the scabbard, then took Sky by the reins, leadin him down and whistlin a tune. Was he expectin me to follow?

"You comin?" He hesitated and glanced over his shoulder. "Sun's settin." Without the gun, there wasn't reason to sit there any longer. I took off after him, just in time to have a branch catch me in the chest when he pushed passed it.

I let out a groan.

"Best watch them limbs."

This Silas Dalton had done begun to make me a little ill. I gritted my teeth and prepared to give him some sass, but then he started up his whistlin again. Took the steam right outa me.

We stood at the edge of his homestead, still up the mountain a bit. He looked down over his place, seemed right proud. The field was wider than it looked from the ridge. "That's my house. Built it myself." He pushed his hair away from his face and pulled his hat tight on his head.

The sight of his nub of a hand give me a start. Before I could mind my manners, my mouth flew open and words darted out like a June bug on a string.

"You only have one hand."

He smiled, then commenced to laugh. "You reckon?" Silas held up his arm, twistin the nub of a hand from side to side.

"What happened? I mean—how'd you—" My face got all hot and I clamped my mouth shut.

"I reckon me and my twin brother, God rest his soul, had us a little battle before we was born. Ain't sure how he managed, but the little dickens broke my hand so bad that my daddy made the doc cut it to a nub. Momma used to tell me Daddy would say, 'A man can't work with a withered hand but he can use a nub.' From then on they begin teachin me to work around what I didn't have."

Silas stared at me until I squirmed inside. I pretended to look around, run my fingers into my hair, and then pulled my scarf over my head, wrappin it to conceal my mark.

"I'm thinkin maybe we need to get to know each other a bit before we move on." He gestured to a rock that jutted up from the bank a few feet away. So I made my way over, pulled my skirt up, and planted my backside on the cold rock. Silas settled down beside me, but he didn't seem in too big a hurry. After runnin for my life most of the day, seemed like I should be huntin to hide out somewhere.

Silas pulled a tiny pouch from his pocket and balanced it against his shoulder. He fiddled with it until he had it snug between two fingers. With his least finger, he stretched his bottom lip out and filled it with a pinch of tobacco. It was somethin to watch a one-handed man do what others needed two to accomplish. Silas cleared his throat and spit.

"Well, little lady, how about you tell me about that mark. Was you born with it?"

He wasn't in no hurry, but he sure didn't beat around the bush.

"I ain't known nothin else. Momma and Poppy raised me, tellin me my real momma had throwed me out to die. Said Poppy rescued me from bein eat by wolves." Once I opened my mouth, seemed I couldn't shut it. Out poured everthing that had happened from the day that Gerald wacked my head with a rock. And a few things from before that too. Silas kept listenin and noddin and uh-hummin, and I just kept right on a talkin. I told him about bein called the Devil's daughter and about not knowin my powers and about Walton savin my sorry hide, and about Edna's good Lord, and about Rita and Joshua gettin hurt on account of me and then runnin off in fear. Eventually I ground to a halt. "I ain't sure if what they say ain't right. Maybe I am a hex on people and conjurin up the Devil."

It was the most words I'd ever put together at one time in my entire life and the sun was hangin low in the sky when I was done.

Silas was quiet for a spell. My rear was turnin to ice and I wriggled on the cold rock.

"Missy, doin the Devil's work ain't caused from a mark on your face." Silas gently tugged the scarf from my face so it fell around my shoulders. "Doin the Devil's work is a choice. And it don't sound like you ever made that choice. Did you?"

I bowed my head. "I've fussed with Gerald somethin awful. Wished him dead plenty of times. The Devil in me flares up whenever I get riled."

Silas about choked on his chaw. "Lands a goshin. What youngin ain't ever whopped up on a siblin? If you ain't conjured up some godforsaken garble of words and throwed out a curse, I'm guessin you ain't been taken holt of by the Devil."

"But what if—"

"Now, the way I see it"—Silas shifted a bit closer to me and touched my cheek—"people don't understand that mark. Most mountain folks live by fear, distrust, and wives' tales. Mostly 'cause they don't know no better. Once they get some understandin, 'specially if the good Lord gets aholt of 'em, they take you under wing and there ain't nothin or nobody who can do you harm."

"I'm scared."

He patted my knee. "Rightfully so. Ain't many folks in your spot that wouldn't be scared. Never knowin if a body will be friendly or turn tail and run. But we're gonna round up Gerald and his posse. You'll see. We'll set things right and you'll be fine."

"It's more than bein chased by Gerald. It's more than knowin he wants me dead. It's findin out my whole life has been a lie. I'm still tryin to make heads or tails out of Walton bein my daddy."

Silas nodded. "I can see your worry. It would be odd to suddenly find out a stranger is your daddy. But I know Walton Grubbs. I'd heard him tell about huntin these mountains for his child. He never give up hope. It was by the grace of the good Lord he run up on you on that mountain. Findin you was the answer to his prayer."

The Devil's daughter bein the answer to Walton's prayer. I let out a laugh from deep inside my belly. Momma wouldn't take kindly to that idea. She'd only ever prayed to the Lord Almighty for protection against me.

Silas stood and offered out his one good hand. "We should get goin. I got a shed with a fireplace in it. We can bed you down there. You oughta be snug as a bug in a rug."

I ignored his hand and hopped down. "What about your wife? Does she know you're bringin home a stray?" Some new fear nudged my insides.

Silas ambled over to Sky and patted his neck. "Just hold to the saddle goin down this hill. That horse has better footin than most billy goats."

We inched our way down the steep bank to the flatland of the valley. A long lane sleeked gently past a plowed cornfield and small garden. Split rails laid along the trail waitin for someone to finish layin them in for a fence.

"You didn't answer me. Is your wife alright with me comin here?"

"Ain't got no wife. Ain't seen a need."

"You ain't went huntin for a wife 'cause of that hand?" I swallowed hard. Seemed around this man I couldn't keep my mouth from runnin.

He stopped and stared me up one side and down the other. A smile come across his lips. "You may be right, little lady. You might just be right."

I could see what Edna was gettin at when she told me my mark was just a mark. They seemed to be people everwhere that had it bad off. Seems we all had our marks of sorts.

Twenty-Three

We turned the bend to Silas's house. It was tall as it was long and right purty. A porch wrapped around it like a warm coat on a cold winter's night. Four pine rockers lined the railin, and empty flower boxes set on the plank porch.

"It's white." I'd never in all my days seen a homestead so bright and beautiful.

"I traded for whitewash. I pull that sawmill round the mountain sawin lumber for folks. Sometimes they pay me in money, but most times they barter. It pays well when you want to build a nice cabin."

Silas showed me round a bit before settlin me inside the outbuildin a few feet from the house. He had a springhouse and a chicken coop full of hens. I couldn't help but think they needed a missus to dance with them like Edna did.

"It ain't much. But I've made it so anybody passin by could at least rest if need be. I figured folks might stay here every once in a while."

I run my hand across the mantel. "It's right nice. Thank you."

"I call it the shed." Silas shuffled his feet. "Well, I got stew simmerin. You can clean up down in the springhouse. That'll offer you some privacy. When you're ready, come on up to the house and grab a bowl. I make the best venison stew this side of the mountain."

"Silas?"

He paused in the doorway. "Yes, ma'am."

"You said Walton was huntin for me?"

He hesitated, then turned. "Ever since I can remember. He'd come by our place to trade and sell with my daddy. I was just a boy, eleven or so. Walt's a good man. He didn't aim on givin up searchin for you."

"I never knew." I set my bag on the table in the corner of the shed. "He said I was stole away."

"That's what we was always told. Your momma come to our place a lot. She'd mourn for hours. Then one day she just quit comin."

I leaned against the table. Feelins welled up in me. Feelins and more questions. The woman who gave birth to me, mourned. I thought I'd lose my breath. The thoughts of everthing I'd ever been told about my momma was a lie. Now, in this very minute, I find out my momma mourned for the infant that was took from her. "What happened? Did she die?"

"No. Don't reckon so. But she went out on her own. Walt went from lookin for his girl to searchin for his wife too. Never found her. She musta hid herself away. Grief can sometimes be worse than regret. Both of them gnaw at the soul."

"I don't understand why somebody would steal a youngin away from her momma."

"There's meanness all over. Greed. Selfishness. Who knows what forces a soul to make bad decisions. Most folks that do evil find ways to explain their actions, tryin to make it alright in their own mind."

Silas tipped his hat. "In the meantime, we wait here for Walton." And he left. I heard his boots clomp along the porch and down the two small steps. Then I heard him call out.

"Now, git cleaned up. You smell like somethin died. Sometimes the truth is the only way to let folks know there's a problem. No offense, missy."

"None took," I shouted back.

I couldn't take offense to his remark. He was right, I did smell like somethin dead. A dead rabbit. I could tell Silas was a gentle soul. *Kindness is from the soul*, Edna had said. *It's gived 'cause it can't help but be gived.* His kindness would probably get him killed or get him a wife that would never turn loose.

I snatched the saddlebags off the table and emptied them. Walton had grabbed a few things he thought I might need to survive. I run my fingers around the waist of my skirt and undid the button. I was grateful I'd put both my skirts on. When it's cold, wearin all the clothes a body has is just plain smart. This time, it paid off, givin me a change of clothes. The nasty skirt dropped to the floor. I'd wear the thin coat Edna had give me as a blouse until mine was washed and dry.

I scooped the clothes into my arms and made my way to the springhouse to bathe. The thoughts of that cold water already had my teeth chatterin, but it was a necessary thing.

A side of pork hung inches above the icy river water that run beneath the springhouse. To one side, a few jars of preserves lined the edge of a wooden flat built to store food. A basket of eggs set next to them. Silas seemed to be right handy in carin for his food. Poppy and Gerald viewed such things as women's work and probably wouldn't survive two days on their own the way Silas lived.

With the sun near spent, it was dark inside, with the kind of chilly dampness that makes your bones ache. I pushed the pork to the side and knelt to douse my skirt and blouse into the water, soakin them enough to scrub against a rock. Once I'd washed and wrung out my clothes, I stripped down to the hide, then dunked my head deep enough into the water to rinse my hair. My face grew numb and my nose commenced to run.

Steppin into the creek, I took a breath and sank to my chin beneath the cold water. My hair floated around my shoulders. "Oh lordy be. Brrr." It took a little extra scrubbin to get that rabbit stench off, but I managed.

Thoughts of home rushed over me. The river by Poppy's house run fairly shallow. In late winter and early spring, Gerald liked to slide across the frozen water. Poppy sometimes let me go play on the ice, if Momma didn't need me.

A memory rose up. Bein on my hands and knees, slidin across the ice. As I was playin, spinnin around on that frozen river, Gerald took Poppy's axe and made his way to me.

"I'm gonna cut this ice and drop you in the river," he'd said. "Maybe we can freeze that mark off your face."

I was just a youngin, but Momma would say I could talk a skunk outa his stripe. "Quit pickin on me, Gerald. I'm gonna tell Poppy you took his axe."

He'd laughed as he reared back and swung. The blade popped against the ice.

I couldn't crawl to the bank fast enough before the cracks reached me and the ice broke, droppin me through. The cold took my breath and the current pulled me under the ice. I'd opened my eyes and peered through the whitish murk, thinkin it was kinda pretty.

I surfaced in the icy water of Silas's springhouse, shakin back my wet hair. Poppy had come for me that day.

I'd pushed my hands against the ice, tryin to escape, when a foot crashed above me, breakin through and pullin me out.

Poppy'd laid me down on the bank. "Wasn't right bright of you, now was it?"

"B-b-but, Gerald—"

Poppy busted in over my talkin. "Gerald hollered for me to help. Said you fell through the ice while he tried to warn you. Bein stubborn will get you killed."

I shook off the memories with the cold springwater and pulled my clothes over my wet body.

How could I have forgot such an act?

Seemed every day that passed, more and more memories come to me. Some good, but most not. Most were the things Gerald had done. Lookin at 'em now, I could see his meanness clear. I could see now how bein too humble 'bout things can be as deadly as braggin. It hadn't done any good to argue, though. Poppy always listened to Gerald, and anything contrary I said came back to haunt me later. Poppy thought I was the one makin up stories. Gerald always managed to make me look witless.

My gratefulness to Momma and Poppy for takin me in and raisin me was somethin I was beholden to. I never wanted to think that the things Gerald was doin was wrong. I was just humbled and grateful they'd saved me, and I reckon that forced me to look over the spite.

But now the pictures in my head was startin to clear. Gerald learned early on to be skilled at lyin. The more I thought on Gerald's meanness to me, the more I started to see his anger come at me after Momma lost that infant. Momma changed that day and Gerald changed because Momma changed. He begun to spin tales to suit hisself and make me a horrible creature.

Hid away like a rat, I was kept by that family to work and not much else. My only times of play was when Momma didn't have me doin chores. Gerald was pretty much free to do whatever he pleased, even nothin at all.

I pulled my hair to one side and squeezed out spatters of water on the hard-packed dirt, then twisted it into a bun and pinned it tight to my head. I slid socks over my frozen feet and pulled on my boots. The faster I tied the strings, the harder my tears dripped. Figurin out there was never any love for me in that family was hard. Watchin Momma hug on Gerald as a youngin but push me away dug at my soul, and the more I had come to know Walton and Edna, the more it hurt. I'd already found more kindness from strangers than I'd ever had from Momma and Poppy. But after Momma lost that infant . . . everthing changed for the worse.

I flung my wet clothes over the line by the house as the last rays of sun streaked the valley. There was remnants of snow on the mountain peaks. Spots of brown peered through the white cover. Soon the snow would completely melt and the trees would begin to green up. I always loved spring, despite its sneaky cold snaps. The air seemed clearer. Fresh. Free.

"See you survived that cold creek water. Feel better?" Silas called from his porch.

I squeezed the fabric of my shawl tight in my fingers and nodded. "I feel clean. Ain't sure better is the right word."

Silas beckoned me toward the house. "Soup's hot. Come on up. We'll get you nice and toasty."

I finished stretchin my wet clothes over the line and trudged my way around puddles of rainwater. My boots sucked into the mud.

"Hate to drag mud in your place."

"Swing out that way. You'll miss the most of it." He drew a line in the air, pointin me in the right direction. "It ain't no problem. It'll scrape."

I circled around the mud and dragged my feet in the brown grass, cleanin the mess from the soles of my boots. When I reached the porch, Silas reached down to help me up the steps. I stared at his hand for a minute.

Silas went to laughin. "What's a matter? Ain't you never met a gentleman before?" He snagged my fingers and guided me up the steps.

"Can't say as I have."

"Well, my momma taught me well. Taught me to say 'please' and 'thank you.' And to *always* help a lady up the steps."

Lady? Before today, I'd never been called a lady. The idea was strange. Come to think of it, I'd never even considered myself a lady. *Reckon I am, though. Reckon I am.*

Silas, actin a might silly, pulled open the screen door and bowed.

I couldn't help but smile. "Your momma did teach you well. Was there nothin she could do 'bout your mind? Seems you're a little on the silly side."

Silas let out a roar of laughter. It was such a sweet sound. Real, honest laughter. And it was a great joy to see such happiness. This Silas Dalton was a big man with a tender heart. Kind. Funny. And happy. It was just enough to make me like him.

Two bowls of stew sat steamin on the table. The scent of coffee made my mouth water. The house was simple, but the little things he'd done made it special. A pantry with carved and polished wooden plates and cups. A mantel with extra hooks to hold hot pots and a piece of square metal hoverin over the fire to put biscuits and bread in to bake. Oil lamps filled to the rim—ready to hang, set to one side of the room.

A body could tell, any woman Silas Dalton chose to be his bride would be well provided for. It was sweet to see how he planned out just how he would care for the one he'd love.

He sat on the stool next to me and took my hand. It twitched but I didn't pull it back.

"Good Lord, thank You for what You've gived me to live on here. Thank You for the food You have blessed to my springhouse and for the wherewithal to cook it into somethin tasty. And thank You, Lord, for this sweet new friend. I pray Your hand of protection over her. Amen." He squeezed my fingers.

His prayer had included me. *Friend. Well, I'll be.* On a day with so many firsts, it was the first day I'd ever had a friend. And like Edna and Walton, this man seemed to know the good Lord well. One thing that rose to the surface with Edna, Walton, and now Silas, was their gratitude and kindness. Despite hard times, they loved people anyway. That was somethin I wanted—to get past the hurt, past the mark on my face, and love people anyway. I think there is happiness in that.

Twenty-Four

SILAS STOOD UP and stretched his long legs. "I'll go start a fire in that shed. Knock the chill off for you. If you have a mind to, wash them few bowls." He clomped across the wooden floor, the door bangin behind him as he stepped into the darkness.

I didn't hesitate. I'm not sure why. Maybe 'cause that was what I was used to doin—gettin up and cleanin up. Or was it 'cause he asked right nice? Not orderin me around. Guess it didn't matter one way or the other.

I poured a few ladles of water into a metal basin and washed out the bowls. They wasn't much to wash, for we'd nearly licked them clean. Silas was right about one thing. He was a good cook.

I wasn't used to chatterin whilst eatin. Silas managed both. While he'd talked, I'd found my mind wanderin off. Tryin to cypher why this man was so kind to me. Silas told story after story of his work around the mountain and things about his growin up the only child of Lucas and Idabelle Dalton. Listenin to him talk was like livin the childhood I'd missed.

I dried the bowls with an apron that hung from a nail on the wall. This man ain't got no wife, but he thinks to put a nail on the wall and add an apron. It weren't frilly, but I still couldn't imagine Silas wearin it. Seems like he'd planned for findin a wife sometime soon.

After the bowls was put away, I pulled the hook from over the fire and rested the pot of leftover stew on the griddle. It would bear itself to stay warm through the night.

The wind howled around the side of the house, sendin an eerie fear through my bones. I walked outside and headed to the shed. A curl of white smoke twisted and danced out of the chimney, and the smell of fresh-cut hickory wood tickled my nose.

"Get in here." Silas slapped his leg. "Them winds has picked up. We get them mountain squalls through this little valley at times. It's like the wind walks across the tops of the mountains then trips and falls into this here valley. Makes for a chilly night in winter, but in the spring and summer a man can sit back and be cooled by the breath of God Almighty."

I closed my eyes and imagined a giant man standin over the valley, gently huffin a breeze across the way. It was a right nice picture Silas had painted in my mind.

"I'm much obliged by the kindness you've showed me. Thank you for helpin me."

Silas tipped his hat. "It's my pleasure, little lady."

He pushed open the door to the shed. The fire had already warmed the inside and, to my surprise, Silas had carried my clothes in from the line and hung them over a chair by the fire.

He lifted his finger and pointed. "Them oughta be dry by mornin. I've filled the wood box and I stoked the fire pretty tight. Hopefully, you can bed down and not worry about throwin more wood on the fire."

"You've been so kind." Tears sprang to my eyes and I turned fast to blink them back.

"I've said more times than I can count that Walt finds all the strays and drags them in. Makes a nice little group of friends. I reckon he knew we'd have somethin in common." He bumped the side of my arm, friendly-like, with his handless arm.

My eye caught that nub and I wondered how Silas had managed so well. He'd even beat the little annoyin things—like rollin up his sleeves one-handed. Nothin seemed to bother him . . . nothin seemed to get in his way.

"Folks like me and you, we look past what's on the outside and dig into the soul."

Without havin to work at it, a smile stretched across my face, and I turned and gave his arm a friendly jab. Silas made friendship seem like an easy thing.

"I'll let you get some rest. I checked your shotgun. It's loaded and ready should you feel the need to shoot somethin that moves in the night. Oh, and so we are clear, that don't mean proppin it betwixt your knees to try to shoot yourself." He went to laughin at hisself. I didn't think I needed to tell him that I'd never actually shot a gun in my life. Even shootin myself coulda been hit or miss. "Oh, and on a serious mind, should somethin happen—and I ain't sayin it will—but should you hear Gerald comin, there's a ground cave out back. You crawl out that window and walk ten steps or so. It's covered by a barrel."

"So I move the barrel?"

"Heavens no. I'm smarter than that. Nailed it to the cover over the hole. Just push it to the side and, once you're in, pull the cover back. Ain't had a soul find that hole yet."

He stuffed a bite of tobacco in his jaw. "I believe you'll be fine. Don't reckon you'll need it, but you got the assurance there is a place to hide. Walt should be along in a few days."

Silas opened the door. "Close up this door now and stay warm. Night, Miss Lochiel." He tipped his hat and disappeared toward his house with a lantern.

I lifted my hand and gently waved. "Night, Mr. Dalton."

When I closed the door, the soft yellow glow from the fire made the shed seem homey. In the distance I could hear wolves bayin at the moon. And though I knew they was wolves, a voice inside me couldn't help but ask that question again. *What if?* So I pushed the heavy pine table across the bumpy plank floor until it wedged against the door. If I should be mistakin that them wolves was really a pack of dogs, that table would at least hold off the monster on the other side 'til I could skedaddle out the window and into that ground hole.

Will I ever be able to close my eyes and rest without frettin?

"Stop it," I said out loud. "Just stop it, Lochiel. All you're managin to do is worry yourself into a frenzy."

I walked round the room takin note of where things was placed just in case I needed to rush out. Trippin over somethin wouldn't make for a quick getaway.

A straw mattress lay to one side of the shed. Two blankets was rolled neatly in the middle. I went to my knees and crawled onto the soft bedding. I spread one of the blankets over the tic and made myself a nice bed. It put me in mind of Otis pawin and pushin at his blanket on the floor next to my bed back at the shack. The pup was good company and I missed him. My body sunk into the covered hay. I took in a deep breath and exhaled.

Reckon my life will ever settle? Will Gerald ever stop huntin me?

I hated livin by lookin over my shoulder. But this was the way things was for now. I wondered what Momma and Poppy were doin without Gerald or me around. How would Momma take to bein home alone when Poppy went out huntin? Who was fetchin water for her? A piece of me felt sad thinkin on her all alone in her chair by the fire.

I snuggled into the mattress and buried my face under the wool blanket. The fire cracked and popped, makin a sweet lullaby. Before long, that wind that whistled through the valley brought along a soft rain. The tin roof on the shed tinged a rhythm as the rain pelted out a song.

Down in the valley, valley so low. Hang your head over, hear the wind blow.

I wasn't right sure why that old song come to mind, 'cept the beat of the rain seemed to hum it. Poppy would sing it to Momma when she'd get to thinkin about that baby that died. She'd cry and wail whilst Poppy rocked her and sang. Before long, she'd quiet down.

I can remember buryin my head in my blanket and sobbin when Momma would cry over that lost baby. Was it really me that took that infant's life?

Poppy had a mighty nice singin voice, and when he'd add the sweet pickin of his banjo to it, a body couldn't help but enjoy theirself. Momma didn't say much, and when she did, it was mostly sharp. But when Poppy would sing, his deep, mellow voice could calm the worst of beasts, includin her.

Silas had told me a few things about my real momma, or at least as much as he could remember. He was just a boy when she come around. Best he could recall, I favored her in the eyes. Walt and Edna hadn't yet worked up to tellin me about her. I'd been fightin the Devil in me from pesterin them about it.

I wondered what she looked like. Was her hair black like mine? Did my fingers look like hers? I pressed my knuckles against my face. Did she have a mark too? And why in the world would a body steal a baby?

When I'd start to study on all them questions, my heart would race and I couldn't breathe. I reckon Walton and Edna was right to only feed me tidbits of news at a time.

This would drive even a sane man crazy.

I climbed outa bed and made my way to the shotgun balanced in the corner. I picked up the gun and rubbed my hand down the cold barrel. *Oh, and that don't mean proppin it betwixt your knees to use on yourself.* Silas's words come back and I realized how silly I must have looked on the ridge when he found me. I figured this much. Endin my life would do just that—never give me a chance to experience the good that could come through the storm.

It felt right to take holt of my own life and decide who would live in my soul. I didn't aim to spend the rest of my days in fear. I would take holt of who I was and the fate I'd been given. I cocked the gun and laid it next to the mattress.

"Come on, Gerald. Come on down that mountain. I ain't runnin from you no more." Nope. No more.

THE DEVIL'S DAUGHTER *makes it her sworn duty to drive me crazy. I felt it. Every time she followed me it was like the Devil hisself was hauntin my steps.*

"Stop followin me," I shouted. "You're on my heels every step I take."

"I just wanna learn how to shoot that shotgun. I might need to pull in a rabbit sometime." She dodged a limb I let loose of. "Just show me, Gerald."

I whipped around and stuck the barrel of my shotgun in her face. "This is how you do it. Point. Pull back the hammer then squeeze the trigger. Boom!" *She squinted her eyes tight and took a step back. I reckon she thought I'd pull the trigger. Lord knows I'd thought about it. Blow that mark off her face and maybe blow her away at the same time. I'd have done it too, if I didn't suppose she'd just as soon haunt me dead as livin.*

"All I wanna do is learn so I can pull my weight. Momma might be happier if I can catch a few things when you all are gone off for days."

I felt the hair on my neck raise. "You listen to me." I took my shotgun barrel and poked her shoulder. She inched backward. "There ain't nothin you can do to make Momma happy. You're the reason she's a mess."

"I ain't done nothin to hurt Momma."

"You hexed her. Killed her baby!"

Fire shot from her eyes. "I did no sucha thing. It was blue when it come out."

I poked her again. "You're the Devil's daughter and you ain't done nothin but brought us grief from the time . . . from the time Poppy saved your sorry hide."

That seemed to still her tongue. Her mouth was open a little but nothin come out. She grabbed my shotgun, yanked the barrel of the gun toward the ground and turned to walk away.

I raised my shotgun to the sky and fired. She took off runnin. I shoulda shot her in the back.

TWENTY-FIVE

THE SUN NUDGED me awake. I'd slept through the night—somethin I wasn't used to doing. This new mornin felt different.

Behind the shed, I heard the crack of wood splittin. When I peered through the window, I stood amazed at how this one-handed man could split wood with the power of two men. Silas would grab up a block of wood, straighten it with his hand, and balance it with his knee. When it was just right, he'd grab that axe and whirl it in one swift, powerful swing, hittin the block of wood dead center, sendin it sailin in two pieces. It didn't look like he'd even broke a sweat.

I walked out to the pile of wood he'd split. "You part bull?"

"Bull?" Silas placed another block of wood on the rack. "Ain't sure what you mean."

"You're bustin through that wood like a bull tearin through a fence."

"Well, ain't you just plumb funny?" He took a step forward and belted the block. It split perfectly down the middle. I picked up the pieces and stacked them in the pile.

"How much you plan on splittin?"

"Hard to say. That sawmill runs on steam. So I need to keep the wagon filled."

I watched as he worked seamlessly, one piece of wood after another.

Silas stopped and swiped his sleeve across his face. "You got somethin on your mind? 'Cause there's plenty a chores around here to be done. Eggs need gathered. Corn set in the ground. Chickens fed. Pigs slopped."

I giggled. "I reckon that's a hint for me to work."

"Nope. More like an expectation, but first things first." He set his axe on its end and leaned against it. "Spit it out. I feel a *but* comin on."

I smiled and pointed my finger at him. "You'd be wrong. No *buts*."

"Well, good. I can take a breath and get on with my work." He turned and lifted his axe to his shoulder. "So what do you plan on doin?" Silas leveled his piece of wood and readied it to strike.

I picked up a basket that set to the far side of the wood pile. "For starters, gather eggs. Fix breakfast. Start us some coffee."

I headed to the chicken coop, spinnin that basket in circles on my arm. "Hey, Missy?"

I stopped and looked over my shoulder. "Yeah?"

"What're you plannin on doin?"

"I done told you. I'm gonna gather eggs."

"That's real kind of you, but you're headin to the pigsty." Silas pointed over his shoulder. "That way to the coop."

My face grew warm. "I know. I just wanted to pet the pig."

Silas threw his head back and roared. "I reckon I done heard it all. Pet the pig!"

He laid his arm on the stack of wood and laughed. I could see his shoulders shakin from where I stood. The harder he laughed, the harder it was for me to keep a straight face. If Silas thought pettin the pig was worth a roar, what would he think if I danced with his chickens?

I turned toward the chicken coop. "Move over, girls. I'm comin in."

———

Five days passed and not a sign of Gerald. Walton either. Not a word. I got so I'd walk up the side of the mountain and peer down over the trail me and Sky had traveled, so I'd be ready, either way.

Silas stood waitin once I come down the steep side of the bank. "What you doin climbin that ridge?"

When I pulled back my shoulders like a cocky rooster and strutted past Silas, my boot caught on a vine, takin me to my knees. There was no grace in my steps at all. He pulled me to my feet and steadied me.

"If you're that sure-footed down here, I'd hate to see what you do scalin the ridge."

I rolled my eyes at his smart remark. "My gut tells me that somethin's wrong. Walt shoulda been round by now."

Silas took me by the elbow and helped me over the stones that lay on the hill. "I figured we'd give ole Walt 'til the end of the week. If we don't hear nothin by then, I'll call on the Mabreys down the way. Get them to stay a day or so with you so I can go huntin for him."

I put my finger in his face. "Silas Dalton, I done decided I ain't runnin from Gerald no more. If you go hunt him down, you wellst be ready to have me tag along behind. I got my own horse. And a gun." I straightened my shoulders and jutted out my chest.

Silas looked at me askance and rubbed his nub across his forehead. "Have you ever shot a gun before?"

"I can load the bullets. Cock it."

"That ain't what I asked you. I asked if you'd ever *shot* a gun before."

I stood starin him in the eye and said nothin.

"That's what I thought. How in the world do you think you'd be one ounce of help to me if you can't shoot?" He started toward the barn.

"I can learn."

Silas stopped, towerin over me. Restin his hand on his hip, he shook his head. "It ain't my best option. But I believe you can learn. But you learn to shoot to protect yourself and that's all. Understand?"

"I aim to protect myself."

"Little lady, you need to let the Lord take vengeance. He says that belongs to Him. Not you. Your job is to learn to take care of yourself."

"But . . ."

Slias took a step then swung around. "I appreciate you wantin to stand up to Gerald, but the tone you take about learnin to shoot tells me you want him dead. Is that right? Do you want Gerald dead?"

I reckon Silas had me pegged. It seemed the only way I could gain my courage was to think about killin Gerald. And I was gettin the feelin from Silas, that wasn't right.

The better part of the afternoon, Silas taught me how to aim that shotgun and, more so, how to brace my feet so the kick from it didn't send me to my tail.

He put his arms around me from behind, correctin this or that. He placed his broad hand between my shoulder blades, holdin me steady as he kicked my feet apart to widen my stance.

I put a hole in more things than a body can imagine, but after a spell I got so as I could aim and hit a target every once in a while.

"You ain't cut out for shootin," Silas said as he stacked a few blocks of wood for me to aim at.

"There's a difference in bein cut out for somethin and bein able to hold your own. I figure if I can hold my own, the rest don't matter."

"There you go." Silas balanced the blocks of wood. "Make your way out in the field. When I holler, turn, take aim, and fire. Let's see if you can hit somethin other than the broad side of my barn."

I walked through the field and waited for Silas's call. Up to now, he'd move my mark back a little further with each aim. I walked toward the ridge, shotgun to my side.

Every mornin that come and went brought warmer days. The trees on the mountain had lost the look of last winter's death and, though the new spring leaves hadn't sprouted, you could see a tinge of green where buds would appear.

I filled my lungs with a breath of good air. The river runnin behind Silas's house made for a fresh, clean smell. A hawk soared overhead, searchin for his next meal. It was a beautiful mornin.

"Now!" Silas hollered. "Whip around here and fire."

I wheeled around and yanked the shotgun toward my shoulder. On the way up, I cocked it and pulled back the hammer. I took aim and when I focused, what I saw took my breath. Silas had stood a scarecrow against the blocks.

I reckon he meant to give me a start. There might come a day when I'd be forced to take aim at another person. The real question that jostled around in my head was, could I do it? When it came down to it, would I have the courage to look a man in the eye and pull the trigger? I saw right quick there was consequence to my decision that I'd never thought of.

My stomach turned and I went to pantin like a dog. I looked through the gun's sight and squinted one eye shut. My mind took away the straw face of the scarecrow and replaced it with Gerald's face and mockin laugh.

I could hear Gerald tauntin me.

Devil's daughter. Come up from hell to do his biddin. Come on, demon girl. Get mad. Let me see that mark get redder than it already is.

I could suddenly see what Silas saw in my threats and it scared the tar outa me. I didn't want vengeance. I wanted peace.

Voices echoed in my mind. Hurt and pain bubbled up from my insides like a newfound mountain spring. My chin commenced to quiver, and the longer I stood there, the more I realized that if this moment was real—if that was really Gerald across the field—he'd already have shot me deader than a door nail. *Do it! Pull the trigger. DO IT!*

I took a breath and held it. Then I pulled the trigger. A shot rang out across the field and the chest of that scarecrow busted open. Straw flew into the air, then floated away on the breeze.

TWENTY-SIX

EACH PASSIN DAY grew warmer. And I grew more comfortable with my chores on the farm. My worries for Walton grew as well. I could imagine all sorts of things happenin to him. Gerald runnin upon him. Poppy maybe. Still, I tried to squelch my worry, knowin Silas was a man that pondered things and before he'd set out to find Walton, he would have thought through all the details.

The midday sun hung high in the sky. My stomach never lied to me when it was time to eat. I shaded my eyes and looked up.

"Silas," I shouted. "You gettin hungry? Sun says it's noon."

I watched as he dropped the reins to his plow horse. He took off his hat and waved, my sign that he'd be up to the house before long. I dipped my hands into the wash bucket on the porch and scrubbed the dirt from under my nails. *Where are you, Walton Grubbs?* It grated at me that we still hadn't heard a peep from him.

Well, Lord, we talk a bit more these days and because of that, I feel like I can ask You a favor. Would You please keep Walton safe?

Silas had put a pot of beans over the fire the night before. It'd take the night and bigger part of the mornin for them hard beans to soften. I lifted the lid and the smell of boiled hambone and beans filled the room. Takin a wooden spoon, I dipped a few beans into the palm of my hand.

Woo-eee, hot, hot. I juggled them from hand to hand and blowed enough to cool them to taste. *Hmmm. That ole boy ain't such a bad cook.*

I pulled a stool to the cupboard and climbed up, stretchin to reach the tin bowls on the top shelf. The door flew open and Silas blew in, singin to the top of his lungs.

"Camptown races five miles long, ohh de do-daaah day." He lifted his hand into the air and waited.

I furrowed my brow. "Good land. You're like a tornado comin in a door. Can't you ever just walk in?"

He grabbed me by the waist and lifted me off the stool. "There ain't no joy in just walkin in a room. A body has to make an entrance. One that folks will remember."

"I guarantee folks'll remember that squawkin."

Silas bowed.

"Them beans smell mighty good." He lifted the pot from the fire hook and set it on a plate in the middle of the table.

"They are good. I done took a taste. Who taught you to cook like this?" I dipped a cup into the pot and poured beans into each of our bowls.

"That would be the fine Idabelle Dalton. She taught her boy well."

"Guess she wanted you to get along by yourself." I blew on a spoon of beans.

Silas's eyes met mine. A sadness I'd never seen poured out.

"Did I say somethin wrong?"

"Naw. Not nothin you'd know about anyhow."

"What is it?"

"Momma grew sickly after she lost two babies. They was twins too, like me and my brother was. Snow was hip deep in the holler and Daddy couldn't get down to the doc at the foot of the mountain."

"I'm sorry, Silas. I didn't know. Won't you tell me about it?"

"Ain't much to tell. Other than them babies come early. Me and Daddy brought them into the world. Little youngins fit in the palm of my hand. We ain't sure what took 'em. If it was the bitter cold or the fact they come early. But Momma never seemed to heal after they was born. We burned their bodies after they died, and Daddy spread their ashes in the Indian River. All that to say, Momma kept growin weaker. Her body just didn't heal. Despite her weakness, she made sure I could mind the house once she was gone. She taught me cookin and mendin."

"She musta been a wonderful momma."

"She was. Heck, she was clever. Momma could use her mind to figure about anything out. I guess she just wanted me to be ready to take care of Daddy."

"Well, she did a fine job." I slurped the last bite of beans from my spoon.

"I reckon she did." Silas ladled a second cup of beans into his bowl. "Them is pretty good, ain't they?"

I smiled, watchin him guzzle down his meal. It was only minutes before I got to hummin the Camptown song. "Now I got that blasted song in my head."

Silas slapped his hand against his leg and laughed. "Catchy, ain't it?"

"You better save some of them beans for supper. I plan on makin a good pan of corn bread to go with them." I wrapped the tail of my skirt around my hand and lifted the pot onto the fire hook.

"Let them stay pulled to the side of the fire and they'll just simmer 'til supper." Silas turned his bowl up and licked the last juice from the bottom.

"Your momma didn't teach you everthing." I yanked the empty bowl from his hand.

The hound under the porch went to howlin, and Silas come to his feet.

"Ole Coot ain't much, but he does let me know when somebody's comin up the lane. Maybe that's Walton. I figured he'd make his way up before long." He pushed his stool under the table and wiped his mouth. "You stay here just in case."

Them words sent a chill down my back. His kindness had took away my fear. For the first time in days the hair on the back of my neck bristled.

Silas lifted his shotgun from the rack. "If this turns out to be somethin we ain't expectin, you tear out that back door. It's behind the curtain in the back room. And make your way to that hole I told you about. We clear?"

Silas walked toward me. He leaned close to my face, and his tone changed.

"I appreciate you wantin to take your part. But this ain't the time. You'll do what I tell you so I can keep you safe. This was what Walton asked of me, and you and nary other scutter on the mountain will keep me from doin what I promised. You understand?"

I knew he meant business. I nodded.

"Good. Then you keep an eye out that window. If that ain't Walt, you do what I told you to do."

My eyes skittered to my shotgun hangin on the wall below where his was. I hated feelin helpless. I hated bein scared.

"Hey!" Silas grabbed my arm and gave me a shake.

"Yeah, I know what to do. Go out the door behind the curtain in the back room. I understand."

He nodded and laid his shotgun on the table. Brushin back his hair, he pressed his hat hard onto his head then snatched up the gun and opened the door. He rested the shotgun against the side of the house and eased the door shut.

Coot commenced to bark long and fierce. It sure as whiz wasn't the simple bark he'd give to me when I come off the mountain.

Silas leaned against the porch rail as three horses come into sight. "There's three horses. Somethin tells me that ain't a good thing. You do ole Silas a favor and head on out to that hole behind the shack."

"But shouldn't I wait a minute or two more?"

"No. You go now so they ain't got no chance of seein you skedaddle."

"Will you be alright?"

"Yep. Grab your shotgun as you go. If it comes to havin to use it, see if you can hit somebody other than me."

I lifted my shotgun from the bottom rung of the rack and headed out the back door to the hole. I pushed the barrel back and stepped inside. A ray of sunshine cast light through the cracks, and I could see a candle and some flint on a wooden shelf. I clicked the flint until a spark caught the wick of the candle.

Silas's *hole* was more like a root cellar. Three steps down, there were a few canned jellies on a shelf and two bags of cut taters. The eyes had growed long and was ready to plant. When I pulled that barrel back over the openin, I could see between the slats.

My heart raced as the three horsemen rode up to Silas's porch. Their voices echoed between the house and the shed as Silas walked out to meet them. I could hear every pound of my heartbeat loud in my head.

"Howdy, there." Silas spoke to the visitors. "What can I do for you?"

I watched as he reached his hand toward one of the men. The man leaned from his horse and shook Silas's hand.

"Name's Barney Stiles. We're lookin for a girl about nineteen or so. Runaway."

One of the men slid off his horse and walked to the edge of the house. "You ain't seen no girl, have you? Her daddy and momma are all to pieces."

I wondered what truth might be in those words. My mind tested out a picture of Poppy rockin Momma as she wept over me bein hurt and missin. More likely they were missin my biscuits and havin someone to do the wash and clean up after the horses.

This Barney Stiles was a man, but the other two was just boys. Maybe in their teens. Likely his sons.

"Ain't nobody on this side of the mountain but me and the Mabreys down the road about two miles. We'd be hard-pressed to see anyone else over here 'til the spring rains end. Rains melt the snow on the ridge and make the mud slide. It's a mess. Folks just don't make their way over here 'til it dries up."

The boys climbed from their horses. "You sure?"

"Sure? I reckon I'm about as sure as a worm on a hook."

"You don't mind if we look around, do you?" Stiles asked.

"Well, I told you I ain't seen no runaway. But if it makes you feel better, have at it. I live alone. My momma and daddy died about a year ago, and I've begun to move Momma's things into that shed over there. I could wear Daddy's trousers and shirts. You still have your folks?"

Silas was sharp. He knew my extra clothes would be in the shed so he concocted some cockamamie yarn to beat the likes. He commenced to babble the gosh awfulest mess of yarns I'd ever heard.

I watched through the barrel crack as the man and his boys split and went different ways. Slippin down the three steps onto the cold floor of the cellar, I blew out the candle so no flicker could be seen from the barrel.

Above me, one of the boys scuffled toward the barrel. He stopped inches from the wooden crate, then hauled off and kicked the side. "Dang old dog. Can't you do your business out in the field so a body don't step in your mess?"

He scraped his shoe alongside the barrel. If I hadn't been so scared, I'd have laughed. I inched up the steps and grabbed hold of the leather strap Silas had fixed inside the barrel as a handle. I wrapped my hand through the strap and pulled hard to keep the boy from movin the barrel as he scrubbed his boot against the side.

Silas eventually walked all three into the house. For all I knew, he offered them a bowl of beans.

Either way, he hogwashed his way through, and I reckon they believed him. It wasn't long before he walked them between the house and the shed. I saw him work his way toward the barrel. The closer he come to the cellar, the more I wanted to jump out and ask him if he was an idiot, bringin them men right to me, but I'd save that conversation for later.

Silas picked up some pieces of wood and started stackin them on top of the barrel. All the time, he was goin on about fishin for trout and how they ought to make their way back mid-summer to fish.

I slapped my palm to my forehead. *He's gonna get me killed.* The longer he stood there and talked, the more wood he stacked against the barrel. The man was blockin me in, keepin me from bein seen and heard, and maybe keepin me from pokin my shotgun out.

The light into the barrel slowly dimmed and the sounds of the men's voices dampened. Once again, what Poppy taught me come back. *Just 'cause you don't hear no noise don't mean danger is gone. Stay still. Be quiet.*

And so I did. I slid to the cold dirt floor and wrapped my arms around my knees. I was good at bein quiet.

TWENTY-SEVEN

HOURS PASSED AS I sat balled up, huggin my knees. Despite the warmth of the spring days, the ground was still damp and cold. My teeth chattered. I rubbed my hands together and blew on my fingers. *Where the Sam Hill are you, Silas?*

I didn't know Silas real well, but I knew him good enough to know he wouldn't just leave me buried in that hole for no reason. *The Lord is my shepherd. I shall not want.*

Miss Edna had taught me some Scripture out of that Bible book.

"Now, Lochiel," she'd said. "You remember these words. We'll say them 'til they stick. And I promise you, one of these days you'll come up on a time when you can say them out loud and find comfort."

That was one time I thought Edna was a tiny bit crazy. But I repeated the words she read until they stayed in my mind. It looked like this was one of them times when she was right 'cause I found some peace in the words.

He maketh me to lie down in green pastures. He leadeth me beside the still waters. He restoreth my soul.

I found it strange that the good Lord's words was so true. Here I was, layin down *under* his green pastures, and right beside the gentle ripplin water of the Indian River. I held on to the good Lord's words and, oddly enough, I stopped chillin. I guessed they was such good words that they warmed my heart.

"We choose what we make ourselves to be," Edna had said. "We can be kind or we can be meaner than a rattler."

Her words filled my heart.

I was fightin hate for Gerald and Poppy. How does a body choose to be kind to others, even when they ain't nothin but hateful to you?

I could tell from the short time I had with Edna and Walton that there was somethin to the good Lord. There was a peace they both had, even in their pain, that seemed to be smoothed over because of what they called *faith*. I wasn't always the smartest bird in the nest, but I was bright enough to see they was happy even when they was sad.

All I knew was I wanted that. I wanted my hate and anger gone, and I wanted to be kind—to choose to see the good in even them folks who wasn't so good. That meant I had to start with my own self. I had to fix me before I could find the goodness and kindness I needed to be like Miss Edna.

I eased my way to the candle and run my fingers along the board, feelin for the flint. Pullin the pieces between my fingers, I clicked them together, catchin a flame once again on the wick. The flame grew to light the cellar, and I cupped my hand so it wouldn't go out.

How much longer, Silas? How much longer?

He must have read my mind, for shortly after I lit the candle, he showed up to the barrel. I could hear him pull a piece of wood from the stack and split it.

"You keep quiet, little lady."

"I ain't sure how much quieter you want me to be. My teeth is clatterin like two squirrels fightin over a nut."

"Them men ain't here. But they're up on the ridge. Watchin. I can't chance them seein you."

"That's fine. By mornin all they'll find is my froze body, stiffer than a board."

He split another piece of wood. "I'm fixin to build a fire next to this barrel. Once I get it built, I'll drop you a knife. They's taters down there you can peel and eat."

Raw taters was never my favorite, but there was plenty of times they was the only meal I got from Momma. "I can manage. But ain't they gonna wonder why you're buildin a fire in the middle of the night?"

"Naw. I told them there was a pack of wolves on the ridge. A fire keeps them off the homestead."

I inched up to the crack in the barrel. "I ain't so sure the good Lord will be happy with your lies."

"I ain't lied yet. There ain't no runaway here. There's a nice woman. And there's a pack of wolves on the ridge. They bay at the moon all night long."

Silas commenced to build a fire with some bite. It was big enough that it warmed the side of the barrel. I snuggled against the wood inside.

"You reckon I'll be here all night?"

"Might just be. I see their fire on the knoll. Don't you worry. I'll be in and out stokin the fire. Hate to leave you in that hole."

"I been in worse."

"That breaks my heart, Miss Lochiel." Silas patted the side of the barrel. "I pray the Lord will have mercy on the soul of that evil brother of yours. I best be goin inside now, so I don't raise no brow."

"I'm much obliged."

"You need to stop thankin me. I do what I do because it's the right thing. I do it 'cause I want to. Now, I'll stoke the fire heavy and hopefully it'll burn the best part of the night. I'll be back later to check on you."

I watched between the slats as Silas walked to the house, and I pressed my shoulder against the barrel so the warmth of the wood could thaw my cold muscles.

"I'm much obliged to You, Lord, for Silas. I couldn't ask for no better friend."

Yea, though I walk through the valley of the shadow of death, I will fear no evil: for thou art with me . . .

My eyes grew heavy, and sleep seeped into the cold darkness of the hole.

———

"Silas! Silas!"

A wagon rolled fast up the lane. The shouts of the driver hung in the misty fog.

I stretched and drew my wits about me. Crawlin to my knees, I pressed my face against the barrel to peer out. I knew that voice. I recognized the sound of that clatterin and clangin wagon. *Walton.*

Coot went to barkin and Silas come rushin out on the porch, pullin his suspenders up on his shoulders. He walked bow-legged down the porch steps. I saw his hand go up and wave.

The horses slid to a halt, and Walton slumped from the wagon into a heap on the ground.

"Silas, let me out. Let me out!" I pushed my back against the barrel and tried to move it, but with the wood weighin it down, it wouldn't budge.

"Walton!" I beat my fists against the side of the barrel. "Silas, let me out."

Silas lifted Walton to his feet. His face was bloody and swollen.

They say when a body gets scared enough they can do things that no other person could do. And when I saw Walton all beat up and bleedin, hidin myself was no longer important. I took in a breath, pressed my shoulder against the barrel and slowly scooted it. Logs toppled off the top and onto the ground. I shoved the shotgun out first, and then squeezed between the barrel and stack of wood and run across the field.

"Walton! Oh, Lord, have mercy."

Silas set Walton on the porch steps and as I come toward him, he snagged my arm. "What in tarnation are you doin? Get back in that cellar."

His voice turned from the gentle, lighthearted man to a man that meant real business.

"No!" I stood toe to toe with Silas. "I ain't hidin when Walton is hurt."

Walton wrapped his bloody hand around the porch rail and pulled hisself up.

"I got in a brawl with a couple of Gerald's thugs tryin to sidetrack 'em. Go on now. I'll be fine. I done lost you once and don't aim to do it again. You do what Silas tells you."

I couldn't bear seein Walton weak and bleedin. I twisted my arm to get free, but Silas wouldn't turn loose.

When I looked at Walton, I could see parts of me in him. Same skin color, same golden eyes. It was the first time in my life I connected to somebody. And this somebody was really my father. Seein him hurt was pullin at my heart somethin fierce.

"I ain't plannin on tellin you again. We ain't got time to fuss over this." Silas pulled me toward the hole. "It's for your own safety. Can't you see that? There's people here who care about you."

People who care. The words seeped into my heart. People. That's more than one. And there was only two others here. Walton and Silas. I tried to take in what he'd said.

When a body spends their life not bein loved, it's hard to understand what love is. I'd dreamed as a young girl, what it must feel like to be cared for—to have someone hold me in their arms when I was afraid, or wipe tears from my face if I cried. I tried hard to squeeze my arms tight around myself so I could understand what it might feel like to be hugged.

And here, Silas was tellin me there was *people* who cared for me. Walton cared for me. And Silas cared. That put a spin on things I didn't expect. My mind was in such a muddle I couldn't figure which was the better thing, to obey them and hide or to stay and fight.

And then Coot went to howlin, and there was no more chance to choose. We could hear the echo of several horses poundin their way up the lane.

Walton set hard on the steps. "Almighty God, show us Your hand of mercy."

Twenty-Eight

"Let's hope that's not Gerald." Silas cocked his shotgun and readied hisself to aim.

Three horses rounded the bend. Shotguns hung from the riders' hands. "Them's the three what Edna took on. They's all bark. I got them." Walton held a pistol.

But more horses come from the river. They splashed through the water and came up the bank behind the house.

One man come over the porch rail and pushed a shotgun into Walton's shoulder. "Drop the gun."

If ever I wanted to leave a puddle around my feet, it was now.

I stood, heels dug into the dirt, and swung my shotgun to point at the man behind Walton. Cocked it.

"Easy, little lady," Silas said softly.

I scanned the homestead. Men circled us. More people than I'd faced in my entire life, all huntin for me. There was no runnin or hidin now. We was pinned tight. If I took a shot, the rest of the men would kill us before we could flick a fly. I eased the gun down.

Poppy walked from behind the house. "Lochiel, you been causin trouble all over the mountain. Folks say you cursed that boy. He died because of you. It's time you come home so I can protect you."

"Protect me? You've hid me away from people all my life. Now you bring a passle of men to *protect me*?" Poppy's words stabbed my heart. "And I did no sucha thing. I never hurt that child. I prayed over him."

"Prayed?" Gerald walked from the other side of the house. "You prayed? Who in tarnation would teach the Devil's daughter to pray?"

My knees shook beneath my skirt as Gerald walked straight to me.

"You been baptized yet? Give your soul to the water? That oughta put the Devil's fire out."

Silas inched toward me, but one of Gerald's men hit him with a shotgun stock. He stood for a second, tryin his best to shake off the blow, but his legs weakened and Silas went to all fours. The man hit him again and he toppled.

"Gerald, what in heaven's name do you want from me? I'm gone from Momma and Poppy's. What more do you want?"

Gerald went to Walton, took his pistol, and hauled him to his feet. Walton was taller, but Gerald was stronger. Gerald turned his face toward me. "I want *you*. I'm gonna make you pay, kill you for all you done. Gotta show that Devil that I'm better—stronger—"

"Meaner." I finished his sentence.

Poppy walked over and stood eye to eye with Gerald. The image of Poppy protectin me warred with the picture of him stealin me away from my momma. Didn't seem right.

"Son, what are you doin here? You told me Lochiel run away. You didn't say you wanted her dead. This ain't right."

"Back away, Poppy. She's gotta die. She's evil."

"Stop this, boy. We ain't killers."

Gerald wrapped his hand around the shotgun and twisted, grabbin my hand. Poppy took a step closer and before I could work loose, Gerald slipped his finger over mine and pulled the trigger.

The shotgun fired and Poppy let out a holler.

The real trial is when you look a man in the eye, can you pull the trigger? If Gerald could shoot Poppy, there was no end to the evil he'd be willin to do.

Poppy was on the ground, rollin round and cussin.

Gerald stared straight at me as he released the gun, leavin it in my hands.

"She shot him!" Gerald's voice rang out. "I was tryin to get the gun away from her and she blew a hole clean through his leg!" The men glanced around at each other, seemed not quite sure what to make of what they seen. "What're you waitin for? Help him!"

Same old tricks. Always layin the blame somewhere else.

Gerald pushed one of the men next to him. "Go! Now!" But the man just stood starin.

It looked like this time Gerald slipped up and his lie come back on him.

One man jumped from his horse and tied his belt around Poppy's leg. But two of the men turned their horses and galloped off.

Gerald's face was as red as I've ever seen it. He was close to Walton now, and his hand eased against Walton's shirt.

I whipped the gun up and pointed it at Gerald. "Get your hands off him or I'll shoot you. Don't think I won't," I hissed.

Gerald's laugh was hideous. He leaned his head toward the sky and roared. I wasn't sure what to do. Silas was laid out cold on the ground. Poppy was in misery. And Walton had a gun pointed at his head.

There was nothin in my mind that was clear at that point. I was numb. Angry. Scared.

My hands shook but this had to be done. *One, two*—

A hand shot out from behind me and ripped the gun from my hands. Gerald's man pulled my arms behind my back and roped them tight.

My chance was gone. All I could think to do was say the words Edna had taught me. Say 'em loud.

"Yea, though I walk through the valley of the shadow of death, I will fear no evil: for thou art with me; thy rod and thy staff they comfort me. Thou preparest a table before me in the presence of mine enemies . . . "

Gerald rushed at me until his nose was an inch from mine. His breath reeked of whiskey. He hauled off and spit in my face. A nasty wad of slobber trailed down my nose and cheek. I struggled to get away from the man that held me, but couldn't.

Gerald grabbed a handful of my hair and pulled my head backward. With his other hand he pulled a knife from his boot and laid it hard against my cheek.

He spoke to me in a low growl. "Still wonder if I can cut that mark off or if it goes clean to the bone." He had my hair at the scalp and I couldn't move. I felt the edge of the knife slice into my skin.

"Would you look at that?" he said, loud, for everone to hear. "She wiggled and I cut her."

Poppy pulled hisself along the ground, leavin a trail of blood. "Gerald. Listen to me. I can't be a part of no killin. Let the girl go."

"You can't be a part of no killin?" Gerald horselaughed. "Ain't you or Momma neither one ever been a part of me. Why would this be different?"

Poppy tightened the belt around his leg then rolled to his back and moaned.

Gerald waved his gun in the air. "Did ya see that? She pulled the trigger. She shot him without even a second thought."

Walton took that moment to muster his strength and run his elbow hard into the man that was holdin a gun on him. He run at Gerald, hittin him in the back and knockin us all down. I rolled and struggled to my feet, but with my hands tied up, there was no use.

"Take them all to the river. Let's baptize this devil. She can speak words from the Good Book. Let's see if the Good Book can save her."

I thought my arms would rip off at the shoulders as Gerald dragged me. His men that stuck by him hauled Walton and Silas. The ones that saw through Gerald, took Poppy, tucked tail, and run. Gerald's posse was shrinkin.

"Gerald, you're actin like a crazy man. Why you doin this?"

"Crazy? You're callin *me* crazy? All I want to do is save your soul. Baptize you and wash your sins away. I been to a reevivayl." The way he said it made my skin crawl like a thousand spiders ran over my body. "We all gotta work to save the sinner's soul."

I tried to kick at Gerald. He threw me to the ground and jumped on top of me. He pressed a hand to my throat. With his face close to mine, he whispered in my ear.

"What do I do first? Have my way with the Devil's daughter or baptize you and clean you of your sin? Put out the fires of hell."

I struggled to bring my knee up. It'd worked once before. But my hands was pinned beneath me. And Gerald was stronger now, stronger with the demons urgin him on. And my breath was givin out.

Silas had roused, cussin and shoutin at Gerald. The truth was, there was nothin any of us could do.

As quick as he'd jumped me, Gerald stood. I gasped air and rolled to my side. He picked his knife up from the dirt and walked to the edge of the water where Walton was pressed to his knees. Gerald walked past Walton and rinsed my blood from his knife.

I crawled to my feet and took to runnin at Gerald best I could. Then Gerald swung around from the water and jabbed the knife deep into Walton's stomach.

I stopped dead still. Walton teetered back and forth on his knees. His eyes met mine and he mouthed the words, *I love you.*

Gerald drew back with his foot and kicked Walton in the chest, sendin him rollin into the icy waters of the Indian River.

Twenty-Nine

My heart and my gut told me to fight like mad, but I couldn't even pick up one foot. I watched as Walton's body floated downstream.

Get aholt of yourself. Don't you show no fear. Don't you let him win. Don't you dare, Lochiel. Over and over, I repeated them words in my head.

"What's a matter? That peddler that rescued your sorry hide not mean that much to you?"

I stared. Not a breath. My eye twitched.

Gerald walked close to me. "Ain't you grateful to him? Ain't you gonna cry 'cause there's no one to rescue you now? I can make you cry." He clasped his fingers around my chin and squeezed. I felt the muscle around my eye throb like a wasp sting. This was one of those times it was best to not answer a word.

Gerald's men didn't seem none too happy about him killin Walton. There was some fuss and two more rode off, leavin only two to answer Gerald's biddin.

A body is made by the choices they make. Either you choose to be good or you choose to be evil. Edna's words burned in my heart as my mind scrambled to find a way to murder my brother.

"Hmm. What am I gonna do now? I think I wanna baptize you first. Let that water wash away the Devil. Ain't that what baptizin does?"

Silas never let up his cussin and rantin. "Don't you lay nary a hand on her. You hear me?"

Gerald went to laughin that evil laugh of his. "What ya gonna do, nubby? You gonna flail me with your nub?"

That found me my tongue. "Leave him alone, Gerald."

Gerald shoved me to the ground face-first, then stepped over me, the toes of his boots on either side of my shoulders. He grabbed me by the hair and yanked my head upward. Pain shot down my back.

"Let me see, what is it the pastor says?"

"I know," said one of his goons. "I know what the pastor says."

"Tell me there, Larry. Share with me. We want Lochiel's baptizin to be . . . special."

"He holds up one hand and looks to the good Lord and says, 'In the name of the Holy Ghost and the good Lord, I baptize you.' Then he dunks 'em."

The Lord is my shepherd . . . My chest was so full of anger I thought I would pop open like a week-old-dead deer.

"I hate you. I hate you. I hate you." My words didn't come out with much sense behind them.

He rolled me to my back, and towered over me like a giant tree in the forest. His stringy hair hung in his eyes. "You hate me!" Spittle flew from his lips. "That's a good one. You hate me. Well, I hated you first." The sounds he was makin was now more animal than man-like.

Gerald's face drew tight. He gritted his teeth, and I could see his anger come to a boil. With his face reddenin up, I could see faint white lines on his cheek from where I'd scratched him. He reached out, and I flinched, sure I was gonna feel the back of his hand again. But he grabbed under my arm and whipped me to my feet and dragged me the remainin steps to the water's edge.

He brought his head close and dropped his voice low, so it was just him and me. I could feel his hot breath on my neck. "You was a curse from the day I found you in that shack. I shoulda left you to die, and now I'm gonna fix that mistake. From the day I brung you home to Momma, you've been a hex to me, to all of us. I shoulda kilt you long ago."

My mind raced to keep up with his words. It was Gerald. He had been the one to take me. Gerald. He would've been just a youngin then. Already bringin misery to everthing he touched. But just a youngin. How could Poppy have let that happen? My stomach churned and I retched.

"You vile woman!" Gerald thrust me away and I fell to my side and rolled, landin my feet in the river. He'd do me in for sure.

My boots commenced to fill with water, and my skirt dampened. With my shoulders propped against the bank, I wrestled to loosen my wrists from the ropes before they got wet.

"Now that you're in the water, maybe you'll get cleaned."

I could see that I was about to meet my maker. Today, if it was my day to die at the hand of a ragin, crazy brother, I hoped I was ready. But I would not give up without a fight.

Gerald turned to command his men. "Bring him over here."

All I could see was Gerald's legs.

"I want Nubby to see this special baptizin."

Edna had told me about the Lord speakin to her heart. I won't never forget her words. *When the Lord speaks, there ain't no question it's Him. So when you hear Him speak to your heart, you answer. You hear? You always answer. Just like little Samuel did in the Good Book.*

"I have the sole privilege of baptizin the Devil's daughter. Ain't that somethin?"

There was no question in my mind that right at this minute the good Lord was speakin loud and clear. *Lochiel, you bite him.* I was sure without a shadow of a doubt what I was hearin in my heart was the Lord.

I found a foothold in the river's edge and pushed myself up with it.

Don't you question the good Lord's callin. You just do what He tells you.

And so I did.

I opened my mouth and latched onto Gerald's leg like a tarpon. I sunk my teeth long and hard into his leg. So hard I could feel the flesh break open between my teeth.

Gerald fell to the ground hollerin as his trouser turned red with blood. He hauled off and kicked at me. The ropes on my hands loosened and it was like the Lord hisself set me free. I scrabbled out of the water and started toward Silas.

But Silas shook his head violently. "No. The river! Run along the river."

I never learned to do nothin more than wade knee deep in the fishin hole.

"Run, I said!"

I got my wits about me and took off like greased lightnin, barrelin downriver along the water. I tripped on the tail of my skirt, but as quick as

I landed, I was up and runnin again. And when I run outa riverbank—I jumped.

———

When my head broke the clear ceilin of the Indian River, I was caught in the rapids, bumpin and tumblin over the rocks. The river run gentle and slow by Silas's homestead, but on down further, the current grew rough. I reckon I was like a bear cub whose momma shoved him into the river to fish. It was sink or swim.

For me, it was more thrash about. My feet touched the bottom just enough to let me shove myself up from under the wash for a breath. Every time my head would surface, I'd suck in a bite of air and a gulp of water. My nose stung and my arms and legs grew numb from the cold water. Around one and then over another boulder, the river spit me up and out of the water, landin me in a crevice and a shallow pool.

I grabbed at a downed tree and pulled myself to the bank. I looked from where I'd come. There was no sign of Silas's place. I listened hard. There was no sound of man nor beast, just the gurgle of the river.

I crawled on all fours to a grassy spot. With no strength left and no ability to hold in my cries, I laid face down in the grass and wailed. Hard long groans and blood-curdlin screams.

I knew now for a fact it was Gerald who'd stole me away from my momma. And now he'd killed the man who called me his daughter. And was still determined to kill me. Stamp out the last bit of reminder of all he'd done.

If only I woulda obeyed right away and hid, he might not have killed Walton. I cried harder, sobs takin my breath and churnin my stomach 'til I retched again.

"If only I woulda hid! I hate you, Gerald Ogle. I hate you!"

As I lay there screamin as hard and loud as I could, I heard the good Lord speak to my heart again.

The choices you make decide the person you'll be. What is your choice?

"You give me this mark." I shook my fist toward the sky. "You made me this way. You give me to the Devil. Why me? Why would You do this to a body?"

There was nothin else left in me. I was spent. I reckon if Gerald run up on me, he'd just kill me. So I laid there. A warm breeze rustled my hair and my eyes slowly closed.

The river sang with the wind. He leadeth me beside still waters . . .

THIRTY

IN THE TIME I laid there on that knoll, my heart was broke. And I didn't rightly know what to do with the pieces but tried to rest in the sound of the gentle ripple of the river.

It was hard to decide which was worse—a broke heart or a broke spirit. I'd had them both. I tried to keep my thoughts on Edna, rememberin how she'd rise every mornin to greet the day. How she lifted her hands to the good Lord and sang his praises, despite the messes that come her way.

I wondered if Edna would raise her hands to the good Lord now. Now that Gerald had killed her son—killed my father. Still in all, what time she had to teach me about the Lord, showed me this God was a quiet sort, movin deep inside me and not outside so I could lay my hands on Him. What I'd learned from Edna was a kind of peace and trust.

"Even when our earthly heart breaks, the good Lord knows it and He lets us lie down in green pastures," she'd said. "Sometimes gettin to them green pastures means passin through the mud. You cinch up your boot strings so the mud don't yank 'em off, pull up your skirt, and step on in, keepin in mind the pasture is a real welcome place."

It looked like from here forward, I'd have to forge my understandin of the good Lord on my own. *So I'm hopin You're listenin. My heart is broke and I'm all alone in a world that hates me. Are You listenin?*

Was I all alone on the earth? I didn't know what had become of my one and only friend, Silas. The men might've killed him for tellin me to run. Another death might be laid at my feet. *If it's not a bother, if he's not already dead, could You maybe keep Silas from gettin caught up in my mess again?*

The breeze kicked up, gently twistin a strand of half-dried hair around my face. I'd swear on my grave, it felt like a hand cuppin my cheeks, like it was wrappin me in a tender hug.

Poppy kept me hid away so folks never saw me. He told me it was to protect me. That people with this mark on them was hunted and killed. All Poppy had managed to do was hide me from knowin. I was ignorant. Ignorant to the world. All my life lessons was hittin me at once.

I was angry. Hurt. Cheated. And all at Poppy's hand.

I'd pondered Gerald's confession whilst I laid there. Gerald might have been the one who stole a baby from its momma, but Poppy, how could he have allowed it?

I'd done figured Momma wasn't right in her mind. It took me a spell, but the truth was, she wasn't. She was just all caught up in the storm of grief that swallowed her over them babies she birthed that died. It didn't make her coldhearted nature right, but I could at least understand it some.

But Poppy? I loved him. I still wanted to think, deep down, he cared for me. But he hadn't made Gerald return me to my momma—or stop him from bein nasty to me—or lift a word up to stop him from killin Walton—and that made him no better, but worse. He let me believe he cared for me, but all along he was trickin me. He wasn't interested in savin me from Gerald at Silas's homestead. He simply wanted no part of Gerald's tryin to kill me. Same as when we was kids. Poppy watched Gerald go after me more times than I had fingers, and all he did was walk away.

I walked the edge of the river for some time, hopin to find Walton's body washed up on the bank or hung up on a branch juttin into the river, but he was gone. Gone forever.

When Poppy had buried the third baby that died, Momma had laid a few fresh-picked flowers on that grave, right next to the other two she'd lost before. She wouldn't let me add on one I'd picked, so I'd buried it under a little dirt nearby, makin a little grave for that flower. I picked a few jonquils from the bank and tossed them one by one in the river. Every one that hit the water and floated around the gentle rapids and spun in the eddies tore out a part of my heart.

Then it come to me. I needed to find Edna. She'd be brokenhearted. I'd heard her talk about my momma after I was stolen away.

"It ain't right for a body to outlive their youngins," she'd said. Walton's brother had died of the fever some years back. "It ain't the way the world oughta turn."

I knew in my soul I couldn't go back to her place, though. If Walton had been at Edna's when Gerald found him, before Walton escaped to Silas's place to warn us, Gerald could be lookin for me there, and my showin up on her porch would put her in danger. Or at least more danger than she was in now.

Here I stood—cryin into the river—truly alone.

Life was gettin shoved down my gullet before I had a chance to swallow. Wads crammed down my throat, nearly chokin me to death.

Right this minute, it was just me. I was left to fend for myself. *So get up off your rear, brush it off, and start fendin.* Brought to mind somethin Walton said—*After all, that's what we do in these hills. We take the mess, pile it up, and then start to shovel it over our shoulders. Clear a path. Move on.*

I pressed my fingers to my lips and gently kissed them, then tenderly waved my hand toward the river. "Good-bye, Walton. Good-bye, Daddy." I swiped the tears on my sleeve and took a step. It was my first step on my own.

I walked a good piece before I saw a tail of smoke twistin and twirlin up and over the tree line. *A house? A camp? Friendly or not?*

It didn't rightly matter. I needed help. I tore a strip of fabric from the tail of my skirt. Runnin my fingers through the tangles in my hair, I managed to pull the mess of curls together and make a braid. The strip of material made the tie. Might as well not be lookin wild.

A small creek forged its way toward the river, so I knelt to wash my face. One thing was for sure, it never mattered how hot or cold the day, mountain water always put a chill to your skin. I cupped my hands and scooped up a palmful of clear water. It trickled through my fingers and down my arms.

Buryin my face into my hands I scrubbed the dirt, blood, and streaks of tears from my cheeks. There was no tellin who I'd meet at the source of that smoke. But I'd do my best to not look homely.

I dampened my hands enough to comb down sprigs of wiry curls that escaped the braid down my back. I stood, threw back my shoulders and took aholt of who I was. Lochiel Ogle.

Then it hit me like a rock. I wasn't an Ogle. I was a Grubbs. I went to smilin. The first chain that held me to Poppy was broke. I was makin my way to real freedom. The search to find out who I was, was bound to be more than in a name. But knowin the name was a start.

"My name is Lochiel Grubbs," I said out loud. "I'm a good woman. Kind by choice, 'cause the good Lord knows I have reason to be bitter."

All right, go. You'll be fine. I tried to convince myself.

In the distance I could hear dogs howlin. It seemed they would always haunt me. But if I could make it to the source of that smoke, I might find help.

I weaved my way through the stand of trees to a clearing. Four small cabins dotted the field. Three stood against the base of the mountain, and the fourth more toward the river that snaked through the land. Three youngins played in the field, chasin and trippin each other. Their giggles echoed across the field. A woman stood to one side of a cabin, pinnin clothes to a line and fightin the wind that snagged at her dress. Down toward the riverbank, two men worked, lashin small logs together, steppin off distances to measure every once in a while. It looked like a peaceful place.

I stood at the tree line, gatherin my courage to walk into the open. In my head, I pretended them children was runnin to greet the stranger with a mark on her face. They wrestled to see who could touch the red splotch first. The men meandered toward me, juttin their hands out to shake my hand and welcome me to their place. And the women, the women made over my fat braid, untwistin it to roll it into a soft bun.

I smiled, anxious to know these families. Hopeful they'd feel kindly toward me.

I shook my head and pushed the dream to the side, conjurin up the guts to walk toward the cabins. I took a step. I'd be calm. Tell them what happened. Ask if they'd seen Walton's body wash down the river. I practiced my words.

"My name is Lochiel Grubbs. I'm Lochiel Grubbs." I wasn't really no Ogle. I was a Grubbs. "My name's Lochiel Grubbs."

The more I uttered the name, the better it sounded. I gathered more courage.

One of the boys spied me across the field and waved. I saw him turn toward the men and shout. His hand pointed across the field at me. The woman at the line pulled her hand up, shadin her eyes for a better look.

There was nothin I could do but keep walkin. I had nothin to cover my mark. The men laid their tools down, clappin the dust off their hands as they started across the field.

I felt naked. I'd hid behind Edna's shawl, underground, overhead, behind slats of wood. Hidin felt safe, comfortable. But then isn't that always what hidin is? A place of comfort, an escape from fear? I rubbed my fingers across the mark. *Oh, Lord, please blind their eyes to my mark.*

A little blonde-haired girl took to runnin toward me.

"Hey, lady. Where'd you come from?" Her voice shook as she trotted across the field. "Where you goin?"

I eased my hand into the air and waved. "Hello."

The child come just feet away. Her hair hung in her face. She pushed her fingers against her head and shoved the long strands of hair behind her ear.

"My name is Lochiel . . . "

The girl stopped. Her smile faded and then it happened. A blood curdlin scream. High-pitched, long, frightenin.

The men broke into a run. I went to my knees and extended my hands. "Don't scream. I won't hurt you. I promise. Please stop screamin."

She pointed at my face, then wheeled around to her daddy. "She's marked." The scream broke loose again. "It's the woman them men said killed that boy."

"I didn't kill anyone. I'm not a killer." My heart went to racin. This was nothin I had imagined. No warm welcome. No kindness. Just anger at the animal folks thought I was. There was never any give to the bad that people thought. It was only fear and hate. Couldn't these people see I was not evil? Couldn't they see there was more to me than this mark?

I tried to calm the child, but nothin I said helped. And when I took her arm, she yanked hard and fell. "Daddy, help me. She's gonna kill me!"

Just as I stood to help the child to her feet, two of the men jumped at me.

"Wait! Please! Let me talk."

"You tried to kill my girl."

"No! I never—"

The two men danced about me, keepin me caged in without actually touchin me.

"That's it. The mark of the Devil. Folks all over the mountain know about you killin that boy. I reckon we found us a murderer."

"You don't know what you're talkin about. Please, let me explain."

"Don't listen, Joseph," the other man said.

"I'm not a devil!"

"She is of her father the Devil, and the lusts of her father she will do."

"Let me explain!"

The man called Joseph drew back and his fist hit my jaw.

I COULDN'T HELP but notice Lochiel had growed into a purty woman. Curves in all the places there should be. I caught myself sometimes eyein her and wonderin if it weren't for that mark, what kind of woman she'd be. From the one side, she looked like her father the Devil, but from the other, a man could be right fooled. I'd set myself to guard against her wiles, but she'd hexed my mind.

Lochiel sat on a rock by the river. I had to keep an eye on her, makin sure no one come upon her. The sun was hot. Her lips parted while she worked. Her raven hair was loose, callin to my hands to play. My eyes were drawn back to them lips like they was a rabbit stew for supper. Her skirt was tied up, showin her bare legs. As she stood and turned from the water, her hips teased me.

"Lochiel, why don't you come sit a minute?" I patted my knee. She pulled her basket tight under her arm. "Come on, Lochiel, you know you want to."

"Don't you have work to do?"

"Ain't you the sassy one?" I took hold of her arm. She twisted loose.

"Don't you lay a hand on me." Her low voice let me know her words was a lie. "What would Momma say if she saw you makin eyes at the Devil's daughter? What's the matter? Can't find a woman who'll have you?" She was askin for it.

I smirked. "Got yourself a sharp tongue." She shrugged and walked away. There she was, beggin me to follow.

I come up behind her, close, and reached my hands to her waist, then slidin them down, feelin her round—

"Poppy!" Her voice rang across the yard. My hands yanked back and Poppy come from the barn, shadin his eyes to see over to us.

"Do you need help?" she called out, all innocent-like.

My stomach burned with anger. She knew what she was doin, settin out to hook me. "You better sleep with one eye open, Devil's daughter."

She turned quick and trotted over to Poppy. There was only one way this was gonna end.

THIRTY-ONE

THE CALL OF buzzards woke me. It had been a long winter, and the scavengers were hungry. The scent of my blood started them circlin overhead. Each lap drew them lower and lower until two lit on the ground and picked at my ankles. I kicked at the nasty birds.

"Git! I ain't dead yet! Git outa here."

I tried to wiggle, but my arms was tied tight to a scarecrow pole. The burlap body above me was stuffed with straw and set in the field to ward off such things. I raised my head upward, starin into the straw-filled legs that hung above me.

"A lot of good you are."

There was no one in sight. The youngins were gone and the men no longer worked.

"Help me! Someone help me. I ain't the Devil's daughter. My name is Lochiel Grubbs."

I must have screamed for an hour, but not a soul answered. The doors to all the cabins was shut tight, and all I had was hungry buzzards peckin at my legs.

I kicked again. "I told you I ain't dead."

I twisted my hands in the ropes, tryin to wiggle loose. When that didn't work, I scraped the ropes against the pole. "Stupid buzzards. You could be useful and gnaw these ropes."

My throat was raw and I was drier than tanned leather. I dropped my chin to my chest and started to cry. *Somebody help me. Please! I ain't what people think.*

The sun rose high into the sky, and my skin burnt from the heat, but the breeze that tossed the new grass was still brisk from winter's end and gave me the shivers. The seasons was still tryin to call a winner in their brawl over who would take holt. The two fightin over who was the strongest.

My cries became parched sobs.

"Help me," I whispered. "Someone please help me."

The door to one of the cabins opened and a woman walked out. She made her way across the stubbly cornfield carryin a bowl. A rag hung over her wrist.

She stopped at my feet and stared down. "Turn your head so I can see that mark."

I did as she asked. "I ain't what people say."

"I don't reckon I asked to hear your story. Just to see that mark."

I bent my head far to the side. "There. You get a good look. And if you want to see more, rip off my dress. The mark trails down my neck and over my shoulder." I reckon my first thoughts was to snap at the woman. *When you get your eyes full, open your mouth.* But quick-like fear grabbed aholt of me. She easily held my livin or dyin in her hands. One scream and them men could give me a hammerin I might not survive.

"Well, ain't you the smart-mouthed one? You ain't set out here long enough to lose your fight?"

"I don't want no fight. I want help. Please just listen. You can touch my mark. You'll see it's just a mark. It's not evil."

The woman leaned her head to one side, peerin at my mark before she spoke.

"That ain't what them men said that come across the mountain. They said you put a curse on a boy. Made him sick because he wouldn't succumb to your ways. They said you hexed him. Killed him deader than a doornail."

"Edna says a mark is just a mark. It don't make the person." I tried to swipe the blood from my face with my shoulder. "Please help me. Please?" I softened my voice, doin my best not to frighten the woman. "I ain't never cursed or hexed a body in my life. I choose kindness, not evil. Please believe me."

"I don't know no Edna, but that ain't what my momma taught me. She said when babies was born with a mark like yours, they was burned by the Devil. Called as his own."

I gritted my teeth and groaned.

"My momma told me them kind of babies was few and far between and if they wasn't cleansed as infants, they'd be marked for life. Marked to do the work of the Devil."

I shook my head. "I'm not doin the Devil's work," I whispered.

The woman knelt next to me. "Looks like my husband give you a good lick on the jaw. It's already black from the hit." She dipped her rag in the water and blotted at the dried blood on my mouth.

"Your husband know you're talkin to me? Ain't you afraid I'll hex you?"

"You're tied under a scarecrow. He's a protector."

I rolled my eyes. "I ain't right bright. But this thing over me is just burlap and hay. It don't do nothin but make the birds think it's a person so they don't light and eat your corn."

She rinsed the rag and worked her way around my mouth, swipin away the blood.

"Open your mouth."

I eased my jaws open.

"Looks like you still got all your teeth. Joseph didn't punch one out." She lifted a pouch and dribbled water into my mouth. "Slosh that around and spit."

I swished the water from side to side in my mouth and then spit. Red-tinted water shot onto the ground. "That burns."

"It oughta. That's a good-sized cut inside your lip."

She dribbled some more water in. Enough to quench my thirst.

"Thank you." I figured it couldn't hurt to ask. "Could you untie me? Please?"

"Can't do that. I got youngins. I don't want you puttin no spell on them."

Tears welled in my eyes again, but I blinked them back. "What's your name?"

She eyed me good before she spoke. "Betsy."

"Betsy. That's a right nice name."

"Hush, now. Let me clean these wounds." She snagged my chin with her fingers and twisted my head to one side to swipe the blood off my neck.

"Do you see many folks up this way, Betsy?"

Her eyes got big and she snatched her hands back. "Don't say my name again. Don't say my name anymore. You might take a piece of my soul with it."

"No, no. I wouldn't do nothin like that. I won't say your name again. I'm not gonna hurt anybody. There ain't nothin about me that can do somethin like that."

The woman gingerly tapped my chin. I figure because she came away without a burn, she grabbed on again.

"So do you see many folks up this way?"

She cocked her head and looked puzzled. "What's that got to do with anything?"

"I just wondered."

"A few. We try to welcome strangers." She dipped her rag again, pressin it firmly against my lip to stop the bleedin.

"You welcome strangers? I take it you mean you welcome them until you see them up close, then you decide whether they're folks you want around or not?"

She dropped her hand to her lap. "You're tryin to trip me up."

"No, I ain't. I'm just askin if you judge everbody before you know who they are. See, your youngins waved at me. And the men put down their work to come out to meet me. Then when that little girl saw my mark, right that minute I was judged to be a killer. Up to then, I was a stranger bein welcomed in."

Betsy dropped her head. "Joseph knows what's best for this family, and what he says goes."

"That boy people say I killed? Well, let me tell you about that sweet child."

"I don't want to know what you did to kill him." She waved her hand for me to hush.

"I found him outside my shack, face down in the weeds. The child was knocked out cold. His head was bleedin. There was a cut the length of your finger in the boy's head. His jaw was swelled and it took two days for that youngin to come around."

"I told you I don't want to know."

"Yes, you *do* want to know. Me and my grandmomma took that child in. We cleaned his wounds, spoon-fed him soup, and when he took on a mean fever, it was me and her who held him in the cold wash of the river, tryin to take down his fever." My voice quivered as I spoke. "I rocked that little boy. Kissed his head. Prayed that the good Lord would protect him. And then his momma come. We took her in too. I kept my cheek covered so she couldn't see my mark. And as long as she didn't know I had this blessed ole mark, she was alright with me helpin her and her boy."

"You knew his mother?"

"Yes, her name is Rita. That boy would be good one day and the next he'd be on fire with fever again. Over and over we fought the heat that burned in his little body. I reckon it was from his head bein slashed open. And when my daddy put me on a horse and sent me runnin from those that wished me dead, that little boy was alive. He was sick with the fever, but that child was alive."

Betsy stared, never blinkin. I could see her ponderin over what I'd told her. She washed out the rag, twisted it until no more water drained, then stood.

"Where you goin, B—, ma'am? Do you believe me?"

Betsy pulled her skirt up and stepped over my legs. "I'll see about bringin you some soup and bread. Joseph's gone after the Ogles, and I ain't one to let a critter suffer."

"*Critter?* Is that what you think I am? An animal? Then you might as well go to your cabin and get Joseph's shotgun. Cock it and pull the trigger. You'd be bein kinder than you are now. I ain't the Devil's daughter. This mark don't make me who I am no more than your long fingers or green eyes make you who you are."

She pushed her hair from her face and dumped the water from the bowl. Tuckin it under her arm, she walked away.

"Wait. I need to know 'bout my daddy. The man who wants me dead"—I couldn't bring myself to say *brother*—"stabbed him in the gut, then shoved him into the river. You ain't seen his body? I mean, dead or alive? I need to know if he's dead. My daddy's Walton Grubbs."

Betsy stopped dead. She turned and shoved her hand into her apron. "The peddler?"

"Yes, yes, the peddler. That's my daddy."

She took a few steps toward me. "Walton's a good man. Even though he's a half-breed."

I snatched at the tiny thread of hope. "Has my daddy ever done you wrong? Has he ever been dishonest with you a day in his life?"

Betsy shook her head.

"Do you still trade goods with him? Barter for things you need on the farm? Does he travel miles at a time to get you the things you need?"

She nodded.

"Walton has always been a kind man. True to his word. Ain't that right?"

"Yes."

"My grandmomma told me. Walton told me. It's the choices we make that makes us who we are. Not what we look like. Not a mark. I reckon you like Walton, trust him, 'cause he's been good to you, brung you what you need, never cheated you. So even though he's a half-breed, you trust him, right?"

Betsy nodded again. She seemed to be thinkin.

"And I'm tellin you this. I have a mark, but I ain't never done nothin hurtful to no one." I decided that whatever I done to Gerald just didn't count now, seein as he aimed to kill me. "You can trust me 'cause I got no plans to hurt anyone. I choose to be kind. If you walk away from me and Joseph comes back with Gerald tomorrow, and they kill me, I ain't holdin nothin against you. I choose to be kind. I choose to be different. That's what my daddy taught me. That's the word of Walton Grubbs. Honest. True."

Betsy turned toward the cabin.

"I choose to be different," I repeated as sobs heaped up from my gut. My wails caught on the wind and followed Betsy across the field. "I ain't gonna be like these people. I choose—to—be—different."

A bloody spit dripped from my mouth and I wondered for a minute if that buzzard would be back. And if he did come back, maybe he would eat around my mark.

THIRTY-TWO

BETSY WAS GONE a spell, and between them buzzards peckin at me and my rubbin the tar outa them ropes around my wrists, I was wore out. Still, there was somethin inside that nudged me on. *Keep scrubbin them ropes against that post. They'll give.*

I sure had the time to ponder whilst I set at the foot of that scarecrow. I kept on doin what that little voice in my head said. Scrubbin them ropes, tryin to break them.

"Well, Lord, I reckon I got the time to talk, so I hope You got the gumption to listen. I understand Edna's believin in You. I don't understand the not seein You face-to-face, but I somehow figure there is somethin to what Edna and Walton says about You. I don't have much understandin. But I'm askin You. For a woman who knows little, but is willin to trust, will You at least give me determination? I ain't askin for You to fix my mess. But give me the gumption to see it through."

I cocked my head to the side and scratched my chin against my shoulder. Why is it a body always gets an itch when they can't scratch it?

"There's more, Lord. Edna was a right forgivin woman. She never looked at me as the Devil's daughter. She looked at me as a young woman. And what's more, she'd tell me she just wanted to be like You. And if that's what it means to be like You, then that's what I want. I want to look at the side of people that might be buried deep. So, Lord, if You'd answer me out loud that would be real nice. But if You choose to keep Your trap shut, then I reckon that's alright too. But I choose to be like Edna. And if that's like You, then I reckon I'm askin to be like You. I just need to be determined not to hate. Not to want revenge. And one more thing. Sir, please don't let me die at the hand of a buzzard. I guess that's all for now."

I rested my head against the pole. My mouth was dry again. My skin burned from the sun, and the breeze had dried my lips 'til they was crackin open.

I ain't the Devil's daughter. I closed my eyes and drifted off.

A hand pressed against my shoulder. "Wake up, Missy. Wake up." My eyes was heavy, and when I cracked them open, darkness covered the field. I closed them again.

"Open your eyes. It's me."

"What? Who are you?"

The ropes around my wrists loosened, and my arms were lifted then dropped.

"You ain't much help. You done forgot I only got one hand? Help me out here."

One hand? I shook my head. The air shoved outa my lungs as I bounced up and down on this man's shoulder. I was weak. Tired. Thirsty. Hungry.

"Here. Take this. It ain't much, but it'll feed you a few days."

I opened my eyes wide enough to see the light from a lantern and Betsy. She brushed my hair from my face. "I'm sorry." Her words choked in her throat.

My body slipped off Silas's shoulder, and he laid me across the saddle of a horse. The leather smelled sweet.

Liftin my head to look at Betsy, I whispered, "I forgive you."

When I uttered them words, it was like a new strength come upon me. I was still tired, still weak, but the strength in my heart grew.

Betsy came close. "You'll be fine. It took me a spell, but I managed to find someone to help you." She seemed to be beggin, but I already forgive her. I didn't know what else to say.

A hand gently twisted my head to one side. "I'm gonna strap you to this horse. It won't be a cozy ride but it'll have to do. I ain't gonna let nothin happen to you." The tender lips of a man pressed against my cheek. Pressed against my mark.

"Silas?" Hope seeped into my soul. Then joy overwhelmed me as the realization that Silas was alive rushed over me. I reckon the good Lord heard my weak prayer. He'd saved Silas and softened Betsy's heart. He had, without a doubt, saved me.

"Shh. We got a long road ahead." Silas took the bag of food Betsy handed him. "What you done tonight has saved the life of an innocent woman. The lie you'll have to tell to protect yourself won't be right, but necessary. I believe the good Lord knows that."

Betsy pulled her shawl tight around her arms. "Take the path up the ridge. At the top, when the path ends, trust your heart and go left across the gap. It ain't marked. But there's a natural break in the woods. Cross the river. It's hard there. Real hard. But once you're on the other side, you can find shelter. There's a village of people like her."

People like me. What did that mean?

"Betsy." I moaned as I twisted toward her. "Thank you."

She patted my head. "Go. Git—before you wake up my youngins. My little one can't keep her mouth shut. Go!"

Silas took the reins of my horse and climbed on his own. "Try your best to hold on."

He kneed his horse and then I felt the animal under me begin to lumber. I watched as the soft yellow glow of the lantern disappeared.

We rode the better part of the night, a golden round moon givin us just enough light to find our way. After a bit, Silas started to yap. I wasn't sure if he was talkin because he was scared or because he wasn't so sure I was alive. But he commenced to yap.

"I mighta never found you. Gerald's goon smacked me with his shotgun. I reckon he thought I was dead since I didn't take no breath or move. I wanted him to think he'd won the battle. Once they cleared out—"

"Stop. I'm sick." My gut tightened and everthing inside me bubbled. "Silas—stop!"

"Whoa, there." Silas halted the horses and jumped down. "What's wrong?"

What little was left in me boiled to the top. I turned my head away from Silas and retched.

"Let me unstrap you from this horse. Hang on."

He released the strap that held me across my horse and lifted me down. I went to my knees and gagged again.

"I'm gettin you some water." Silas flipped open the saddlebag and pulled out a soft skin pouch. He unknotted the end and raised it to my mouth. "Drink slow."

The taste of the cool water was like a refreshin rain. It dribbled down my chin and onto my dress.

"Ease up, gal. Here. Sit down." Silas helped me to sit, then slipped up close to me. "Rest a bit. We can't tarry long, but we can stop long enough to catch a breath."

Silas rolled a blanket from his saddlebag, hunkered down right in front of me, and propped it behind my head.

"You rest against this tree for a minute."

"What are we gonna do?" I whispered.

"Ain't important right now." Silas stroked my hair.

"Is too important. And what about Walton? We have to find his body."

"The only thing we have to do right now is find us a place to hide 'til we figure a plan."

"But Walt—"

"Shh, shh. Ain't nothin we can do about Walt now."

"I know'd Gerald was mean, but I never—"

"Will you just hush? Rest a minute. Get enough strength so you can sit on that horse instead of hang over its back."

"You come after me." I tried to see his eyes in the darkness.

"I reckon I did."

"Why? Didn't I cost you enough?"

Silas laid his hand on the curve of my cheek. "I reckon that all depends on what you weigh out as cost."

I rested my hand over his. "Nearly cost you your life."

"*Nearly* ain't enough, now, is it?"

I had to think on what he meant by that. I dropped my hand to my lap, feelin awkward, not wantin him to know I didn't understand what he was sayin.

Silas patted my cheek, rose, and stepped back. "We'll figure this out. Gerald will get his. He will. My momma used to always say, 'What goes around comes around,' and it will."

I tried to stand but my knees was wobbly. Silas steadied me. "What about Edna?"

He took my chin in his hand and turned my face toward the moonlight. He dabbed his sleeve across my busted lip. "That's a pretty nasty lick you took."

"Yeah, well, I still got all my teeth." I spread my lips in a big smile. "You didn't answer my question."

"Can't you just hush for a few minutes?"

I asked again, right harsh. "I *said*, what about Edna?"

Silas hesitated.

"You think she's dead, don't you?"

"I don't know. How would I know?"

"You don't have to know to have a gut feelin."

"Alright, yes. My best guess is those men have done killed her. But you understand, I got no way of knowin. It's just a—"

"Gut feelin."

"Yes. A feelin. I'm figurin Gerald is clearin away anything and anybody who might stand in his way of seein you dead. Them Ogles has been hidin you for years. Gerald's guilt finally turned to anger, rage. And now he blames you for his own doin. He ain't right in the head."

I turned the water pouch to my mouth again and drank.

Silas took it from me. "I told you to go easy. When's the last time you ate?"

"Supper—at your house."

"Well, that's goin on two days now." He dug into the saddlebag and pulled out a biscuit. "Here. Start slow."

It didn't much more than hit my stomach 'til it found its way out. Silas used his foot to dig in the dirt, kickin it over my vomit. He scooped up an armful of pine needles and buried the mess, then took a branch and swept the spot, spreadin the damp dirt all around. "That oughta put off any scent of us."

"There has to be a way to settle this without any more people dyin."

Silas held the stirrup and looked me over.

"Think you can ride?" When I nodded, he said, "Here. Use my shoulder to lift up."

I grabbed his shoulder with one hand and the saddle horn with the other. He shoved my foot into the stirrup. "On three. One. Two. Up you go."

"Do you think we can stop Gerald?"

Silas tightened the saddle and patted the horse "Here." He handed me the reins.

"Do you think—"

"I heard your question. You done asked it a slew of times. Just worded it a little different. I don't know 'bout Gerald. I don't know what we can or can't do. What I do know is that the most important thing is to get you somewhere safe. After that, I'll ponder on what to do."

Tears sprung to my eyes and I was glad for the cover of darkness. Silas was nice enough but his tone told me he was tired of me pressin him. There was one thing that was clear. This man was kind beyond what any person should be. He took me into his home and now he was protectin me without even really knowin me. And he seemed to care about me. That was a new experience—to have Edna and Walton care . . . and now Silas.

He climbed on his horse and we made it up the ridge 'til the trail ended. The sun was just breakin light. The ridge was steep, slick. Betsy was right. It was gonna take a heap of trust to turn down the mountain toward the gap when there was no forged path.

"You ready?" Silas asked.

The sound of the river roared below us. I swallowed hard as my horse took a step and slid. "Shouldn't we walk?"

"Nah. These horses was raised in the mountains. That's why they got two short legs."

He chuckled. A beautiful, deep, throaty sound.

It took a minute for Silas's humor to sink in. Then I laughed a little bit.

And Silas belted out more laughter. And the sound of that made me laugh again, louder this time. And then we couldn't stop. I laughed 'til tears streamed down my face. It was the first time ever I'd cried tears of laughter.

And it felt good. Really good.

Thirty-Three

THEM HORSES SLIPPED and slid, but their legs was strong as we tried to snake our way down the slope.

Halfway down, Silas pointed out a small clearin. It wasn't much more than a flat spot, but it was level. Rocks jutted out from the side of the mountain, and small, spindly trees hung tight, their roots stretchin into the dirt against the ledge. Vines hung from the trees like water rushin over a fall and when the breeze blew, they danced gently to and fro.

"That looks like a good place for us to get some rest." Silas pointed toward the overhang. "We'll stop here. The horses can mosey into the woods a bit and gnaw at the new grass and vines."

He climbed from his horse and wrapped a strong arm around my waist, liftin me gently to the ground. My knees give a little, but I managed to stand straight.

"You do good for havin only one hand. I don't reckon you need a second one." A grin stretched across my face.

"Man has to manage. Has to survive. Or die. I've learned to get along purty well."

"Do people talk about you? I mean, do they look at you different?"

Silas pulled his hat to the back of his head and run his one hand through his hair. He spit, then ground the slobber into the grass with his boot. "I reckon some folks do. But once they know me, I don't guess they even notice that one of my hands is gone."

"You think that will happen for me? You think folks will quit seein this mark and just see me?"

Silas lifted the strands of vines and nodded for me to climb under. "It don't rightly matter what folks see or what they think. What matters is you findin happiness in who you are. I ain't pleased to be missin a hand, but I know it don't make me less of a man. It just makes for a bump in the road."

We sat under the ledge, and both of us got quiet. As I looked out over the ridge, the sun peeked through the clouds. I didn't have much at Poppy's, but I did have a small window in the loft. It looked across the river to the mountain on the east.

A thick, white mist stood between the river and the sun, turnin the yellow ball into a white circle. Lavender splashes bubbled through open spots in the mist and pink strands dribbled over that. As the sun climbed higher into the sky, it edged above the fog, boastin bright orange that faded into yellow.

I'd seen some beautiful sunrises, but there was somethin special about this one. Not only was the colors somethin else but it was different. Maybe it was seein it from above instead of below. Or maybe it was seein it with the eyes of someone new—someone whose eyes was open wide now.

Chills raced down my spine.

Silas laid back and propped his head on his arm. "Ain't that a sight?"

"Ain't it though?" I whispered.

"Ain't nothin a body could ever wish for that could hold a candle to this."

"Silas, I got no home. No place to even lay down and call my own. This here is somethin alright, but I can't help but wish for somethin more."

"We all feel lost at times. But, well, home is where you make it, little lady."

I wondered for a minute if I was just feelin sorry for myself and Silas aimed to make me see these mountains was my home.

"I suppose you're right. I'm just tired. Tired of bein hunted. Tired of bein called somethin I ain't. I want peace. Is that wrong?"

"Naw, peace ain't somethin bad to want for. But it is somethin we have to figure out. Best I can tell, you're in good company." Silas bumped my arm with his elbow. "I recall the pastor preachin a sermon 'bout the good Lord havin no place to lay His head. No place to call His own, neither. Good company, I reckon, bein in the same spot as the good Lord."

He sat up and nudged his shoulder against mine. "One other thing. You may have a mark, but you know what I see in you every time I look?"

I shrugged, but my heart was hungry for his words.

"I see eyes that's as yellow as that new sun." He pointed to the sky. "Eyes that spark with life. Eyes that burn into a body's soul with compassion."

My heart was doin strange things as I hugged the blanket to my middle. He was talkin about my eyes but I couldn't bring myself to look at him. My cheeks were feelin warm.

"I know it ain't right for a man to lay with a woman before they's married. But we only got one blanket. It's a bit nippy and I'm wore out. My intentions is nothin but good. So lay down here next to me. Cover us up, and I believe the good Lord will allow us some rest. The horses is in the woods, and we're hid under these vines. We both need to sleep."

Now the warmth spread to my neck and shivered down my spine. There was somethin especially sweet about Silas. His heart was kind, and he made mine beat a little faster. I stretched out next to him and spread the blanket across us.

"I don't 'spect I'll be fightin you for this cover, will I?"

"I reckon not." Silas rolled to his side. "Rest now, Lochiel. Rest."

He barely got the words out before he was sawin logs. But me, well, I couldn't take my eyes off that sunrise.

I watched as the fog burned away and the river below come into sight. The birds that soared above was hawks, not buzzards. Graceful. Masterful. Dippin and divin, catchin on the breeze. They didn't seem to have a care in the world. My eyes grew heavy as I drifted into sleep.

We slept the better part of the mornin before Silas roused. He sat up and stretched, his yawn louder than a bear growlin. I had my balance back, so I rounded up the horses and brought them to the rock ledge.

"Miss Betsy give us two big loaves of sourdough bread. I think she put jelly in there too."

Silas flipped the saddlebag open and dragged out the food. He pulled one loaf to his nose and sniffed. "My, my. Nothin makes a man's mouth water more than fresh sourdough."

I shook my head and smiled at his pleasure. Silas took his knife from his boot and swiped it clean. He pressed the blade through the bread.

"Look at that. Cuts like hot butter." He had one of them curious possum grins that made me smile as he handed me a portion.

"It does smell right nice. But you ain't had sourdough 'til you've had mine. The key is in the kneadin. Knead a minute, sprinkle a tad of flour, knead some more. But not too much. Elsewise it won't rise right." I took a bite of the bread.

"Jelly?" Silas stuck the rag filled with jelly at me. The juice seeped through the cloth. "We need to eat this so we don't draw ants."

I giggled. "Like ants is the biggest problem we have."

"Oh, yeah? Them critters'll be all over you before you can say Jack Sprat. Can't brush 'em off fast enough. Them rascals are little, but they is the stubbornest varmints I ever seen."

I caught myself spittin out a laugh. Seemed Silas had grown good at makin me laugh.

The bread was so tender it melted in my mouth. "Mmm, good stuff," I said as I took a second bite. "So, what's next?"

Silas scrubbed his chin. "Well, we find this village Betsy talked about. She said it was just over the river."

I pondered before I opened my mouth. "The one where they say there's people like me?"

Silas's chewin slowed. He swallowed hard. "I guess. It don't matter, does it?"

"I guess not." *They take care of their own*, Walton had said. When he'd said it, I didn't know that meant me.

He rolled the sourdough tight into the rag and stuffed it into the saddlebag. "You ready?"

I climbed to my feet and walked around my horse. "This is the steed Walton give me."

"Yep. I figured since you rode him across the mountain to me, Walt would've give you the horse he thought you'd bind with. They grow to know you, understand your intentions."

"That was mighty kind of you. I named him Sky." My voice cracked as I fought back tears.

"Aww, now look. Walton was a good man. He loved you. Loved you for years before he'd ever laid eyes on you. Loved you despite everthing. He called that mark a blessin, not a curse, 'cause it helped him run you down."

"But he's dead." I swiped at my cheek. "And I never got to tell him it was Gerald. Gerald's the one who stole me away."

"He died a fulfilled man, even without knowin. He found his daughter. Give his life for her. There ain't no greater love."

It was my fault Walton was dead. That was a guilt—a curse—I'd have to live with the rest of my life.

I remembered Edna talkin about the love of the good Lord and how He give up His Son for man. I thought it sounded a little hokey. A God you can't see, givin His youngin for us. But Edna was convincin. And it wasn't long before she'd done explained the love of the Lord right plain-like.

She told me, "They's one thing you need to know about the good Lord. He's bigger than all of us. It ain't for us to question. Just for us to believe." I reckon I started then to see the strong love of a father. Walt's love proved mighty strong.

Silas helped me mount up and patted my knee, then pulled hisself onto his horse and made his way to the slope. I followed. The river didn't look deep, but it was fast and its voice rumbled up the mountain.

"How do you reckon we get across?"

"My best guess is, if there's a village of people, there's a rope stretchin over the safest place to cross."

My stomach turned. I couldn't swim. And even when I jumped into the river runnin from Gerald, the current did the carryin. I just had to keep my head up enough to breathe. There was times it didn't look deep and I figured I could put my feet down, only to find it was a lie, yankin me under 'til my toes touched. Then I got plumb lucky when it landed me in a shallow spot.

"I ain't keen on takin to the water." I leaned to one side to dodge a limb.

Silas turned in his saddle. "Me neither. So we're gonna hope these horses are mighty swimmers. Come on, missy girl. It's gonna be fun." He let out a laugh that echoed across the pass.

The horses slipped a few times, but we managed to make our way down the side of the mountain to level ground. The river's roar was so loud we had to shout. The rush hard and heavy.

"This way!" Silas pointed upriver. "I see smoke risin."

All I could do was trust he knew what he was doin. I kneed my horse and we made our way along the riverbank. Every step my horse took, I could feel the soft dirt of the riverbank give. The mountains rose high on either side of the river, formin a gorge and forcin the river to run tight between its walls. I'd never seen the river this narrow or this bold.

Silas kept us movin until the river twisted around the side of the mountain. In the distance, several trails of smoke twirled and climbed into the sky.

The village.

Silas raised his hand and motioned me to stop. He climbed down from his horse and walked to the edge of the river. "Well shoot, there ain't no rope."

I eased next to him. "No rope? There ain't no rope? We can't cross?" I swallowed hard.

"That puts us betwixt a rock and a hard place. We'll have to make our way across on a prayer." He paced up the river bed lookin for a shallow spot. "This'll have to do."

Silas took a rope from his saddle and tied it around his waist, then around mine.

Right away my mind latched to bein tied to the porch.

He leaned toward my ear. "So here's what we do. The water looks about knee deep, but you know the river. It ain't always what it looks like. This here rope will keep us together. If one of us slips, the other can hold on."

This rope was to keep me safe, just like Poppy used to say. My heart raced as hard as the water, but I was gettin mighty good at trustin that Silas knew what he was talkin 'bout. This rope was different. It wasn't tyin me down to leave me behind, it was helpin bring me along. Silas wasn't fixin to leave me.

Silas mounted his horse.

"These horses is natural swimmers. So you hold on. If they hit a deep spot, they's gonna start to swim . . . I hope."

"You *hope?*"

Silas grinned, then leaned across and kissed my cheek. "I hope!" He took the middle of the rope and wound it around my saddle horn. "Only got one hand. Can't hold the reins and your horse too."

Oh, Lord. Jokin ain't what I need right now.

We eased the horses slowly into the rush of the river. They snorted as they fought against the wash. My knuckles was white, holdin on to that saddle horn, but them horses pushed across that river like they was pullin a plow.

The bank was in sight and I started countin my blessins. Silas's horse stepped up into ankle-deep water. Silas threw his leg across the saddle and slipped into the river.

"Shouldn't you stay on that horse 'til we're out of the water?"

"Nah, we're good now." The words had hardly made it to my ear when he stepped and sank beneath the water.

"Silas!" The rope wrapped around my saddle horn tightened.

His head bobbed up, and I saw him gasp for air just as the current sucked him back into its grips.

"Hup, horse. Hup!" Sky leaned into the wash and stepped forward. Silas's head rose above the current.

"Stay with me!" Every time his head sunk beneath that rush, my heart sunk with him. "Lord, have mercy. Silas, stay with me!"

The horse struggled as she fought the current and the pull of Silas's weight. He didn't come up a third time, and my horse couldn't move any further. Silas must be snagged on somethin under the water. I tried to knee my horse in Silas's direction, but she wouldn't budge.

Three men appeared through the forest, headin toward the river.

"Help me!" I flailed an arm. "Oh, please help me."

They dropped their goods and rushed to help. One dove headfirst under the water whilst one tried to yank me from my horse. Seein what held me up, he pulled his knife out and sliced the rope.

"No!" I flailed at him as he pulled me down. "Silas is on that rope."

The rope popped and unwound from the horn, then disappeared into the water.

"Silas! Oh, my Lord. You cut him loose." I struggled with the man pullin me from the river even while I knew I couldn't jump back in to save Silas The horses climbed from the river, water streamin from their shiny sides.

"Silas is in the river!"

"Hoit'll get him." The man released my arm. "You stay here. Outa the way."

It felt like hours, but it was only seconds before the man broke the ceilin of the wash with Silas across his shoulder. The three men dragged Silas onto the bank and rolled him to his stomach to press on his back. Water blew from Silas's mouth as he coughed and gagged.

I pulled him into my arms. "Silas, you fool! You nearly drowned. And you woulda, had it not been for these men." He mumbled somethin but didn't open his eyes.

I lifted my head and brushed the wet hair from my face, fully exposin the mark. The men took a step back. Then another.

"She's marked."

"It's the Devil's mark."

I stood. They backed away, eyes wide. All I could think to do was admit what I was.

"Yes, I got a mark." I pulled my dress off my shoulder and took a few steps toward them so they could see the purplish streak that run down my cheek, neck, and onto my arm. "But I ain't no devil."

I dropped to my knees, folded my hands, and prayed like there was no tomorrow.

THIRTY-FOUR

I RECKON I ain't never prayed no harder than I did on that riverbank.

Lord, I need help here.

The men stared for a minute before one of them jabbed a stick at me. "Get up. Come on now. Get up."

I come to my feet 'bout the same time Silas struggled to all fours.

"Please. Let me help him—" My voice broke.

There was a long pause as the three was apparently decidin what to do. The man with the stick nodded, and I rushed to Silas.

"You alright?"

Silas pulled against my shoulder to stand. "I reckon I got a tad cocky."

"Reckon you did?" His weight pressed on me.

He shook his head and pointed toward the men. "These folks is your kind."

Had it been anybody other than Silas, I'd have got my hackles up. But I understood what he meant. I looked like these people. Copper skin, dark curly hair, golden eyes. I could see some of these folks in Walton. More in Edna.

One of the men turned back and ran toward the village. The other two seemed to be standin guard.

Silas eased closer. "Lochiel, do you trust me?"

I furrowed my brow. "What?"

"You trust me, don't you?"

"I reckon after all we been through, I got no choice."

"Just no choice?"

Here we were, maybe gonna be tied to another scarecrow pole in a field, and he was challengin my words. I couldn't help but sigh. "Alright, Silas. Truth be told, I believe I do trust you."

"Good."

For a man who just nearly drowned, he looked purty pleased with hisself.

Before long, we was circled by a crowd of people, hands shadin their mouths, whisperin amongst themselves. Fingers pointed to my face.

Silas reached and turned me toward him, liftin my chin and gently brushin the mark on my face, seemin to ignore all those people round us.

Then he pushed my hair back, leaned down, and tenderly kissed my cheek.

A hush come across the crowd. He pulled back and smiled at me. Then he come close again, and when he pressed his lips against mine, you could hear the gasp echo across the valley.

You coulda toppled me with a feather. My eyes was wide open, and when he backed off again, he give me a sassy wink.

He stepped toward the man that had pulled him from the wash.

"I'm obliged, sir. Me and the little lady here is lookin for some help. We just didn't imagine it would come like this."

He stuck his hand toward the man in a friendly gesture. Water dripped from his nub.

"I lost it in a fight with my brother. Broke it so bad the doc had to cut it off. This here is Lochiel Grubbs. She's—"

"Marked." The man took a step back.

Silas eyed the man, then smiled. "She's marked with beauty. Look at them eyes. They look like the sunrise. A lot like yours." He pointed at the man's eyes. "She's one of yours. Born with this mark, not given it. See for yourself. Touch it."

Silas took my hand and pulled me closer. "Go on, touch her. She won't eat you."

The man's hand eased to my cheek. I knelt so he would see my intentions was good, to let him see I wasn't aimin to hurt him. As I looked upward to him, his fingertips touched the mark that covered the side of my face. I never took a breath.

I felt like a wild animal, waitin for folks to either feed or kill me. A tear dripped, and the man caught it on his finger.

"I'm Hoit. They say folks who is marked by the Devil has a raised mark. Like a burn bubblin from the skin."

I shook my head. "I don't know nothin 'bout that. I reckon folks judge me be it raised or not. A mark is a mark. Ain't nobody wants one." I bowed my head and waited.

I sure could use that help now, Sir.

That thought no sooner run through my head than the crowd parted. A woman walked toward us, bracin up a man all hunkered over, holdin his gut. He looked familiar. I wasn't sure, but he looked like—like—

"Walton! Oh my Lord in heaven above." I jumped to my feet and run to him. "Walton, I thought you was—"

"Dead?" He pulled me into his arms and kissed my head. Again, the crowd gasped. "Seems Hoit here has spent the last two days pullin men from the belly of the river."

I couldn't say nothin. Tears I didn't think I had left were runnin down my face. I hugged him, my head to his chest, his coarse jacket soakin up my tears.

When I pulled back, the front of my dress was soaked. I laughed through my tears. I hadn't been cryin *that* much. I touched the damp fabric and my fingers come away bright red.

I sucked in a breath. "You're still bleedin."

"Well, that idiot Gerald did ram his blade into my gut. I ain't in the best of shape, but thanks to that icy river and ole Hoit here, I'm still breathin."

A young woman slipped her arm around Walton's waist. "You need to rest. Come."

Walton's knees buckled and I grabbed at him. "He needs to lay down."

Walton straightened hisself. He wiggled his finger for Hoit to come closer. "Hoit, this here is my girl. She was born with this mark. It ain't because of anything she's done. Just like your boy's legs, the scars he got. Wasn't nothin he done to cause that brush fire and nothin he done to cause hisself to get burned. There ain't nothin Lochiel done either. You understand?"

Hoit nodded. "I do."

Walt lifted his hand and waved it at the crowd. "This is my girl, and there ain't no Devil in her. Anyone wants to judge her, they got me to deal with."

Despite his weak legs, Walton's voice demanded respect. No one challenged his words.

I could see Hoit was the man the people looked to. If he approved of me, there would be no problem. Walt stared straight into Hoit's eyes. After a minute, Hoit waved his arm and nodded. The crowd slowly went about their business.

"Mr. Walt, you need rest so we can stop the bleedin." The young village woman nudged him toward a lean-to.

Silas slipped his arm around Walton and helped the woman move him toward a makeshift shack. She slipped her shoulder under a hide that covered the entrance. "Here, lay. Rest."

"You're a tough ole bird, ain't you?" Silas teased.

"I'm much obliged that you took in my girl. That you put to stake all you have to help an ole peddler."

"Aw, you ain't just a peddler. You're a friend. Besides, I've done took a shine to that girl of yours."

Walton smiled and winked at me as they lowered him onto a pallet. The village women stuffed fine wads of dried moss and root herbs into the wound and wrapped his stomach with cheesecloth.

I eased his head onto a folded sheepskin as gently as I could, but his tight grimace let me know he was feelin poorly. "I can't believe you're alive."

I laid my head against Walton's chest, careful not to put weight on him. He wrapped his fingers around my head.

"I know. That Gerald is plumb crazy. I knew he was harborin some anger, but I never realized his vengeance could be so violent."

His fingers slipped to the bed and I sat up. "It was Gerald. Gerald told me so hisself. Gerald was the one to steal me away."

"Leastways, you're safe. You and Silas are safe." Walt's voice was weak.

"For now, anyway." Silas shook his head like a dog, tryin to dry his hair. "Gerald ain't more than a day behind us. We somehow have to end this before he kills our girl."

"Ain't rightly sure what to do." Walton shifted on the pallet and moaned. His face contorted again and he shut his eyes against the pain.

"Ain't there somethin else we can do to help him?" I dabbed a bead of sweat from his forehead. "There has to be somethin."

Silas took hold of my shoulder. "He needs to rest. Let him sleep."

Hoit poked his face in. Seemed to avoid my eye but nodded at Silas. "Just came to check on Mr. Walt."

At the sound of his voice, Walton stirred. "Will you do me the kindness of seein to the needs of my girl? Would you do that for me?"

Hoit eyed me then. After a few seconds, he grasped aholt of Walton's hand and wrist. "I'll see to it."

"I need to stay with him."

"No." Silas still had his hand on my shoulder and he steered me to the door. "You need to get into some dry clothes and put a little warm food in you. We need to come up with a plan to stop this mess."

"Follow me." Hoit led me to a cabin where he exchanged quiet words with a woman and a girl, then turned and left us. Folks was scared of me, that was easy to see. They kept their distance. But even in their fear, seemed they trusted Walton, and that trust allowed me safety. His years of peddlin proved to be my savin grace.

Turned out this woman, Esmeralda, was Hoit's wife, and the girl was his daughter, Junc. They brung me to a shed where they allowed me a hot bath—somethin I hadn't had since I'd crawled out from under Edna's cabin covered in mud—and they brung me clean clothes. The skirt was the prettiest I'd ever worn and I almost cried again when I slipped into it. Seemed to be the year for cryin. I'd cried more since I left the Ogles than I'd cried my whole life with 'em. Funny how kindness can make a body shed tears.

When I was cleaned up, I found Esmeralda had left a corn pone and some soup beans. I picked up the wooden bowl and run it under my nose. The smell of soup beans and sweet corn bread made my mouth water, and I wasted no time tippin it to my lips. The soup beans was so good, I just closed my eyes and savored the taste.

"You best slow down and chew." A woman pushed open the shed door. "Mind if I come in?"

I slowed my eatin, careful not to say somethin that would frighten her. "You can come in. It ain't my place to kick you out of."

"This here is my shed. I ain't much in the way of possessions. So I expect everthing to be in its place once you're gone."

"No need to worry. I ain't one to pry and handle other folks' things."

"See that you don't." The woman walked around me, eyeballin my mark. "'Bout how old are you?"

I shoveled another bite of beans into my mouth. "Nineteen or so."

"Did you ever know your momma?"

I swallowed, then cleared my throat and looked up. "Not my real momma. Just the woman that raised me."

"She name you?"

I cocked my head. Odd questions for a body to be askin, but the way I saw it, it was someone talkin to me. Not runnin away screamin at the sight of my mark.

Without waitin for my answer, she turned back to the door. "You need anything, you let me know," she said.

"Hey." I called out before I'd figured on what I was gonna say. "So . . . you got a name?"

"Roseland." Roseland opened the door. She stuck her hand outside and motioned to someone, then turned back to me. "There's someone here who wants to say somethin to you."

I filled my mouth with another bite of beans. "Alright. I'd like to talk to anybody that'll talk back."

Roseland stepped out and another woman stepped inside. Her head hung low as she stared at the dirt floor.

"Come in. You want some beans?"

"No. I don't want nothin 'cept my son."

"Your son?"

She lifted her head.

"Rita?"

THIRTY-FIVE

I NEARLY SPIT my mouthful of beans across the table. "Rita!"

I swallowed hard and come to my feet. "How are you?"

Just as I reached toward her, her hand come up and she took a step back.

"Don't you come one more step closer. You touched my boy and look what happened."

"I didn't do nothin to that youngin. He was a sweet child."

Rita gritted her teeth. "All I want is my boy and he's dead"—she pointed a finger at my face—"because of you."

"I'm sorry 'bout Joshua. But I didn't have nothin to do with his dyin. I didn't even know he died and, I promise, I only tried to take care of that little feller."

"I know what you say you did. But that ain't the result, now is it? My boy is dead. Dead!"

My heart sank. Poppy used to always say you couldn't reason with a mad woman. I reckon he was right about that. Rita had it in her head that I was the cause of little Joshua's dyin. And I needed to set her straight.

I pressed my hands against my hips.

"Rita! You look at me and you get this one thing straight. I never laid a hand to harm that child."

"You done your damage." Her voice rose.

"It was Gerald that smashed his head, not me." My voice matched hers. "All I ever—"

I stopped mid-sentence. It was like someone proddin at my soul. I coulda swore someone spoke in my ear.

It's the choices you make . . .

"All you ever did was kill my boy!" Rita continued her claims.

The hair on the back of my neck stood. *What do you choose?* I could choose to be angry or I could choose compassion. I reckon the right thing was compassion. I had to stand against what was natural—fight against the things I wanted to say, and choose to be gentle. Choose to be kind. Choose to love despite the worst.

It might only get me a slap in the face, but in the long run it would be what was right.

"Rita." My voice softened. I made my way to the stool by the table. Suddenly, the sweet smell of the beans turned to alum, and it felt like my mouth would pucker.

"I know there ain't no convincin you anything other than what you have in your head to believe. That's the way of things. But I would've never hurt Joshua. And I would never hurt you." I touched my neck. "People judge me by this mark. If I could take it away, I would. But I swear, I never laid a harmful hand on that youngin. You believe what you will, but the truth is the truth."

As I walked to the door, she edged away from it. "I ain't mad. I ain't hurt. I'm a woman stained by this mark. That's all I am. And that boy, he saw past the purple stain on my face. He wasn't scared at all. For that, I'll always be grateful."

I walked out the door, leavin Rita in the shed. She followed me outside, rantin and sobbin. Squallin that I killed her boy. I tried to close my ears to her threats and accusations, but they dug clean under the skin and stuck me like a splinter jabbed under a fingernail.

"Don't you walk away from me!" Rita screamed. "Turn around here. I want to see your face when I tell you what I got to say. I want to see you suffer like I've had to suffer." Her words blistered like scaldin water. I made the choice to turn back to her. She balled her hand into a fist and shook it at me.

We were drawin a crowd. More folks than I'd had mind to see in my whole life gathered round us. It was mostly women, carryin their youngins on their hips or carryin pots of water on their heads. The wind caught the ends of my hair and twisted them round my face. I took in a breath and slowly let it out.

When Rita was sure she had my attention, she hollered so the whole village could hear her.

"It was me. Me! I was the one told Gerald where you was. I give him every detail I heard when Walton put you on that horse and sent you away."

It was like the icy river water begin to run through my veins. I turned cold all over, and my legs give way. I fell to the ground. Not a soul offered to help me. Her words cut to the core.

Rita had set Gerald and the others on Silas's place. She was the reason Walton was stabbed and Silas knocked out cold. The reason I sat tied to a scarecrow with the buzzards pickin at my flesh.

Things wasn't addin up. Why would she do that? Even if she thought I'd hurt her son, why would she talk to Gerald—the man who'd busted up her son to begin with? A stranger who'd knocked her around too?

What do you choose? I was beginnin to get right agitated at that voice, but I could see that now wasn't the time to ask Rita those questions. She'd lost her son and her anger was lookin for a place to land.

"Did tellin Gerald bring Joshua back to life?" My voice was quiet, almost timid.

With fists still curled and body rigid, Rita was pantin and red-faced. But not comin at me. I took that as a good thing.

"Did tellin Gerald get you the revenge you wanted? 'Cause I can tell you what it did do. It brought the Devil hisself down on innocent men. Walton was nearly killed and his friend Silas was hurt. And them was two people that had nothin to do with your boy. Is that what you wanted?"

Tears left trails over her dirt-smudged skin.

"I know you're hurt and I'm sorry. But this ain't the way to bring you peace."

I took just one step toward her. She didn't budge.

"I'm sorry Joshua died. I'm sorry your boy is gone, and if I could change that, I would."

I took one more step. "You must miss him somethin awful. He was so brave and sweet."

I inched closer to her, then finally reached my arm around her and pulled her against me. Kept my voice calm. I felt her pain and I held her tight, suckin in her wrath and tryin to love her through it.

Rita broke into heart-wrenchin sobs as I held her.

"My boy!" she cried over and over. Her wails caught on the wind and carried across the mountain pass, and her shoulders shook as she cried.

Sadness crept into my heart and I took on tears as well. I held her fast, swayin back and forth, her face pressed into my shoulder. And when her knees grew weak from grief, we both sank to the ground. It was one of them times when a body could feel their heart split like a piece of firewood. I brushed my fingers down her hair and she sobbed, my anger toward Gerald boiled.

A sound made me look up. The village women had gathered closer, now offerin Rita their love. They could see she was broken. And I reckon, for once, the real blame wasn't on me.

Thy rod and thy staff, they comfort me. Them words Edna taught me from the Good Book ate at my soul. For a minute, I did find comfort in them. As hurt as I was at Rita for callin Gerald down on me, my soul cried for this woman eat up with grief.

Several of the women started to cry. Moans of sadness rose to the mountaintops. They led Rita to the fire that burned in the center of the village. Any men that had been around before had disappeared now. Two women dipped their fingers in the black ash from the fire, then drew lines down her face. A gentle drum thumped, and the women swayed to the beat. They lifted their arms into the air and cried deep, agonizin moans—slowly movin around the fire. Seemed they were helpin her mourn the loss of her little boy. As they passed by her one by one, they marked her with ash until her creamy skin was covered in black. They held her. Sobbed with her. Wailed with her. And when the drum finally stopped, they took her to the river.

I had never witnessed anything more lovin than the gentleness of the native way. The women gathered around Rita, stripped her, then tenderly laid her across their arms, just above the wash of the river. Her body rested in their arms as one washed the dirt from her hair, then braided it. They dried her and dressed her, then walked her to her home. It was over. Her grief could slow now.

My heart ached. I understood loss.

Silas appeared next to me.

"You alright?" His arm draped over my shoulder.

I swiped at my cheek. My chin quivered. There was no real words for the pain I felt deep down in my gut. Like the bitter taste of alum that would draw your mouth tight, and dry your tongue so dry that even water couldn't quench the thirst, this was a taste I'd never forget.

Rita passed by me, her eyes red and swollen from her tears. She first said nothin. A few steps past me, she turned and come back.

"I'm sorry," she said, sobbing.

"I'm sorry," I echoed.

She hung her head like a whipped dog. "I was angry and I wanted revenge, however that come. I wanted you dead. I wanted Gerald to come back to me. And he didn't want nothin to do with Joshua or me. He just ranted on about you."

"You wanted Gerald to do *what*?" I pushed her away enough to see her face.

"I wanted Gerald to come back. Come be with me and his boy."

"His boy? Are you sayin your boy belonged to Gerald?"

Gerald would be gone huntin or whatnot for days on end, but I never knew—I was sure Poppy never knew—Gerald was a—

"Rita, is that what you mean? Gerald is Joshua's *daddy*?"

"When I happened upon your place lookin for Joshua and I saw that mark, I knew you was the one Gerald was goin on about. I knew then, you was the secret he'd been keepin. He'd told me about hidin the Devil's daughter, but he had a loose hold on truth, and I never really believed him. Leastways, not 'til that day when I saw you with my own eyes. Exactly like he said you was."

There was a lump the size of a rock in my throat. Rita's tellin Gerald where I was, was nothin more than beggin to get him back. Gerald. Hateful, vile, violent Gerald. I remembered Edna tellin me that the truth was sometimes more hurtful than a lie. I felt I'd been hit in the gut with a stick.

One of the women took Rita by the elbow and led her away.

I stood there. Silas was still there by me. I'd forgotten he was there. I had no words for him. My head told me to be angry, but my heart spit back the words Edna taught me from the Good Book.

And now abideth faith, hope, charity, these three; but the greatest of these is charity.

I pushed the loose strands of hair from my face. Silas took me in his arms and tucked my head under his chin. "Folks want a body to be truthful, but when they hear the truth, it's a bitter taste," he said softly. "The truth ain't always what we thought it would be. It stings sometimes. But choosin the truth is always better. Relief comes when truth sets you free." His words was right. Even though the news Rita shared pained me . . . the truth was better. Silas pressed a kiss to my hair and I released all the air left in me.

Seems the Devil had been snuffed out. Nothin boiled inside. *I choose love.*

I HAPPENED ON her outside the Indian village. She was alone, scroungin up kindlin. It didn't happen often, to find one of them women alone. She looked up at me with a bit of fear. Fear in a woman is a good thing. Desire came on me strong and I had to grip the saddle tight to keep my hands from shakin.

She'd come to me easier if I talked sweet to her.

I slid off my horse and hung back, not givin her reason to run off. "What's your name?"

She backed up a step.

"Oh, don't worry, I ain't gonna hurt ya. Just want to talk a bit. What's your name?" I wondered if it'd be one of those crazy names the natives mostly used.

"Rita." Her voice was soft, like the wind brushin the tops of the trees.

"That's a right purty name. For a purty woman." She looked like Lochiel but older. Her dark hair hung in tight curls. Her skin was the color of chestnuts.

She smiled a little bit. Gave me some hope and set my body aheat.

It didn't happen easy though. Took a couple visits before I'd talked enough for her. I had to promise her I'd take her as a wife. I told her stuff I never meant to tell. About Momma, about huntin, about hidin the Devil's daughter. I promised I'd build her a proper cabin and show her off to all my friends. I about run out of words. I was gettin tired of waitin, tired of talkin, and finally twisted my fingers in her hair and brung her to me.

Her skin was soft. She squirmed a bit but didn't have any real fight in her. I could tell she wanted all we done, same as me.

I'd had a taste, and was more than hungry to have more.

I found her a few more times after that, and each time we'd lie together a little longer. She grew happy to see me, didn't have fear in her eyes no more. But then she started hangin on me, not wantin me to leave. Havin her was comin at a price, and she weren't the type a woman I could make a family with. Best I be done with her. Wasn't worth the trouble no more. I could find me another woman. A better woman.

THIRTY-SIX

"WHY DO YOU need to go back?" I asked Silas.

It'd taken me some time to take in Rita's news. Things was comin clear and, though everthing didn't make sense, at least some of it did. Gerald had taken me right outa my Momma's arms. Poppy and Momma musta known that, but made up a story, the good Lord only knows why. Gerald had told at least Rita the truth, though he spent most of his breath in lies. Secrets and anger and anger and secrets. Round and round 'til his lies commenced to fall in on theirselves and Gerald decided to kill me.

It's odd how the decisions we make cause ripples in our lives down the road. That's what we had here . . . a ripple that started long ago in the middle of the river was finally makin its way to the bank.

"Answer me, please. What if—"

"Hush, missy. Life is full of what-ifs. A man can't stand around and wonder when they is gonna happen. Now I got things to do on the farm, but I'll be back." He cinched his saddle tight on his horse. "I figured I'd make my way across the mountain and see about Edna. See—"

I butted in. "See if she's alive?"

"We've talked about this. There ain't nothin that says one way or the other. But me and Walt was talkin and he wanted me to check on her. Put an end to the wonderin."

"Walton ain't sure either?" I rubbed away the tears that was seepin.

"Missy, none of us is sure of havin tomorrow. But if there was ever a woman who could take care of herself, it's Edna. She always said, where there's a will there's a way. So if there is, you can bet Edna's found it. For now, we'll hope for the best." He gently tapped my nose with his finger.

"You think Gerald's give up his hunt for me?"

"I don't know, just don't know. When Walton's mended, he'll start back over the mountain, listen to the talk—"

"But—"

Silas pressed his finger over my lips.

"Lochiel, trust me. You're safe here. If somethin is gonna happen, it's gonna happen if I'm here or if I'm checkin on things at the house. Good Lord says worry don't fix things." He slipped the reins over his horse's head. "I'm a man of my word, little lady. I'll be back." He climbed on his saddle and started right off.

"Silas!" I hollered. He turned in his saddle. "Don't cross the river. Go the mountain trail. Remember what happened last time."

He busted into an all-out laugh. It was good he laughed 'cause I shed my share of tears as he faded from sight.

———

I still wondered if Gerald had give up his hunt, prayed that was so. Didn't seem like him, hot-headed as he was, to let grass grow under his feet. If he wanted me dead, he'd get to it. But I was startin to feel like I might just belong with these people. Every day it growed easier to live and work alongside them.

Over the last few weeks, Esmeralda and June took me with them into the fields to plant corn, and they spent a good amount of time teachin me to make dye for the fabrics they weaved.

Rita and me, we'd become friends—me holdin Rita when she cried over her boy, and her tellin me the tales Gerald spun about me. Together we'd took some evergreen branches and tied them together, makin a grave blanket to cover Joshua's restin place.

"Rita, why wouldn't you let the villagers burn Joshua's body?" I asked as she laid the blanket of evergreen over his spot.

"I couldn't bring myself to allow it." Tears wet her face and her voice quivered. "He feared fire somethin awful. Now I just wanna keep his little body as warm as I can."

When I hugged her, our tears run together.

Walton was still mendin but doin his best to be a daddy to me. "After I get on my feet good," he told me, "I'll get some men together to build you a hut of your own. Would you like that?" Yes, I reckon I'd like that just fine.

"You goin down to the river with the women today? Wash day, you know." Roseland set her tin cup on the table. Steam twisted and turned from the coffee.

"Yep. I reckon any woman worth her weight ain't about to miss wash day." I rolled my eyes.

Roseland was lettin me stay in her hut while she come and went about her business. She was gettin ready to head up the mountain for a few days. "Just 'cause you stay here don't mean this is your home to keep. You're still moochin. As long as you mooch, you work. We clear?"

I smiled to reassure her I understood this was not permanent. "I know."

"See that you do."

Roseland was gruff in her ways, but I could tell she had took a shine to me.

"You want me to braid your hair before I go?" The women here often did each other's hair, but not Roseland. Rita told me she'd never seen Roseland do anyone's hair before I'd come. She didn't usually stick around very long at a time.

"I'd like that. Reckon while you're gone, it'll just run wild like it used to." Roseland pulled a chair over, and its legs drew crooked lines in the dirt floor of the hut. When she pressed me down to sit on it, I remembered Edna's gentle hands doin the same, twistin my hair up and securin it with a cloth and a stick. First Edna and now Roseland was more mother to me than Momma had ever been. Food and clothes was easy enough to come by, but hands to do hair, that was real lovin.

"Didn't your momma ever do your hair?" Her voice sounded angry.

"No. She hardly ever touched me that she didn't have a cross in her hands."

"A cross?" Roseland's fingers sunk deep into my hair and separated the strands into three parts to braid.

"Momma used it to fend off my hexes. I never even understood what hexin was 'cept that it was bad."

"Hogwash." Roseland's hands worked swiftly. "Youngins should be held tight, loved hard, protected. She weren't no momma." She dropped her hands to my shoulders and gently squeezed.

"Roseland?"

"What, girl?"

"I was thinkin about Rita, her losin Joshua and all. You reckon she'll ever heal?"

"Lordy child, you worry over things. Your questions take more time than I got right now." Roseland's hands worked swiftly. "I reckon you've heard it before. It ain't right for a momma to outlive her youngins. It just ain't the way of the world. Unnatural." She pulled a stool next to me and sat. "Still, time has a way of patchin a hole." Her eyes looked far away, into the past, it seemed. "Don't suppose she'll ever heal, but she'll be patched. She'll learn to live with the loss." Her rough fingers wrapped mine. "Yea, Rita will harden."

Roseland got up and pulled her coat on.

I didn't want to let her leave just yet. "I reckon Rita did her best to help Joshua. She tried. Didn't she?"

She pushed her leather rim hat tight. "Rita did all a mother could with what she had to do with. I'd kill anybody who tried to hurt my youngin. I reckon she did her best to protect hers. I don't judge her one way or the other and neither should you.

"Now, we need some of them rugs made for tradin." She pulled her long, thick walkin stick from the corner and pointed it toward the basket of long pond grass and reeds. "Reckon you can manage weavin a few before I get back?"

"Maybe Rita will sit and weave with me."

"Washin first. Rugs second." She paused and ran her eyes over me. "I . . . I'll be back in a few days. You get them rugs made."

Then she opened the door, and walked out. As the door closed I heard her commence bickerin.

"They don't make 'em much more stubborn than you, you old cuss." Roseland's voice rose a notch.

"What's got your goat?" Walton snapped back.

"Blessed ole coot. Won't stay down long enough to heal proper." She grumbled as she walked away. I pulled open the door. Walt stood waggin his head from side to side watchin Roseland walk off. I come outa the hut and wrapped my arms around Walt's waist. He kissed my temple.

"She don't mean nothin by it." I gently tightened my arms around him. Instead of walkin toward the river, like I expected, Roseland was walkin the other way. Must be somethin she still had to do before she set out.

"Oh, I've know'd Roseland long enough to know her ways." He watched where she was goin, then squatted to sit on a log. "Hoit's got some men settin to raise you a hut on the far side of the village."

"They're already workin on it? But I thought you . . ." A stream of excitement shot through me, catchin my voice like a coon in a trap. I'd never had anything outside the clothes on my back. Havin a place of my own meant more than I could say.

"It won't be nothin fancy, but it'll be yours. And I promise you'll know what it means to be cold in the winter. These huts ain't real warm." He grinned. "I got a pot or two on the wagon. A blanket or so you can have."

Tears welled in my eyes. "Walton, what if you'd never happened on me in the woods? How can I thank you for all you done for me?"

He tenderly rubbed my shoulder, then brushed his knuckles across my mark. "Tell you what you can do. You can decide to be happy with the days you are blessed to have."

I waited a minute before I spoke, then had to clear my throat first. "Now you sound like Edna."

"Uh huh."

"You think she's alright?"

He patted my knee as he stood. "Worry don't fix nothin. What will be, will be."

"Lochiel!" Rita come runnin down the middle of the village wavin her arms. "Come on, Lochiel. Come on now."

I turned to Walton.

"We better find out what's got her riled up," he said.

I slipped my hand under his arm to steady him up but he brushed me away and walked alone. "You're as bad as Roseland. I'm slow but I can manage."

Rita clapped her hands to speed us along.

It took us a spell, but the three of us made our way to the edge of the village. A fire blazed to one side. The smell of roastin meat filled the air. Blankets were spead all around and baskets filled with bread and vegetables laid ready to eat. The villagers stood, chantin a blessin round a hut. Drums thumped a gentle beat, like my heart.

I saw Roseland standin a little off from everone else. Watchin. She hadn't left yet. She caught my eye and smiled.

"Lordy mercy, what's all this?" I took Rita by the hand.

Walton grinned with knowin. "Guess maybe your hut will be done sooner than I let on."

"This here is what we call a poundin. Everbody brings you a pound of somethin to help you. A pound of corn, a pound of flour, lard . . ."

I gasped and covered my mouth.

Oh my goodness. They was gathered here for me. Welcomin me as part of their village. Women hugged me, handin me pouches with fruit, bread, and dried corn. The children handed me sweet yellow dandelions and jonquils.

For the first time in my life, I had a place where I fit. Folks had stopped judgin me for my mark. They'd learned I was just like them. They protected me. Provided for me. Called me one of their own.

I hugged Walton tight, then released him to look for Roseland. She musta known, but seems she'd vanished again. That was her way.

People shifted around to settle on blankets, and I could finally see the hut clear. And there stood Silas with Edna.

Thirty-Seven

Roseland was gonna be right proud of me when she returned. Even though I'd spent time gettin my hut in order, I'd also made up all her pond grass and reeds into rugs. Course Rita helped me.

It was her idea that we gather more so that we could also make a ground cover for my hut. I liked the idea of somethin underfoot instead of just the bare dirt. And maybe I could make one for Edna to take home with her. It wouldn't be fancy like somethin Walt could bring her, but I thought she'd like it if I made her somethin.

It was a daily chore, gatherin wood, so we'd gathered the makins for rugs at the same time. Esmerelda and June had come along, bringin round baskets to fill. The more time I spent in the village, the more I learned about how they was all connected. Esmerelda's momma had died, and her daddy had taken another wife, Rita's momma. They was sisters of sorts.

With baskets full, we was headin back. June was carryin on about some silly somethin. Her smile could light a fire.

I leaned my face toward the sky and laughed. It felt good to be . . . happy.

"Well looky here."

The nightmares that haunted me grabbed at me like a bear snaggin a trout. Gerald.

Rita and I both stopped mid-step and dropped our loads.

Rita whipped around, fists balled and ready to fight. As she run past, I tried to grab her, but she wiggled loose.

Oh, Lord, have mercy. She's gonna face him down. I run after her.

If there was anyone more angered at Gerald than me, it was Rita.

Gerald was just after me but Rita aimed to make him pay for Joshua's death.

"Gerald Ogle!" Rita shouted. "You come to see your boy?"

Gerald pulled his horse around, stopped up short. He sat starin down at Rita.

"Woman, what are you talkin about? I don't have no boy. All I want to see is that Devil woman there. Move outa my way."

"Don't you act like you don't know what I'm talkin about. Your son. The youngin I birthed for you. The one you as good as killed."

I stepped up beside Rita. Gerald's eyes flicked over to me. "That Devil girl's filled your head with lies. You ain't thinkin clear."

He lifted his foot and kicked her in the chest. Shovin her into my arms. Memories flashed in my head of a time he had done the same thing to me. I was familiar with the heel of his boot.

"Your son is dead because that Devil girl done her black magic. You told me so yourself."

"It was you that killed him. You killed him just as if you'd put a gun to his head and pulled the trigger."

As Gerald came off his horse, Rita sprang forward, clawin toward his face. Gerald drew back and slapped her hard enough to drop her to the ground. Then drew his gun on her.

"Run, run right now back to the village. Don't stop for nothin." Esmerelda's words to June brought Gerald's gun around to them. I edged toward Rita. Esmerelda's body shielded her daughter's. "Go on," Esmerelda said firmly and calmly. "Get your father to gather the men."

This was nothin but a try to get Gerald to run off. Most of the men were off huntin. Maybe Gerald knew that already and that's why he come now.

Rita leapt up to come at Gerald again, but I grabbed her waist and swung her around.

June took off like a deer across a clearin.

Rita struggled somethin fierce. "Rita, no! This ain't bringin Joshua back."

"This ain't your battle. It's mine, and I'll fight it on my own," she hissed. She struggled against me, but I wasn't about to turn her loose.

"This won't help."

"Well, I never. Devil's daughter had a change of heart? She must be hungry for another soul." Gerald stepped one step toward me.

He pointed at me and pranced around like a proud rooster. "I told you she had powers. You can't kill her. We tried, me and my boys. And looky. Now she's done drove you crazy."

I held tight to Rita whilst she screamed and fought, but my curiosity got the best of me. "Where are your men now, Gerald?"

Esmerelda's movements rustled the undergrowth.

"Sit down, woman," Gerald roared, and backed toward his horse. Maybe he was thinkin better of takin the three of us on.

"Gerald, I got no more fights with you. What's past is past," I said.

"Past?" He laughed a snide, nasty laugh. "I ain't got no past with you, Devil girl. I just want you dead so the people here on the mountain can live without the fear of you killin 'em. Drinkin up their souls."

"That ain't true and you know it ain't. Leave these people be. If it's me you want, then here I am. Take me wherever you want to and do what you want. But leave these people alone."

Gerald edged around behind me as I hugged Rita close. The cold barrel of his gun pressed against my neck. All the time Rita sobbed horrible, heart-wrenchin sobs. I figured this was my end. I'd already escaped it twice before. I just hoped the good Lord would have mercy on me and make it fast.

"This what you want, Gerald? You wanna kill me like you killed Joshua? Will that please you?"

The bristles of his beard brushed against my ear. "I want to take you. I want to dance with the Devil and win."

His nearness churned my stomach, but I didn't dare move. A memory of him with a boyish face flashed across my mind. His smiles when Poppy'd brought him a new gun. His excitement while he showed it off. "I'll shoot better'n Eckert now," he'd said. How'd my brother become this?

A rustle from Esmerelda, and Gerald swung around and shot the tree right above her head. "Move again and I won't miss, woman."

Rita ceased her wigglin. I swallowed hard. "Well, here I am. You think

I'm the Devil, then here I am. Do what you will." His hot breath damped my neck and I shivered. "But you answer me this one thing."

"What's that?"

"What lies did you tell Rita to coax her into your grip?"

Gerald run his gun against my cheek. The end was still hot and I fought not to pull back. "I never told that woman nothin. She's lyin. I never laid with her."

Rita commenced to holler. "You're the one lyin, you filthy beast."

"You're a half-breed. I don't mess with no half-breed." Gerald's words stung me, but for Rita it was more than she could bear. She twisted around in my arms and screamed one last time.

"Liar!"

I held her face tight against my shoulder and I felt the gun barrel slip away from my neck.

"It's alright, Rita. It's alright."

Gerald's gun popped.

"Noooo!"

Rita slipped through my grip and fell limp to the ground.

Thirty-Eight

I couldn't move. Gerald had shot Rita while I held her tight against my chest.

In my good intentions to try to save her, I held her still so he could shoot her dead.

My ears rang somethin fierce from that gunshot. My head was spinnin, and my stomach started to rumble. I gagged from the blood splattered on my face.

"Oh, Lord, have mercy!" I cried.

"Yea, though I walk through the valley of the Shadow of Death, I will fear no evil, for Thou art with me." I mumbled the words over and over, searchin for the comfort Edna had promised I would find. Rita lay at my feet, her eyes wide open, fingers touchin my legs. I felt the warmth leave her hands. *"Thy rod and thy staff, they comfort me."*

My body begin to shake.

Gerald hauled Rita's body and flung her aside. Next thing I knew he was bindin my arms to my sides with a rope and I was powerless to stop him. I couldn't force any part of my body to fight him off. Esmerelda was on her feet, pummelin him with her fists, but now there was just two of us and I was already bound.

Anger bellowed inside my stomach like a wildfire burnin out of control. This must be how the fires of hell burned, and if that was so then maybe Gerald was right on one account. If I could have called open the gates of hell to suck him in, I would have.

"I will fear no evil, for Thou art with me." I repeated the words again and again. Gerald left me standin there and he mounted up. Esmerelda pulled frantically at my ropes but couldn't get the knot to move.

"You wanna ride, Lochiel? Let's go for a ride." He kicked his horse. As the animal bolted and broke into a run, Esmerelda's hands fell away, my feet left the ground, and my body come down hard.

If I'm gonna die, Lord, make it quick.

I'd never felt such pain as my body scrubbed over the rocky ground and bounced off a tree. Shouts, poundin hooves, and screams became a single roar in my head. Then we was splashin through the river, shallows first, then deeper. First the water felt better than the ground. A comfort. Until water rushed over my head and into my mouth. I struggled, spittin and coughin. Then my body was pulled back under. Then out again, draggin across the ground. And turnin, my body flipped, thrashed on every side.

Suddenly the motion stopped.

Silas was there, cuttin the ropes away. *Where'd you come from?* I don't know if I said the words out loud or not. He didn't answer.

I rolled to my side and tucked my knees to stand. A long moan sounded. I reckon I'd made the noise.

"No. You stay still, little lady. You need tendin to."

I pushed up off the ground. Everthing spun around me. Watery blood drained down my arms. Gerald was backin toward the river, gun fendin Silas off. He wasn't on his horse no more. I took a step toward him. Then another. Every piece of my body screamed out. I took another step.

"Lochiel, no." It was Silas's voice. "Just let him go."

It hurt even to breathe in and out. I didn't turn away from Gerald. My eyes stayed fixed on him. "Why did you take me from my real momma?" I held my arms out to him.

Gerald had backed right to the river's edge now. His horse danced in the river, waitin to carry him off. Back home to Momma.

I kept puttin one foot in front of the other. I couldn't see no one else but knew at least Silas was there. Givin me strength to move. Couldn't be sure, but it seemed like maybe them angels Edna talked about too.

"You comin to let me send you back through the gates of hell? There won't be no gettin away from me this time." Gerald pointed the gun at my face. "Look at her. She bears that mark that makes her the Devil's daughter." He staggered and his words was like a drunk man. He was hurt but it didn't stop his rantins.

Gerald's body begin to quiver.

I was standin so close now, the tip of his gun pressed against my chest bone. He pushed the barrel harder. The sharp pain made me gasp. I rested my hand on his and he flipped it away with his barrel.

"Why did you steal me away? Answer me! You was just a youngin. A child. What made you do that?"

"Shut up!" He turned his head slightly, kept his eyes on me. "Can't you hear her whisperin a curse on me? Can't you hear her?" His voice sounded like he'd run the mountain. Couldn't tell who he was talkin to.

I lifted my hand to touch his cheek.

He smacked my hand away, joltin the gun against my chest as he did. My breath sucked away.

"I finally got you right where I need you. I can kill the Devil's daughter and be free of your curse. Stop you doggin my every step and hauntin me night and day."

"You made one choice as a youngin that brought this mess into bein. You can decide now to walk away. We'll just let things end. Go home, Gerald, go home. Take care of Momma and Poppy. Please?"

"You took the life outa my momma. You was supposed to give it back. That's what the mark of the Devil can do. Give and take life."

"This mark is just a stain on my skin. It ain't got no power. I didn't do nothin to your momma." I wanted to holler at him but all I could muster was a whisper.

"Shut up! You hear me? Shut up!" He shook his head like he was tryin to rid his mind of my words.

He restoreth my soul. People is odd creatures. They is easily broke. Them that manage to survive is creatures who find hope in the darkness. The rest live beneath the weight of hate and bitterness. My heart opened wide and the only thing I felt was love—love and pity, for a man who longed to be loved hisself. That's what drove his anger. A hunger for love. Whether I lived or died at the hands of my brother, he would know I cared for him.

"Put the gun down, Gerald. Let me hold you in my arms. Let me hold my brother." I raised my arms toward him. "Let me offer you the love you never felt. I want to. Please let me?"

Gerald backed away from me, stumblin down into the river. "I ain't your brother. I ain't nothin to you!" He shifted to keep his balance.

I stepped after him, the pain of the water rushin on my legs droppin me to my knees.

In a flash, I'd toppled over and Gerald's foot was pressed into my chest. It was all I could do to hold my head above the water.

"Gerald, don't do this," I gasped. "Please don't do this." Rushin water sucked up my nose.

I saw in my mind the hundreds of times I had pleaded those very words to Gerald as we was growin up. Moment after moment rushed through my head, and I figured this was my life runnin by me before I died.

"Please . . . don't." As I got the last word out, he slammed his foot on my head and shoved me under the water.

It's odd what happens when a body goes beneath the water. Your eyes open and things that was fuzzy, clears. The sound—even over the growl of the water—causes a person to hear better than ever. I could see the blur of Silas's boots and hear his screams, but when that gunshot rung out across the mountain and the blood spurted into the water and over me, I heard and saw everthing clearly.

The weight of Gerald's foot lifted as his arms flew into the air. His body careened into the river next to me and I shot up from the water, gaspin, pullin him out of the wash and against me.

Silas yanked against me, tryin to pry my hands off Gerald, but I pulled my arm loose from his grip.

"Lochiel, let him go!"

"No!" I shouted, pressin Gerald tighter against my chest. "Don't you die on me! You hear me? I don't want you to die. Please, Gerald." I pushed the strands of wet hair from around his face. "Look at me. You're my brother. Please don't die. I . . . I love you."

Gerald mustered the strength to draw in a breath and spit at me before his body went limp. I wrapped my arms tight around him and wailed. Sobs poured from me as I caressed his face in my hands.

Gerald's eyes was wide open. His pupils was tiny dots, starin at me. As his slobber dripped off my mark and down my neck, I understood what it meant to make a choice. My heart was breakin and though Gerald was nothin short of awful to me, I chose to love him anyway.

And I'd told him so. I'd done all I could do.

I turned toward Silas. "Did you do this? Did you shoot him?"

He shook his head and opened his arms, showin he only had a knife.

My eyes searched around. I turned a full circle.

On the far edge of the bank stood Roseland, tears streamin down her face, shotgun snugged under her arm. She traipsed into the river and took Gerald by the collar, then yanked his dead body outa my arms.

"I told you I'd kill anybody who tried to hurt my youngin. Let him go. Now!" She rolled his body over and pushed it into the wash, a trail of red twisted and turned in the water as his limp body caught in the current and floated toward an eddy.

And there it was. One last answer I'd been lookin for.

Roseland was my momma. She couldn't protect me as an infant but she could now. And true to her word, she did.

She wrapped me in her arms. After a minute, she looked up, over my head, and said, "Them Ogles give her a name that ain't got no meanin. *Lochiel* don't have no meanin."

I turned to see who she was talkin to. Walton was workin his way to us in the water, his hand on June's shoulder for support.

"I know, Rose, I know," Walt said.

Women and children lined the bank behind him.

"I give her a name. I held her in my arms long enough to give her a name. You remember the name we picked, Walt?"

He nodded. "It was a name we picked out together."

Roseland lifted her head into the air and shouted to the women, "Alonna! Her name is Alonna. You hear me? Her name is Alonna, not Lochiel."

I could hardly speak between the chill of the mountain river and the lightnin bolts of pain at every touch. "Wh-what does it mean?"

She buried her face against my head.

"It means *beautiful*." Her sobs echoed across the water. "It means beautiful. And I still give it to you even after I seen that you had that mark. You was nothin but beautiful."

Walton pulled Roseland close. Silas and one of the women lifted me from the river and helped me to the bank. When I looked downstream, Gerald's body had washed up against the rocks.

Gerald had lost it all. Poor Gerald would never know peace. Never know love. He was all alone.

Epilogue

Thunder Mountain—Five years later

THE SUMMER COME into itself, bringin a bounty of color and beauty across the ridge. Betwix the dogwoods and red maples, I'd never seen such a sight. The air was filled with the sweet smell of honeysuckle, and daisies dotted the fields at the foot of the summit. Soft clouds scraped the tops of the mountain peaks as the breeze carried them away. The sun dried the dew like a momma wipin her youngin's tears.

I sat on that bank above Silas's farm, gazin down on the valley nestled between the two mountains. The mornin breeze rustled the knee-high grass from side to side while Silas run the goats out of his freshly planted garden. I leaned my face to the sun and took in the warmth and peace of the mountain. The sunshine has a way of soakin the muck from a body's soul.

I gazed over the valley, rememberin how peaceful it seemed first time I seen it. I'd never felt such peace. This was home. *My home.*

Silas kept his promise, and when Preacher Samuel Stone made his way across the gap to Thunder Mountain, he married us on the ridge overlookin a sea of mountains. It wasn't nothin fancy, though what was different about that day, was my family—Mother, Daddy, and Grandmother. Those was the names I'd chosen to call them. Names with honor. Names with meanin.

When Preacher Stone said them words, "Do you, Alonna Grubbs, take this here man to be your husband?" there was no mention of the name Lochiel or Ogle. My name had meanin. It fit what Mother and Daddy

241

wanted me to be. My name meant somethin special to the people who loved me.

That name was *beautiful.*

If I'd learned nothin more over the last few years than that, then I'd learned a passel. Grandmother Edna kept right on teachin me, and betwix her and Silas, I learned to read the Good Book on my own. I even learned to write my name. *Alonna Grubbs Dalton.* I never wanted to learn how to write Lochiel. There was no point to it.

I've come to figure I ain't never gonna understand the good Lord and His ways, but I'm findin there is a nice friendship in this power I can't see. I was a woman who was lookin for somethin in her life that made sense. A woman judged, lost, and now found. I reckon, despite the things I don't know about the good Lord, the workins He does in me every day makes me a better person.

Edna taught me to never judge someone by their looks. "You never know the hardships others carry. Looks is deceivin so you love and respect everbody. Even the ones who do you wrong." I reckon I couldn't have learned a stouter lesson, since I had walked in the shoes of one judged.

And about them desires of my heart that Grandmother Edna was convinced the good Lord would give me. I suppose He has. And if you was to ask me what I've really gained from the Almighty, I'd say this—He give me eyes to see the best in folks, even when it looks bad. He give me love and I know now that love changes everthing.

I remember the first time I met Walton. I asked him where I would go from that cold mountaintop. I didn't realize the wisdom in his words when he said, *Start here and go there, but my best guess is, you'll know home when you find it.*

I'd come a long way from havin no real home to this. I looked across the field and took in a deep breath of summer air. I found my home.

Strangers pass by our homestead, and I see the joy in their company. When they's hungry, I feed them. I show them my mark and tell them what it's like to have people judge me by somethin that ain't true. The good Lord's allowed folks to give me a fightin chance to show 'em it's only a mark. Doesn't always stop their judgin me, but I'm at least able to smile and move on. What I hope is when folks see my mark they see love that passeth all understandin. When they're cold, I wrap them in a quilt and sit them by the fire. When their hearts are sad, I love 'em despite their sadness. I love 'em for who they are and from whence they come. Despite their marks. That brings me great joy and peace.

I can't argue with Grandmother Edna's words, *The choices we make are what makes us who we are.* When the good Lord sends a wanderin soul to our home, they will never leave without knowin they are loved.

As Edna growed feeble, I made Walton bring her to us and me and Silas watched over her 'til her soul passed over the mountain. The day we buried Edna, the daisies in the meadow danced in the breeze and my belly was big with a youngin. The drum of the villagers played in a long steady heartbeat, and the wooden flute of the Indian nation sang a soft eerie melody into the sky.

When I looked to the peaks of the Smoky Mountains, the mist that named them separated like a door openin into the heavens, and I was sure I saw the good Lord's hand reach down gently and motion Edna in. Her soul took flight like the eagle. Just like the words in the Good Book. They was like wings on eagles.

Edna changed my life. Taught me how to pray, how to live. I owed her. I reckon the best way to repay her was to be what she taught me to be.

Before they left, Walton kissed my forehead and Roseland tenderly rubbed my belly. They would be makin their way across the mountain, and it would be a spell before I'd see them again. They were takin to care for Edna's place. Somethin else she would have wanted.

My life was with Silas. I couldn't ask for more. He was like a gift—a second chance at livin.

And that suited me just fine.

Acknowledgments

I AM CONTINUALLY amazed at God's timing and how He gently works His plan in our lives. This story began a number of years ago, and yet, in today's world—amidst the conflicts and cries of racism, bullying, and prejudice—its message speaks at the perfect moment.

It is my hope and prayer that this story will move in your heart to encourage you to follow the commandment Jesus left us . . . *Love your neighbor as you love yourself.*

I cannot be credited for this work alone, for the words belong to the Father who creates each sentence. For my gift, for this story, for what is to come from the words, I am grateful to the Lord God Almighty. Without Him, there is no story.

To my husband, Tim, who supports me fully, encourages me without fail, and loves me just the way I am: thank you is not good enough. You are my prince.

To my children: it is my biggest desire that you see it is never too late, you are never too old, to follow your dreams. When life tosses you a curve, a hard curve . . . forgiveness will always trump even when it doesn't make sense. And despite it all, love prevails.

To Glen Moody and *I Love Books Bookstore*: you are the most amazing book retailer ever. I cannot express how grateful I am for what you do to share not only my books but the books of so many others. Your kind heart to be a determined sharer of good words more than blesses authors like me. Thank you.

A special thank you to my agent and friend, Diana Flegal, for her work and support, and to my friends Kathy Moffitt, Andrea Merrill, Gloria

Penwell, Eddie Jones, and Edie Melson, who believe in me even when I struggle to believe in myself. Thank you so much.

Finally, to Kregel Publications, Steve Barclift, and the amazing Dawn Anderson, whose beautiful ways help to shape my words from a story into a work of art. These novels are *our* novels, Dawn—yours and mine. To the awesome staff at Kregel who work faithfully, believe in me, and encourage me, a special thank you.

Without these people, I would not be standing in success. I am grateful.

Finally to those of you who choose to read these works, my gratitude and thanks. My prayer is that the words move you into action when you see others mistreated, and that through your own example, the love of Christ will shine through.

When my children were small, I taught them the one thing I thought could help them make wise choices. "When you have a decision or a choice to make, when in doubt, Philippians 4:8 it. Is it true? Is it noble? Is it right? Pure? Lovely? Admirable? Is it excellent or praiseworthy? If you can answer yes to these things, you will always make good choices."

Our choices make up the stonework for our pathway. I am learning to continually seek the kingdom and trust that God's way is always greater than mine. May your example stand strong and your choices be led by the wisdom and discernment of the One who is greater than us all—the I Am.

With love,
Cindy K. Sproles

"Cindy writes from the heart."

—ADRIANA TRIGIANI, *New York Times* best-selling author
of *Big Stone Gap*

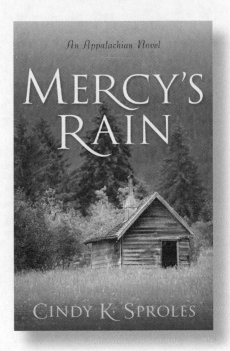

Mercy Roller knows her name is a lie. But the other side of this merciless mountain might have room for her stained and shattered soul to find shelter—and even love.

"At once chilling and compelling in its honest portrayal of nineteenth-century mountain life, *Mercy's Rain* is a beautifully written story of man's depravity and God's mercy."

—ANN TATLOCK, Christy Award winner and author
of *Promises to Keep*

Kregel
Publications

www.kregel.com